PLAYI.   .∧ ΓY

A DARK ENEMIES TO LOVERS FORBIDDEN MAFIA ACADEMY ROMANCE

THE SYNDICATE ACADEMY

BIANCA COLE

Book cover design by Deliciously Dark Designs

Photography: Wander Aguiar Photography

BLURB

Archer Daniels is the biggest flirt at the academy, and he's determined to have me.

Coach Daniels has a history of sleeping with students.

Now I'm in my senior year, he's determined to add me to the list.

I'd rather die than end up another notch in his bedpost.

But the man is persistent to a fault.

He's not someone who gives up easily, pushing harder the more I reject him.

I fear that Archer will stop at nothing until he gets what he wants.

A fear that quickly turns to reality as he digs up dirt about me I don't want people to know.

He says the whole school will find out if I don't hand him my virginity.

As if it's some trophy to be claimed.

I'll give him what he wants, but I won't make it easy for him.

I've never been good at losing and I'm going to make him wish he never pursued me.

He may be ruthless and insistent, but I can be just as mean.

We'll see who the true winner is when we both play dirty.

I'll claim his heart and make him wish he never set eyes on me.

And then, I'll walk away and leave him broken.

Finally teach him a lesson.

At least, that's the plan.

As long as I make sure I don't fall for him in the process...

AUTHOR'S NOTE

*H*ello reader,

This is a warning to let you know that this book is a **DARK** romance much like many of my other books, which means there are some sensitive subject matters addressed. If you have any triggers, it would be a good idea to proceed with caution.

As well as a possessive and dominant anti-hero who doesn't take no for an answer, this book addresses some sensitive subjects. A full list of these can be found here. As always, this book has a HEA and there's no cheating.

If you have any triggers, then it's best to read the warnings and not proceed if any could be triggering for you. However, if none of these are an issue for you, read on and enjoy!

ADRIANNA

*T*his is our last year at the academy. It's hard to believe that in less than ten months I'll be saying goodbye to the place that has been my home since I was ten years old.

The grand hall is full of returning students and staff, gathering at the front of the hall, but there's no sign yet of Camilla or Natalya.

"Hey loser."

I smile at the sound of Camilla's voice behind me and spin around as she runs into me, wrapping her arms around my waist.

"I've missed you so much this summer," she says.

I arch a brow. "Tell me about it. I couldn't wait for it to be over."

Camilla laughs. "Only you would wish away summer break." She sits down in her usual seat and I sit next to her. "What did you get up to?"

My summer break was terrible. Father paraded me

around to potential suitors as he intends to have me married the moment school is out. "Not a lot," I say, swallowing hard at the thought of even recounting how terrible it was, especially as Camilla always has the best summer breaks. "What about you?"

"I went with Mia to Saint Kitts for a month. It was glorious." She holds a hand against her chest. "I want to be back there. The weather was to die for."

I nod in response. "Sounds lovely." My brow furrows as I glance around, noticing that Principal Byrne is getting ready to start the welcome back speech. "Where the hell is Natalya?"

Camilla shakes her head. "No idea. Maybe she's late."

I shake my head. "That would be unlike her." Natalya is always on time for everything, it can get annoying how organized she is.

"Everyone, take a seat," Principal Byrne says over the microphone.

My attention moves to the front where all the staff are congregating. And a shiver races down my spine as I notice Coach Daniels is watching me intently. The man is painfully gorgeous, with a chiseled jaw and straight nose and dark eyes like coffee. And perhaps rightly so, he's also the biggest man whore at the academy. Some students can't resist his good looks and charms, even if they are just being used by him.

It's amusing that a staff member can get away with openly propositioning eighteen-year-old students, but then this isn't a normal academy.

Camilla nudges me in the ribs, forcing my eyes away from the coach.

"What?" I ask.

"I said Natalya still isn't here. Do you think she's okay?"

I swallow hard and glance at the back of the hall, wondering if that bastard, Elias, has done something to her. "Is Elias here?"

Camilla's brow furrows as she searches the hall for him, but it's too big. "Who the hell knows?" Her eyes widen a little. "Do you think he's stopped her from coming?"

I shudder at the thought, as Elias Morales has done some pretty terrible things to Nat in the past. If he got her alone without witnesses, it wouldn't surprise me if his hatred for her would drive him to physically harm her again.

"I'll text her and find out."

Camilla nods as I pull out my phone and type to Natalya.

Me: Are you okay? The welcome back assembly has started and you're not here.

Once it sends, I stare at the two ticks intently, waiting for them to turn blue and signal she's read it. And yet nothing happens.

"Anything?" Camilla asks.

I shake my head. "No, she hasn't even read it."

When I glance up from my phone, my eyes catch on Coach again because he's still watching me. The look in his eyes worries me to no end. It's full of sinful intent and my stomach churns, as I wonder if he might consider me as his next conquest, which will never, ever happen.

Camilla nudges me in the ribs. "Adrianna?"

"What?"

She shakes her head. "I said we'll have to find her as soon as this is over."

I nod in response. "Sure." I glance back at Coach Daniels to find that he's still staring at me, making my stomach twist with nausea. Forcing my eyes away from him, I focus on Principal Byrne, but I can hardly hear a word he's saying.

Coach always sets his sights on one or two senior students a year to have his way with, and I don't like the way he's looking at me.

The mere thought of him touching me makes me sick to the stomach, no matter how gorgeous he is.

Finally, Byrne wraps up the welcome back speech, and it feels like my skin is on fire. The entire time, Coach watched me like a dog staring at a bone. A shudder begins at the top of my spine at the thought of Coach Daniels propositioning me. He may be sinfully gorgeous, but there's no way in hell I'd let a man like him take my virginity.

Camilla hooks her arm with mine. "Come on, let's find Nat. She's got to be here somewhere."

I nod and glance one last time in Coach's direction to find his eyes are finally elsewhere as he speaks with the principal. Following Camilla, I try to forget the way Coach was looking at me. Perhaps it was a coincidence. Only time will tell.

We walk out of the hall and search the corridors, until finally we see Nat coming out of Nitkin's classroom.

"Nat!" Camilla shouts her name.

Her cheeks are flushed as she turns to face us.

"You missed the welcome back assembly. Where were you?" Camilla asks.

"Yeah, I text you."

Nat's throat bobs as she swallows. "Morales strikes again. He locked me in Nitkin's classroom."

Camilla balls her fists. "Bastard."

I shake my head. "What did he want this time?"

Nat's cheeks darken. "I honestly don't know, other than forcing me to miss the welcome back assembly."

Camilla frowns. "I didn't see him in it either."

Nat shrugs. "Maybe he slipped in late at the back?"

I don't believe what Nat is saying. There's something that she's leaving out from her story, but I don't question her. Nat can be ridiculously stubborn. If she doesn't want to tell us the full story, she won't.

"Fair enough." I check my rota. "We've all got gym first, right?"

Nat nods.

"Yeah," Camilla says, glancing at her watch. "And we're going to be late."

I stop in front of my locker next to Nat's, punching in the combination. "At least Coach is pretty chilled out about people being late."

We both grab our bags and then make a stop at Camilla's locker to get hers.

We are five minutes late for gym when we get to the

changing room and quickly get changed, rushing into the gym.

Coach notices us the moment we enter and crosses his arms. "Good of you to turn up, girls." His eyes land on me and they linger for too long, making a shiver skate down my spine. I don't know if I'm being paranoid, or if he's actually looking at me as I'm his next conquest, but he'll be disappointed if it's the latter. There's no way I'd sleep with that man.

"Adrianna, since there's an odd number of students, you'll be my partner today." He gestures to stand in front of him with the two tennis rackets in his hands. "Tennis this month. How do you like your chances?" The smirk on his face is irritating as I take my position, swiping a racket out of his hand.

He is without a doubt the cockiest person I have ever met. "I think they're pretty good, since I took tennis lessons from three years old." I snatch the racket from his hand. "You should be worried."

His eyes narrow. "Is that right?"

"Let's do this," I say, cracking my neck.

"Everyone gather around and see how it's done when I whoop Adrianna's ass."

Some of the students snicker at that, but I'm confident that Coach may be good at a lot of things, but he can't beat me at tennis. "We'll see."

"You serve first." He bats a tennis ball at me and I catch it with one hand.

"With pleasure."

I volley the ball in the air and serve it wide in his

service box, taking him by surprise with the speed, as he struggles to reach it, brow furrowing.

"15. Love," Elias calls, taking the role of score keeper. "Come on, Coach. You've got to do better than that."

I twirl my racket in my hands, smirking at him. "Yeah, at least hit it once."

His eyes narrow as I grab another ball and get ready to serve.

Throwing the ball in the air, I bring my racket down and slam it in the same place, but this time he reads my move and volleys it back. We send each other racing across the court back and forth, until finally he catches me out and I can't stretch to send it back, hitting the top of the net.

"15 all," Elias calls.

"Not bad, Vasquez." He claps his hands. "Right, all of you get playing."

I glare at Coach as we've always had a fierce rivalry since I'm the only one who can give him a run for his money in any sport or combat.

"Now, let's see what you've really got, Vasquez."

I twirl my racket in my hands. "Gladly."

We keep playing, matching each other point for point. Until finally, I steal the win in the first game.

"My turn to serve. Let's see how you fare not seving."

My eyes narrow as I watch him throwing the ball in the air repeatedly, but not serving. "Get on with it," I snap.

He smirks. "All in good time." On the next throw of the ball in the air, he brings his racket down and serves it at a ridiculous speed right at the back of my service box on the opposite side to where I'm standing.

I don't reach it despite using all of my strength to push myself over there. "Fuck," I murmur, quiet enough so he can't hear.

"15. Love," Coach calls out, twirling his racket in his hands.

I glare at him, knowing that it's going to be tough to beat him at tennis with him serving, particularly since he almost beat me on my serve.

The game continues on and I lose by a few points, giving us one game each, when the bell finally sounds.

"Time to wrap it up," Coach announces, never once taking his eyes off of me.

I shudder, as the way he's been looking at me since this year started makes my skin crawl. Coach's reputation with the girls at this school is disgusting, and I fear that the dirty looks he's been giving me suggest he has his sights on me this year.

There's no way in hell I'm losing my virginity to the biggest man whore at SA.

Forcing my eyes away from him, I gather my things and leave hastily into the changing room behind Natalya. "What have you got next?" I ask, trying to push the thoughts that Coach might be interested in me out of my mind.

"I've got law. What about you?" Nat asks.

"interrogation for me."

Nat nods. "Fair enough. I'll see you at lunch, then?" She says as she pulls on her blazer.

As always, Nat is the fastest dresser ever.

Camilla rocks up. "Aren't you going to wait for me?"

Nat arches a brow. "And be late for class?"

She pouts. "I'll be quick."

Nat and I both laugh at that. "You don't know the meaning of quick," I say.

"I'll wait for three minutes, but if you aren't ready, I'm leaving," Nat says.

For the first time, I witness Camilla dress fast. By the time I'm buttoning up my blouse, Camilla is too. "Wow you can move when you want to," I say.

She shrugs. "I'm always fast."

Nat and me exchange glances. "Yeah, right," Nat says.

I feel a sense of sadness sweep over me, knowing that this is our last year here together. I have to make the most of it, as I know my life is going to take a very different turn once I leave SA.

2

ARCHER

*T*he time of giving Adrianna suggestive looks is over, as I watch her as she walks across the gym hall in her too tight top and short skirt It's impossible to stem my desire for her. It's been just over five weeks since the semester started, and I can't wait any longer.

Adrianna Vasquez.

The girl I want this year more than any girl I've ever wanted in any other school year. Biding my time is finally over, as patience isn't my strong suit and she's ignored all of my subtle hints.

She's brilliant in every single way.

Beautiful beyond compare and the top of combat class, even better than any of the guys in the class. The only person she can't best is me.

After this lesson, I intend to make my proposition. I will have her in my bed sooner rather than later. However, there's a niggling doubt in the back of my mind that Adrianna might not be so easy to win over.

13

In past years the girls I've had affairs with have been eager and almost tempting me with their come fuck me eyes. Adrianna is as cold as ice, but I intend to melt that ice and turn her into flames of passionate desire that match my own by the time this year is out.

"Good afternoon, Seniors," I say, drawing the class's attention to me, including Adrianna. "And welcome back to combat class. Today, we will work on disarming techniques." I nod to the cabinet in the corner. "Everyone select an implement."

There's a rush, as there always is for the best weapons, Adrianna effortlessly getting there first and grabbing the ever popular long sword.

"Ms. Vasquez, come here and let me show everyone the moves we will be learning." Even before this year, nine times out of ten, Adrianna was the one I always picked for demonstrations.

Her jaw works as she stands in front of me, wielding the blunted long sword. "I am going to disarm Adrianna. Come at me with a jab and I'll take it from you."

A whisper of a smile graces her beautiful lips. "I'd like to see you try, Coach."

I ready my stance and watch her carefully, as if anyone in this class can best me it's Adrianna.

She swings her short sword around before lunging toward my left. It's an excellent move, but I see it coming and move to the left enough so that the sword swipes past me, giving me the chance to grab her wrist, bending it and forcing her to drop the weapon.

She grunts in frustration.

"That move there is one of the easiest yet least expected. Allow your opponent to think they're going to get you and then flip the table when you disarm them." I smirk at Adrianna. "Care to try again." I throw the short sword in the air and she catches it effortlessly.

"Definitley."

"Everyone in position and take turns to disarm your partner," I say, never once taking my eyes off of Adrianna. "Give me your best shot."

Adrianna's eyes narrow, and her grip tightens on the hilt of the sword. She watches me with such intensity that I can't help but imagine her looking at me like that from the flat of her back while I fuck her for the first time.

And then she moves forward gracefully, shifting her weight from one foot to the other and trying to make me guess which side she'll strike.

Her only give away is her eyes, which shift multiple time to my right, warning me before she makes the move.

I block it and twist her arm behind her back, forcing the blade out of her hand and pulling her close. "Nice try, but you give your intentions away with your eyes."

She grunts and pulls away from me. "Why don't you try, then?"

I throw the short sword in between my hands. "Gladly."

Her eyes narrow as she readies her stance, watching me carefully.

Everyone has tells and I know mine, but the key is to hide them as best you can.

Lunging forward, I fake leaning toward her right, but

shift my weight at the last minute, forcing Adrianna to correct herself suddenly.

Instead of striking her left, I bring the short sword right to her center, the tip resting against her throat.

"Nice try, Vasquez, but you're no match for me." The tip of the blunt sword teases against her skin as she glares at me.

And then she moves suddenly, knocking the sword upwards with force and taking me by surprise.

I lose grip of the sword and she swipes it from the air, spinning around as she grabs it and bringing it up at an impressive speed to my throat.

"You were saying?"

I smirk. "Nice work. This is exactly the initiative I want to see students showing in my class. Again."

Her eyes flash with determination as she returns the sword to my hand. The lesson continues in the same way, each of us winning a round until we're at a draw by the end of the class.

The bell sounds. "End of class. Everyone may leave. See you all on Thursday."

People grumble and pack their bags, as everyone loves combat training. It's refreshing to be a teacher of a subject students are genuinely passionate about.

My eyes land on my target and I move toward her as she packs some of her things into her bag.

"Adrianna, can I have a word with you?" I ask.

Her dark, chestnut brown eyes meet mine and it feels like fire shoots through my veins. "What about?"

The other students filter out of the gym into the

changing room, but Camilla lingers behind, waiting for Adrianna.

"Leave Morrone." I clench my jaw.

Camilla looks a little hesitant, lingering on the spot.

"It's an order." I glare at her, until finally she gives up and heads into the changing rooms.

Adrianna's nostrils flare and I sense she knows what's about to come, as the look she gives me could kill. Once all the students have left the gym, I move toward her, although she's staring at me with what I could only describe as hatred.

Setting her hands on her hips, she asks, "What do you need to speak to me about? I have torture next with Professor Niktin, so I can't be late."

I arch a brow. "Is that anyway to speak to one of your professors?"

She grunts and narrows her eyes. "No, but if I'm late, you know what happens."

I do indeed know what happens to students that are late for Gav's classes. "If you are late, I'll write a note."

Her jaw works. "So, what do you want to talk about?"

Adrianna already knows why I want to talk to her, as I've made it clear the way I've been looking at her and she knows my reputation. I move closer to her, the need to pull her against me driving me fucking insane.

Adrianna glares at me. "What do you want?" She crosses her arms over her chest, defensively.

"I want you," I murmur, reaching for her hip and trying to yank her against me.

17

"Over my dead body," she says, stepping back from me and putting distance between us.

Adrianna is going to be more of a challenge than my previous conquests, that's for sure. And I've always loved a challenge.

I arch a brow and step closer to her again. "I wouldn't be so dismissive."

She keeps stepping away until her back hits into the wall and she's got nowhere to go. Exactly how I want her, trapped and powerless.

"I'm warning you, if you come any closer I'll—"

"You'll what, Adrianna?" I slide my hands onto her hips and yank her against me. "Tell me what you'll do to me."

"This," she says and then slams her fist into my gut, knocking the wind out of me as I double over in pain. A move I should have seen coming if wasn't thinking with my dick.

Adrianna slips free from my grasp and darts around me at the speed of lightning, rushing to grab her bag off of the bench.

The fucked up truth is that her resistance is only making me want her more. "Fuck. Ms. Vasquez, that was uncalled for." I straighten up and turn to face her, striding over to the bench where she's packing her bag as quickly as she can. "Do you want me to give you detention with Nitkin after school today?"

She glares at me. "Uncalled for?! It was self-defense, for fuck's sake. Your behavior is uncalled for."

"Language, Adrianna." I arch a brow. "And what behavior is that?"

Her mouth falls open. "Coming onto me when you're my fucking coach."

I lick my bottom lip as she uses the same dirty word again. "What did I tell you about your filthy mouth?" I keep on closing the gap between us until I'm a foot away from her. "You know that you can't resist." I reach for her hip, but she sees it coming this time, darting out of my grasp.

"Stay away from me, Coach. I'll report you for harassment if you don't leave me alone."

I tilt my head, smirking at her. "Who are you going to report me to?"

Adrianna glares at me. "You may be friends with the principal, but if my father knew that you were trying to get in my pants, I'm sure things would change massively."

Her reluctance, I expected, but she's irritating me, threatening me with her father. "Is that right?" I move toward her and grab her throat, yanking her into me.

Adrianna's nostrils flare. "Let. Go. Of. Me."

I flex my fingers around her throat, enjoying the softness of her skin against my calloused fingers. She's delectable, and the rivalry we've shared over the years only adds to my desire to have her. The idea of Adrianna submitting to me is enough to drive me insane. "Listen to me, Adrianna. I don't take kindly to threats. And I'm not a man who backs down from what I want."

She glares at me hatefully. "I don't give a shit what you

want. There's no way in hell I'd ever get into bed with you."

I smirk. "Who said anything about a bed?"

Her jaw works. "I'd rather die than be another notch on your bedpost."

"We'll see how long you can keep up your resistance, baby girl."

Her eyes blaze with rage. "Don't call me that."

I tilt my head. "Why? Because it turns you on?"

She sighs heavily. "You are unbelievable."

Releasing her throat, I take a step back. Adrianna will not fold as easily as I expected, but forcing the issue may not be the right course of action with her. "I don't intend to give up, Adrianna."

"Well, you should, as there is nothing on this earth that could make me reconsider having sex with you." She shudders as if the idea makes her feel sick. "The man who takes my virginity will be my choice."

My eyebrows hitch upward. "Virginity?" Anger rising inside of me at the thought of any man taking her virginity except for me. "You've never been with a man?"

She glares at me. "No, and that's why there's no chance I'll ever sleep with you."

I'm surprised how unashamed she is of the fact she's never had sex, as a lot of girls get embarrassed about it. But Adrianna isn't like other girls.

"I think you'll eat your words, as I have every intention of being your first, baby girl."

She growls. "I said, don't call me that."

I smirk. "Go on, now, or you'll be late for Nitkin's class."

Her jaw works. "What about the note?"

"Fuck the note. You've got five minutes. I'm sure you can make it."

"Bastard," she grumbles under her breath.

"What was that?" I snap.

"Nothing." She shoulders her bag and then rushes into the changing rooms to get back into her SA uniform.

I watch her as her hips sway from side to side, my cock as hard as stone.

A virgin.

It's hard to believe such a beautiful, confident and sassy girl hasn't already been deflowered.

But I can't deny that I'm glad she's untouched, because it makes me even more determined to ensure I bury my cock inside of her by the time this year is through.

She'll be hooked on me the way I'm already hooked on her.

3

ADRIANNA

"*T*he man is a complete and utter pig," I finish, shaking my head as my blood is still boiling over Coach Daniel's attempt to get me into his bed.

"What are you going to do?" Nat asks.

She shrugs. "I'm going to keep telling him to fuck off."

I bite my bottom lip. "Not sure Archer takes rejection very well."

Camilla nods. "I heard he can make girls' lives a living hell if they reject him."

Red hot anger coils through my veins as I wonder if my friends seriously suggest that I should just lie down and spread my legs for a man whore because his ego is going to be hurt. Crossing my arms over my chest, I glare at them. "What are you saying? I'm not sleeping with him because he'll get angry about being rejected. He can fuck himself for all I care."

Nat nods. "Fair enough."

"He's hot, though. Don't you think?" Camilla asks.

Camilla is insane to even bring it up. He may be hot, but he's had so many students over the years it's disgusting. "Yes, and a complete and utter man whore. There's no way I'm giving my virginity to a man like him."

I'm surprised Nat doesn't back me up as she turns silent, gazing down at her bowl of pasta. The fact is Archer Daniels just wants to add me as another notch on his bedpost, and I won't be reduced to that. I've got too much self respect, unlike his past conquests.

"I'm going to the bathroom," Camilla announces, standing and walking out of the cafeteria, and my attention lands on Nat, who I think is hiding something about that kiss with Elias.

The boy who has spent years tormenting her. He was seen kissing her a few weeks ago, and now he's claiming that she's his. I've been thinking about what he said after that.

Perhaps you should stop lying to the people closest to you, or you might end up with no one.

I sense Elias has something over her and she doesn't want to tell us. It's all very odd. Elias' torment is taking on a new form this year.

"Are you sure you don't want to talk about it?" I give her a pointed look.

Nat clenches her jaw. "I told you, I don't." She grabs her garlic flatbread and stuffs it in her mouth. "Just drop it."

There is no way Nat will talk to me about it if she doesn't want to. "I know you well enough to know you

24

won't tell us if you don't want to. I just worry about you is all."

Nat forces a smile. "I know you do, and I love you for it." She squeezes my hand. "This is something I don't want to discuss."

I hold my other hand up in surrender, knowing when to call it quits. "Got it." I mime zipping my mouth shut to lighten the heavy mood. "I won't say another word about it."

"Thank you," Nat says, relief clear in her expression.

Camilla returns and sits down. "What did I miss?"

"Not a lot," I say, giving Nat a wink when Camilla isn't looking. "How's the pizza?" I ask, glancing at it. "I kind of wish I'd had that instead of the pasta. Maybe I'll get it as well."

Nat laughs.

Camilla shakes her head. "You eat more than any girl I know and yet you're so damn skinny."

I take offence to being called skinny, holding a hand against my chest. "I'm not skinny. I'm toned and athletic."

"Right, I agree. Skinny isn't the word to describe Adrianna's physique," Nat adds.

Camilla sets her hands on her hips, shaking her head. "Whatever. She's not curvy like me." She nods at Nat. "And you can't speak because you are just as slim."

It's amusing, as so many girls would kill to have Camilla's figure.

Nat shakes her head. "I've always envied your physique, Camilla. It's feminine and beautiful."

Camilla blushes. "You wouldn't say that if you had my hips."

"Everyone envies your shape. Stop being an idiot. We're all beautiful as we are in our own rights," I say, as the fact is we all have our unique qualities.

"Agreed," Nat says.

"What have you guys got next?" I ask, shoving my last spoon of pasta into my mouth and eyeing up Camilla's pizza. My stomach still rumbles a little.

"I've got a free period next. What about you?" Nat asks.

I smile. "Same."

Camilla groans. "Lucky for you, I've got extra math with professor Jameson as I'm lagging." She pulls a face. "The fact is, I'm shit at math, so why bother with extra tuition?"

I laugh, glancing at Nat, who seems to be in her own little world. "Do you want to go to the library to study?" I suggest.

"Sure," she says, nodding.

"Right after I grab some pizza."

Camilla and Nat laugh, rolling their eyes. My appetite is enormous, but I do a lot of sports to combat the effects. I jump to my feet and approach the food counter.

Anna, behind the counter, arches a brow. "More food?"

I nod. "Yeah, pizza please."

She laughs and dishes me up three slices. "To save you another trip up."

"Thanks." I take the plate and return to my friends,

who both arch their eyebrows when they see three slices on my plate.

"Did you get us one each?" Nat teases.

I shrug. "Anna dished up three and said she was saving me another trip up." I grab a slice and shove it into my mouth. "She knows me so well."

Camilla laughs. "Well, enjoy. I've got to get to math. I'll see you in anatomy after?" she says to Nat.

"See you then," Nat says.

"I'll see you guys at dinner, since I have a free afternoon."

Camilla frowns. "Lucky bitch."

I shrug. "Perks of taking torture."

Camilla shudders. "I wonder why we're even friends."

Smirking, I take another bite of pizza. "Because I'm the best."

She rolls her eyes and walks away. "See you losers later."

Nat glances at me. "What are you doing in the library?"

I shrug. "I've got a shit assignment for interrogation due in two days' time. I need to get it done."

Nat nods. "Fair enough. It's weird how we hardly have any classes together except the mandatory ones, isn't it?"

Nat and I are very different in our skill sets. She's smart, whereas I'm better physically. Torture, interrogation, assassination classes are all right up my ally, whereas Nat sticks to the brainier subjects like anatomy and Law.

"You've got the brains and I've got the brawn," I say.

She nods. "True."

"We'd make the perfect team." I wink.

Shaking her head, she nods toward the door out of the cafeteria. "Let's get going then."

I stare at my last piece of pizza. "I'm not finished."

Nat shakes her head. "Surely you don't have room for that piece?"

I smirk and pick it up, taking a bite.

She pretends to puke. "Honestly, watching you eat makes me full."

I roll my eyes. "That's impossible."

"Not sure it is impossible."

I stuff the last slice of pizza into my mouth and wash it down with a large gulp of water. "Okay, I'm ready. Let's go."

We grab our bags and head toward the exit of the cafeteria, only for Elias to block our way.

"Where do you think you are going?"

Nat glares at him. "The library."

"Yeah, get the fuck out of our way, Morales. Or I'll deck you."

He chuckles. "Not sure you can after your shitty performance against Daniels in class earlier."

I clench my fists. "What? You think you can do better?"

His cocky smirk drives me wild with anger. "Perhaps." He glances at Nat. "As always, you are a complete and utter nerd, spending your free periods in the library."

I grab Nat's arm and drag her around him. "Come on. We don't have time for bullies like him."

"That's right, run away," he calls after us.

"I hate that boy," I say.

Natalya just looks a little flustered, nodding in response. "Yeah."

Not looking where I was going, I barge straight into someone.

When I look up, it's Coach looking down at me. "You should really look where you are going, Adrianna."

I glare at him. "Perhaps you should too," I say.

He smirks. "Maybe I wanted to bump into you."

Nat shakes her head. "What the fuck?"

He narrows his eyes at her. "Keep your beak out of this, Gurin."

I glance at her and nod softly. "Don't worry. I can handle this. What do you want?"

"You know exactly what I want."

"And you know my answer and it hasn't changed since an hour ago."

His smirk widens. "It will."

"You need to be reported to the police for harassment," Nat says, glaring at Coach.

He chuckles. "While you are at it, we can report every damn student here because of their ties with organized crime." Stepping to one side, he pins me with his glare. "See you around, Vasquez."

I huff and link arms with Nat, pulling her away from him.

"Don't dream about me too much."

I grind my teeth, knowing he's trying to get a rise from me, but I ignore his comment.

"Way to go, being the bigger person," Nat says, shaking her head. "He really is a pig."

"I know," I say, shaking my head.

"Hot as hell, but a pig," she adds.

I glare at her. "It doesn't matter if he's the hottest man on this planet. He's an asshole. A misogynistic asshole."

"Admit it though. If you weren't a virgin, you'd sleep with him, right?" Nat asks.

"No fucking way."

Her eyes widen. "Really?"

I nod in response. "There's nothing on this earth that would get me to sleep with that man, virgin or not."

Nat's brow furrows. "Not going to lie. I would if I wasn't a virgin. He's gorgeous."

There's no denying that Coach is the embodiment of masculine beauty, but it changes nothing. The fact is he's slept with way too many girls at this school.

"I have standards."

Nat laughs. "Are you saying I don't?"

"You don't have standards if you would sleep with Coach knowing how many girls he's fucked at this school."

She opens the library door and lets me in first. "But his experience probably means he's amazing in bed." She lifts her brows comically.

I laugh. "You're crazy."

"I only speak the truth." She sits down in her usual seat at our usual table in the library, and we both get our work out of our bags.

"Thank God Camilla's not here. I can get nothing done with her yapping."

Nat nods. "Agreed. Let's get to work."

We both fall into a comfortable silence, working on our assignments, but I can't shake the issue with Coach, as I know it won't go away. He is about as stubborn as someone can get. I know that he'll hound me until the last day of the year, making my life a living hell, but there's no alternative.

I won't lie down like all the other girls and take his shit.

4

ARCHER

I stride into the staff room to find Elaine and Sophia chitchatting together at the back. They both fall silent as I walk in.

"Don't stop on my account."

Sophia blushes the moment my eyes land on her. The interrogation professor has had a crush on me ever since Oak employed her two years ago. She's attractive, but not my type. Although when I told Oak that, his response was that's because she's not eighteen.

The truth of it is that Sophia is going to be at this school permanently. Seniors come and go and therefore there're no strings attached, exactly how I like it.

"Morning, Archer," Elaine says, glaring at me over her spectacles. "Are you behaving yourself this year?"

"Behaving myself?" I ask, tilting my head. "Don't I always?"

She shakes her head. "No, you do not. I hope you

haven't set your eyes on another young and impressionable girl."

I have, although she's definitely not impressionable. Stubborn as a mule is the better description.

"Not sure what you're talking about."

Sophia looks a little disappointed as she swallows hard and looks away.

"Have you seen Gav?"

They both shake their heads. "No, he's not been here in the last half an hour."

I glance at my watch, as he's usually always on time. We're supposed to be going off campus to grab some dinner and drinks with Oak, who is meeting us at the restaurant.

"That's unusual."

"What is?" Sophia asks.

"For Gav to be late."

Her brow furrows. "Maybe he's been sent a student to discipline last minute?"

"Perhaps." I pull my cell phone out of my pocket and send him a message.

Gav has been a bit off lately, but I can't understand why exactly. As if the dark chaos he harbors inside is becoming impossible to control.

He worries me, especially since I know loosely the circumstances in which Oak found him.

I dial his number, and he picks up on the third tone. "What?" he barks.

"Where are you? We're going in to town to meet Oak for dinner."

There's some rustling on the other end. "Fuck, sorry. I lost track of time. I'll be there in a minute." He ends the call.

I tap my foot on the floor and glance over at Elaine and Sophia, who are both now staring at me. "Is there a problem?"

They both shake their heads. "No, we were just having a private conversation," Elaine says.

I cross my arms over my chest. "Are you suggesting I leave the communal staff room?"

Sophia bites the inside of her cheek. "No, Elaine wasn't saying that. It's just... how long will you be?"

I shake my head. "How long is a piece of fucking string? Gav is on his way."

They continue to stare at me, so I breathe out a deep breath. "Fine, I'll wait in the corridor." I shake my head. "Fucking ridiculous."

As I come out of the staff room, I bump straight into Adrianna.

Although this time she's alone.

"We keep bumping into each other, and that time I didn't plan it," I murmur, my hands firmly on her hips before she can move away.

"Coach, get your hands off of me."

I grind my teeth, my cock throbbing in my briefs as I look down at the beauty before me. "What's your problem, baby girl?"

She growls like the feisty tiger she is. "I told you not to call me that."

"And I told you I'll call you whatever the fuck I want."

Adrianna pushes against my chest, trying to get away. "This is becoming beyond creepy."

"And I think deep down you love the attention."

She pushes harder, freeing herself from me. "I think deep down I want to slit your fucking throat."

I laugh. "That's a little harsh, isn't it?"

"Do you not know who my family is? We're fucking insane, so stop messing with me or I'll set my brother and father on you."

"Oh, I'm quaking in my boots," I say sarcastically.

Adrianna doesn't have the guts to rat me out to her father, as she's too scared of him. At least, that's what I gleamed from my research into her and her family.

There's something off though about Adrianna and her relationship with her family, and I haven't finished digging. If I can find some dirt on her, I can use it against her.

"You should be. Don't come near me again." She spins around and storms down the corridor, hips swaying temptingly.

A part of me just wants to hunt her down like an animal and stake my claim now.

Adrianna Vasquez brings out the fucking caveman in me, but I have to play this smart.

"Hey, sorry," Gav says as he approaches from behind.

I turn to face him. "Don't sweat it. It's just odd for you to be late."

He nods, swallowing hard. "Right. Sorry."

From the look in his eyes, I can tell he's not in a good place. He hasn't been since the start of school five weeks ago.

Oak and I discussed it. We both think he needs to go back to see a shrink, as his punishments have been harsher since we returned.

"Is Oak meeting us there?" he asks.

I nod. "Yeah, who is driving?"

"Fuck driving. I've ordered us an Uber."

"Good shout." I clap him on the back.

His brow furrows as we walk toward the exit of SA. "Why were you standing outside the staff room?"

I roll my eyes. "Sophia and Elaine were having a private conversation. They practically kicked me out."

Gav laughs. "I wouldn't have taken that shit from those two."

"Yes, but you aren't me. And they wouldn't have dared try to kick you out. Everyone is too scared of you."

He cracks his knuckles. "Good."

Both of us are relatively quiet in the Uber to the diner, but once we get there, I can see Gav relax a little. He's always loved our weekly dinners here, as if they take his mind off of the sickness that plagues him, if only for a short time.

Gav is a sadist through and through. I don't know what exactly happened to him as a kid, but Oak reckons it was very dark and disturbing. No one can get him to open up about his life in Russia. He just says he doesn't remember.

Oak is already sitting at the table in the diner where we eat weekly, a beer in hand.

"You two are late," he says as we approach the table, eyes fixed on me.

BIANCA COLE

"Don't look at me." I glance at Gav. "I had to call Gav to find out where he was."

We sit in our usual seats, and the waitress, Jenny, comes over, batting her eyelids at me. "Hey Archer," she says, twirling her hair around her fingers.

I've flirted with her a lot and even got close to asking her out until Oak and Gav banned me from going anywhere near her. They don't want a reason not to come here, as they do the best ribs and burgers in town.

"Hey," I say, as she sets down three menus.

"I'll be back to take your orders in a minute." She twirls around and walks away, glancing over her shoulder at me.

I shake my head. "She doesn't want to quit, does she?"

Oak sighs. "It's your fault for flirting with her constantly."

Gav nods. "Yeah, that was always a bad idea."

I swallow hard and look at my menu, even though I already know I'm going to have the ribs. They are delicious.

"How's your week going?" Oak asks.

I run a hand across the back of my neck. "It's been okay." It would have been better if Adrianna hadn't refused my advances.

Gav clears his throat. "So, who is it this year?"

I glance at him, as I'm surprised they haven't asked me already, to be honest. "No one, yet," I lie, knowing that it is too embarrassing to admit that Adrianna isn't falling at my feet like the other girls.

38

If she continues to reject me, I know they'll tease me to no end.

Oak narrows his eyes. "We're five weeks in. You have always got your eye on someone by now."

Unfortunately, my friends know me too well.

"And I saw you getting close to Adrianna Vasquez when I met you earlier. Don't deny it."

Fuck.

I thought that he hadn't seen us together. "She was gone by the time you arrived."

He smirks. "But was she?"

"Vasquez?" Oak asks, shaking his head. "She doesn't seem like the type that would go for you."

I clench my jaw. "She's being reluctant at the moment. In what way isn't she my type?"

Gav chuckles. "She actually has a brain."

"Hey." I punch him in the shoulder. "I don't go for idiots."

He arches a brow. "You go for ditsy blondes, and Adrianna is basically the polar opposite."

"Bullshit. I go for girls that are beautiful and athletic, and Adrianna is both."

Oak laughs. "She's as stubborn as they come, though. So if she's resisting now, don't hold your breath that anything will change."

I narrow my eyes. "She may be stubborn, but so am I. I won't give up."

"Whatever, let's not talk about school or students," Gav says. "Did you see the game last night?"

Football. It's one of the few things that Gav and I

really have in common. We both follow the New York Giants.

"Of course. They were fucking exceptional."

Oak sighs. "I don't get why you two love football so much." He glares at Gav. "Especially you. I expect you to be into MMA or something."

Gav winks. "We all have guilty pleasures. Although I do like MMA as well, especially when it gets really bloody."

I shake my head. "You are sick in the head."

"And proud of it," Gav says, glancing around. "Where the fuck is Jenny? I need a drink."

One of the other ladies who doesn't normally serve us obviously hears Gav whining as she comes rushing to the table. "Apologies for the wait. What can I get you?"

"Whiskey neat and a full rack of ribs," he answers.

I nod. "I'll have the ribs too, but with a beer."

Oak clears his throat. "I'll have the burger and fries."

She nods. "Sure thing. Coming right up."

I rub my stomach. "I'm starving."

"When aren't you starving?" Oak asks, shaking his head. "You ate an entire plate of pasta for lunch, followed by three helpings of dessert. Where do you even put it all?"

I shrug. "I burn it off. That's what happens when you are active." My stomach grumbles. "See, starving."

Gav rolls his eyes. "You don't know what it is like to be truly starving."

"And you do?" I ask.

He nods, a dark look in his eyes. "Yes," he says simply.

I don't know what my friend went through to make him as fucking sadistic as he is, but it couldn't have been good. "Fair enough. I'm just hungry. It's a saying."

"One that is said far too flippantly."

Jenny comes over with our drinks.

"Thank fuck for that. We need to get drunk and liven this conversation up."

Oak shakes his head. "You know my plan is in motion now."

I sit up straighter at the mention of the sole reason Oak bought the academy. "Right. I forgot Eva had arrived, since she's not been in any of my classes." I run a hand across the back of my neck. "How is she doing after those bitches fucked her up?"

Oak's jaw clenches. "Fine. I'm taking advantage of the fact she's not going to gym or combat classes to use her to bring down her parents."

I nod. "All the boys are talking about how hot she is. Is she hot?"

Oak clenches his fists. "She's alright. I guess."

From the look in his eyes, he thinks she's more than alright, which would complicate his plans if he wanted her in that way.

"Anything like her asshole parents?" I ask.

He runs a hand through his hair. "Practically the opposite."

Gav frowns. "Don't tell me you're getting cold feet?"

Oak shakes his head. "Of course not. She's just not what I expected."

Gav's about to speak when Jenny comes over with two plates of ribs and a burger.

"Thank God, I'm sta—" I notice Gav glare at me. "So hungry."

She smiles as she sets my plate of ribs down in front of me. "Sorry we're very busy, but I hope you enjoy your ribs." Again, she gives me a look and I ignore it. Oddly, for the first time, I'm not even tempted by her flirting.

"Thanks." I pick up a rib and devour it, getting a disgusted look from Gav, as she hasn't even put his ribs in front of him yet and I'm already eating.

"What? I'm hungry."

He rolls his eyes as Jenny walks away, looking a little deflated at the lack of reciprocation. Despite knowing I couldn't go there, I've always been a little flirtatious, but I'm not feeling it today and I know the reason.

Adrianna Vasquez.

She's deep under my skin, and until I get her into my bed, I won't want anyone else.

5

ADRIANNA

*N*atalya's new friend, Eva, notices me in the library, where I'm trying to complete my interrogation assignment.

It's a little strange having a newbie in our group. And I can't help but feel like Nat is trying to replace Giorgia, which I don't like. Eva seems nice, if not a little judgmental about people like us, because she wants nothing to do with the world she was born into.

"Hey Adrianna, can I sit?" she asks.

I nod in response.

She smiles and takes a seat next to me. "This place is crazy. You know, I just witnessed a sword fight in the quad."

I arch a brow. "Your point is?"

Eva shakes her head. "I never knew a school like this existed, that's all." She runs a hand across the back of her neck. "How is it that they keep any governing body out of this place?"

"They don't," I reply, still skimming the book in front of me that I'm meant to be reading for interrogation class. "School inspections are carried out now and then. We have to attend normal classes and put on a show for the inspector."

"Really?" Eva's brow furrows. "How do they explain all the weapons in the gym?"

"They hide them." I play with the end of my hair. "You'll probably see what happens sometime this year. There's always at least a visit once a year."

Eva nods. "Fair enough." There's an awkward pause as she taps her fingers gently against the table. "It's really kind of you, Nat and Camilla, to befriend me."

I glance up. "I hate Jeanie. You know she used to be friends with Nat?"

Eva's eyes widen. "Really? What happened?"

I shut my book and sigh, knowing I won't get any work done now. "Elias Morales happened."

Her brow furrows.

"He arrived here in sixth grade and took an instant dislike to Nat." I think back to the time, remembering Nat was just one of the bitches that hang out with Jeanie and her crew. "She was as thick as thieves with Jeanie, but Elias was the hot new guy who everyone had a crush on. So, naturally Jeanie invited him to sit with them at lunch, and Elias insisted he wouldn't eat with them if Nat was there."

"He didn't even know her and made that judgment?" Eva confirms.

I nod. "Yeah, weird isn't it?"

"Very."

"So Jeanie, being the bitch she is, kicked Nat off their table and out of their friendship group."

Eva shakes her head. "I hate her."

"Something we have in common. So, I invited her to sit with us as we knew each other from class and the rest is history."

Eva smiles. "Best friends ever since?"

I nod. "Yeah, me, Nat, Camilla and Giorgia."

"Nat has mentioned Giorgia. Why did she leave?"

"None of us really know the full story, but her family live in Sicily and they pulled her out of school the end of last semester. It's weird not having her here." I put my pen down. "We think that they were freaked out by the war in Boston, since her father's boss, Fabio, has made a deal with Milo Mazzeo."

Eva looks confused. "I don't know who any of those people are."

I chuckle. "You must have been living under a rock. Are you sure your family is mafia?"

"Positive." Eva clears her throat. "But I've never had any interest in it."

I nod in response. "We're like the polar opposite."

Eva nods. "Yeah, I guess."

"I don't remember a time in my life that I wasn't involved in some kind of criminal activity, even as a kid."

"That must have been difficult. Not being able to just be a kid growing up?"

I think about it and I guess my family did force me to grow up early. I shrug. "Never really thought of it like that."

"Hey," Camilla says, approaching the table. "What are you two up to?"

I sigh. "I was trying to get an assignment done." Chucking my book into my bag, I sit up straighter. "But the likelihood of that happening with motormouth here is zero."

Camilla holds a hand to her chest. "I'm not a motormouth."

Eva laughs. "In the short time I've known you, I'd say you could take the prize for the amount you can talk."

She gasps. "I am offended." And then she takes a seat, leaning over the table. "Have you heard the news?"

"What news?" I ask.

"Nik and Rosa are officially over. I thought it would never happen."

I swallow hard, as for a while now Camilla has been harping on to me about how we'd make a cute couple. Nik isn't my type. He's attractive, but a complete asshole.

"The guy treated her like shit," I say.

Camilla nods. "Yeah, but only because she let him. He needs a stronger woman." She arches a brow suggestively.

"I've told you I'm not attracted to Nik."

Camilla sighs. "But you don't have a date for the winter formal. Nik would be perfect. Why don't you ask him?"

I grunt in frustration and turn my attention to Eva. "Has anyone asked you yet?"

Eva's cheeks flush a little. "Not yet. Do you think it's too late for anyone to ask?"

Camilla shakes her head. "Of course not. It's early to

be honest. Alek asked me last week though, but as friends." She purses her lips together. "I'm pretty sure he's gay, but too afraid to come out. After all, Elias is his best friend, and we all know he's not exactly kind."

"Are you going to go with him?" Eva asks.

She nods. "Yeah, I'd rather go with a friend who I know won't grope me inappropriately than some guy I don't even like."

"Makes sense," I say.

"Has anyone asked you, Adrianna?" Eva asks.

"No, thank God." I shake my head. "These dances aren't really my thing."

"Even though you are a fucking national salsa champion in Mexico." Camilla makes a frustrated sound. "If I had half the talent you do for dancing, I'd be on that dance floor as much as physically possible."

"Well, that's where you and me differ. I don't like to draw unwanted attention to myself."

"Wow, are you really champion?" Eva asks.

I nod. "Yes, five times."

Her eyes widen. "Impressive."

I don't comment on that, as it's just another achievement for my parents to tout about when they talk about me. It's all they care about, making sure I'm the best at everything, so that when they want to marry me off, they can brag about how amazing I am and secure the perfect match, not for me, but for them.

"I don't really want to talk about it." I stand, intending to leave, as I'm not in the mood right now for dealing with Camilla's overly happy attitude. "I've got to get going."

Camilla checks her watch. "The next class doesn't start for twenty minutes."

"I have some things to get from my dorm room."

Camilla stands. "Okay, I'll come with."

I shake my head. "No. I want to go on my own."

Her eyes widen. "Alright, we'll see you at dinner later, then?"

I nod and shoulder my rucksack before walking away without a word. I know that it's not their fault that I'm in a bad mood. It's Coach Daniel's fault. He won't stop trying to get me into his bed practically every single time I see him, and it's already tiresome.

If he's going to keep this up for the rest of the year, I'll probably end up murdering him.

SOMEONE KNOCKS on my door and I go to open it, frowning when I see Natalya standing there in a dress, looking ready for a night out. "What's up?"

"We're going out," she says.

It's not often that Nat wants to go anywhere. "Where?"

"Town," she says, barging her way into my room. "Camilla wanted to get ready in here."

Camilla clears her throat. "Town with Elias Morales and his group of asshole friends, she forgot to mention." She throws her dress on my bed and strips out of her joggers and shirt.

"And why the fuck are we going out with them?"

48

Camilla rolls her eyes. "Don't even go there. Just pick a dress and let's party."

Elias Morales is a fucking asshole and I don't really want to go out with him, but the idea of getting off campus for a few hours and having a few drinks is appealing.

I walk into my closet to get a dress, selecting a red mid-length dress with a low neckline. As I walk out of my closet, I see Camilla is already dressed, which has to be some kind of record for her. She's wearing a stunning lilac max dress with a high neckline, which makes me rethink my revealing choice.

"Wow, you look gorgeous," Nat says.

I nod. "Doesn't she always?"

Camilla shakes her head. "You two are just being nice."

"Nope, if I was dude I'd definitely fuck you," Nat says.

Camilla laughs. "Don't be an ass, Nat." She notices my dress. "Let's see then. What are you going to wear?"

Camilla wolf-whistles the moment I hold it up. "Now, that is hot as fuck."

I roll my eyes. "I haven't even put it on yet." Sliding my sweatshirt off, I get undressed. Before slipping the dress on and turning to Nat when I realize it zips up from the back. "Can you zip it up?"

She nods and zips me up and I walk into the bathroom to check it out since Camilla is hogging the dressing-table mirror. The dress looks good and I'm not afraid to admit it.

I grab my makeup and put some on, not a lot, as I prefer not to go out caked in it. Once I'm finished, I head back into the bedroom and sit next to Nat. "How long do you think she'll be?"

"I can hear you, you know?" Camilla says.

"God knows. We might be waiting for days," Nat says, winking.

Camilla grumbles something under her breath but continues working on her makeup.

"So why are we going out with Elias, exactly?" I ask,

Nat's jaw clenches. "Because he can get us out and I wanted a night on the town, that's all."

I'm very good at knowing when anyone lies to me, but Nat has tells that are unmissable. For example, she always clenches her jaw when she's about to lie. "I see, well who else is going?"

Nat shrugs. "Not too sure."

"Are we going to get Eva?"

"Of course," Nat says, as if it's a given that Eva is a part of the group now. I guess she is, but I still can't shake the feeling that Nat is trying to replace Giorgia.

"I miss Giorgia," I say.

Nat's expression turns solemn. "So do I. Have you heard from her at all?"

I shake my head. "No, not since the start of summer break. You?"

Nat shakes her head and we both fall silent.

After at least thirty minutes, Camilla says, "Ready." Standing and grabbing her clutch.

"At last, now we just need to get Eva ready." She glares at Camilla. "Let's hope she doesn't take as long as you."

There's no way in hell Eva is going to be alright with going out with the three girls that stabbed her on her first night here. "She isn't going to want to go out with the three bitches."

"None of us do, but we won't tell her they're coming," Nat says.

Camilla makes a tutting sound. "So devious at times, Nat."

All she does is smile and nod toward the door. "Come on, or we'll be late."

Eva will be pissed when she finds out Jeanie and her minions are coming, but it's inevitable when going out with Elias. They're always with him.

We walk down the corridor, and I can't deny that despite the company we're going out with, I'm thankful to get off campus for a few hours. Far away from Coach Daniels.

6

ARCHER

"Is this really the best place for us to grab a drink?" Gav asks. As always, he's his usual grumpy self.

Oak nods. "It's a little loud."

I shake my head. "Sorry grandpa, but this is the hottest place in town."

"In case you forgot, we're professors at a nearby school, not frat boys," Oak says.

I laugh. "Both of you need to lighten up." I shake my head and make my way toward the bar. "It's not like we'll run into any of our students." A lie if ever I told one. The sole reason I brought my two best friends here is because I know a group of academy kids are coming here tonight. I also know that Adrianna should be with them.

"Usual?" I ask Oak.

"Yeah, whiskey, neat."

"Never can change it up, can you?"

Oak looks irritated. "Why should I? I like whiskey."

I order our drinks and get cash out to pay, but Oak stops me. "Put it on a tab." He passes the bartender his credit card.

My brow furrows. "Why didn't you let me pay?"

He arches a brow. "You know I'm loaded. And I know what you earn, considering I pay your wages."

Gav clears his throat. "Lets find a booth, preferably somewhere we don't have to shout to hear each other,"

Oak spots one. "Over there."

Gav leads the way, literally bombarding through students as if he's wading through a jungle and pushing aside overgrowth.

"Agreed," I hear Oak say as I get to the table.

"What did you agree to?" I ask, sitting on the opposite side of the booth.

"That this is the last time you choose where we go for a night out." Oak glares at me.

"Both of you need to chill." The only reason I chose this shithole is because of a certain Mexican beauty who is somewhere here right now, but I've yet to spot her.

Oak is looking contemplative, even though he's here to unwind. "Hey, you are here to unwind and not think." I clap him on the shoulder. "Stop thinking about the Carmichael girl!"

"Eva?" Gav asks, sound surprised. Oops, turns out it wasn't common knowledge that Oak has the hots for the girl he wanted to ruin to get revenge on her parents.

"Yeah, it seems the girl I intend to ruin to get to her parents is irresistible," Oak replies.

Gav laughs. "She's cute, for sure, but I wouldn't have expected her to be your type."

Oak's eyes darken as he straightens. "And what exactly do you think my type would be?"

Gav rubs the back of his neck. "Older than twenty-one." He glances at Archer. "Clearly, my two closest friends are perverts."

I hold a hand to my chest. "How dare you?"

"It's true."

"Are you telling me you've never found a student attractive?" Oak questions.

Gav takes a little too long to reply, making me think that he has found a student attractive. "No, they're all too young, too immature."

"I thought that too," Oak mutters.

"Has anything happened between you two?" I ask.

Oak's Adam's apple bobs as he swallows. "I kissed her in my office."

Gav basically chokes on his vodka, but I'm not surprised. Oak has had it bad for her since the moment she stepped onto campus.

"You did what?" Gav shakes his head. "I thought you want to ruin her family. How does that work if you ruin yourself as well?"

"Hence why I called off all of our one-on-one discipline classes and chucked her out of my office," he replies.

"Sounds like you did one thing right," Gav says.

Gav is wrong in my opinion. If you are that drawn to

someone, then fuck rules and appearances. I'm not so sure, actually.

"It's clear that you like her, so why don't you just be the one to ruin her reputation?" I tilt my head to the side slightly, wondering if what I'm about to say could be true. "Or is it because you actually care for her?"

"Perhaps." He shrugs. "I'm not sure. All I know is she's not what I expected. She's not a spoiled mafia princess." He inhales deeply. "She's nothing like them."

"Are you forgetting what her parents took from you?" Gavril asks. The anger in his tone is clear as day.

Oak knocks back the rest of his whiskey, slamming the glass down. "Enough of this. I agreed to come out because I want to forget about it, not talk about it." I wave a server over and she takes my order for another round. "Let's get drunk and forget about the Carmichaels."

Gav doesn't let up, watching Oak over the rim of his glass.

I nod, downing my drink. "Here, here." I smile at Oak. "Let's get drunk."

Finally, Gav relaxes. "Sounds good to me." He polishes off the rest of his vodka, just as the next round arrives.

Oak stops the server before she leaves. "Keep them coming, every twenty minutes, and put them on my tab." He hands her a fifty-dollar bill.

Oak is loaded because of the insurance pay out on the fire at his company's premises. I glance around the bar, trying to find any signs of the students.

"I'm going to dance," I say, hoping I'll get a better

view from the dancefloor.

"Have fun," Gav says, sarcastic as ever.

I move onto the dancefloor and instantly a girl makes eyes at me. Being that I would look like a fucking fool out here alone, I move toward her. "Care to dance?" I ask, even though I have no interest in her what so ever. She's attractive, but ever since I set my sights on Adrianna, no other girl will do.

"Definitely," she says.

I pull her onto the floor and her arms wrap around the back of my neck. Her eyes alight with desire that I can't match, but I have to pretend to be into her just to keep dancing.

As I spin her around, I keep looking out for Miss Vasquez and come up empty handed. If they don't turn up as expected, I'm not sure I can stop myself marching into her dorm and barging into her room. I need to see her.

While I'm distracted, the girl I'm dancing with yanks me down and slams her lips into mine. I'm stunned for a moment by the suddenness of it, and it feels so oddly wrong that it's not Adrianna's lips.

Someone taps me on the shoulder. "Arch."

I break away, thankful for Oak's intrusion. "What?"

"We have students at the bar who Gav and I are going to join and torment." At last. Who would have thought it'd be Oak to see them first? "Wondered if you wanted to tag along?"

"Where?" I ask, finding it hard to believe that I've missed them after all my searching.

"In the back. About fourteen of them." Oak tilts his head to the left. "Do you want to join us or not?"

No wonder I didn't see them if they're at the back of this place. I glance at the blonde girl, who's looking rather irritated by the interruption. "Sure." I peel myself out of her arms. "Sorry, sweetheart. Maybe another time." I give her a wink and follow Oak back to our table.

Gav's fist are clenched. "Ready?" he asks Oak.

Oak nods. "Follow my lead."

The three of us walk toward the back and the table where the students are. At first, I don't see Adrianna and all my hope deflates. Until some guy who had been standing by the table moves and it feels like my world slows to a halt.

A mix of fierce desire and intense possessive rage hit me all at once. The dress she's wearing is as sexy as sin. It's a hot red, which matches her red-hot attitude and the neckline plunges way too low to be appropriate. She's sitting at the table with a bunch of adolescent boys dressed like that, and she shouldn't be seen like that by anyone but me.

Elias notices us first.

Oak clears his throat. "I didn't realize all of you had clearance to leave the grounds." There's a lethal calmness in his voice. "Who gave you permission?"

I kick Alek off his stool, sitting down. All the while, my eyes are pinned to Adrianna in that hot as hell dress.

"I did." Elias lifts his chin. The cocky son of a bitch. "After all, we're eighteen years old. We can do what the fuck we want."

Oak arches a brow. "That may be so, but you are all too young to legally be here."

Elias laughs. "Who the fuck gives a shit about legal? The academy is all about teaching everything that isn't legal."

A few of the students laugh, and I must admit he has a point. The law means nothing at SA. "Can't argue with that," I say. "How about we join you?"

"If you think you can handle it, old man," Rizzo says.

Old man. It's a pathetic attempt to wind me up. "You know I could kick your ass even after sinking two bottles of scotch, Rizzo."

Rizzo laughs, sliding a bottle of vodka over to me. "Help yourself."

I'm not going to say no to that, grabbing the bottle and pouring some into my now empty glass.

The waitress who Oak asked to keep the drinks coming approaches, placing a hand on his shoulder. She whispers something to him before placing a glass of whiskey in his hand.

Oak leans toward her and whispers something, giving her another fifty dollar bill. She nods and winks before heading off to get more drinks.

"So, how the fuck did you lot sneak off campus?" Oak asks.

Elias, as always, is the only one to speak up. "I'm afraid if we told you that, professor, we'd have to kill you." What I would do to smack that fucking smirk right off his face?

Now and then, I glance at Adrianna, who is glaring at

59

me hatefully. Ever since my first attempt to get her into bed, she's icier than the fucking Antarctic.

"I'd like to see you try, Elias," Oak replies. "A few have tried, none have succeeded."

"Yeah right, old man."

Adrianna's nostrils flare as I refuse to let up, staring at her like a hungry animal staring at a steak it's about to devour. She will be mine, one way or another.

"Dimitry," Oak barks, forcing me to break my gaze.

His eyes widen. "What?"

"Did you forget what happened the last time you whispered something inappropriate to Miss Carmichael?"

I smirk as it's clear Dimitry is trying to get into Eva's pants, which Oak won't like one bit.

"I haven't said anything that Eva doesn't want to hear," Dimitry says, glancing at Eva. "Have I Eva?"

There's a tension in the air, one you could cut with a knife. Eva stands. "I need to get some air."

Dimitry says something to her, but she shakes her head and rushes away.

Oak's eyes track her as she moves through the room. And within thirty seconds, he's up and following her. The man has lost his shit over that girl. It's inconsequential when I sleep with a student, but Oak is the principal. He's the man in charge, so it's risky getting close to her, especially considering the truth about his past with her parents.

I focus all of my attention back on Adrianna, knowing that there's nothing I can do to stop Oak. He's a big boy and has to work out this shit for himself. Her cheeks are flushed a pretty pink as she glares back at me, never once backing down.

"Relax, all of you. We're just here to have a good time, too." I can't take my eyes off of Adrianna. "How are you doing, Miss Vasquez?"

"Fine," she grits out, her nostrils flaring. "At least I was fine until you arrived."

I arch a brow. "That's not a very nice thing to say to your coach, is it?"

She glares at me with a fire that turns me harder than stone.

I groan, as all I want is to have her beneath me all night long and show her what she's been missing.

Gav claps his hands. "As fun as this has been, I'm not all together comfortable drinking with underage kids in a bar. Now, all of you need to head back to the academy."

I stand, knowing I'm not letting him cut this short for me. "Ah, cool it Gav. Let the kids have some fun." I wink at Adrianna. "Care to dance?"

As expected, she shakes her head. "No, thank you."

"Arch, you can't be serious. Where the fuck is Oak?" Gav asks.

I shrug. "Fuck knows. I don't care." Knowing he's probably getting stuck in to the student he was supposed to be forgetting about tonight, since they're both missing. "Dance with me, just once."

Adrianna sighs in frustration before taking my hand, sparks shooting through my veins the moment our skin touches. I will have her, one way or another.

7

ADRIANNA

*M*y skin crawls as I take Coach Daniel's hand. It was give in or have him badgering me the entire night. He wants me to dance with him for one dance. I guess I can make it through that, even if it makes me want to puke.

"So, Adrianna. Am I finally wearing you down?"

I grind my teeth. "Not a chance in hell."

He chuckles and yanks me against his chest. "I'll wear you down eventually, baby girl."

"Don't call me that," I snap as he spins me around and then yanks me against his chest.

"Or what, Vasquez? Are you going to test out your combat training on me here in the middle of the dancefloor?"

I sway my hips to the beat, remembering my salsa training that my mother enrolled me in when I was five years old. "Perhaps."

His nostrils flare as he spins me away. "You're a good dancer."

"Did you expect anything else?" I ask, as he brings me back toward him.

"No." He tilts his head. "It seems you're good at everything." His eyes narrow. "But everyone has a weakness and I intend to find yours."

I swallow hard at the threat in his tone. I don't have a weakness as such, but I do have secrets. I don't want him to find out, or anyone, for that matter.

My way out of the shithole of a life my parents have planned for me after graduation, which involves betraying my own family. It could all go wrong if anyone gets in the way.

"I don't have a weakness."

He smiles, and it's a smile that sends butterflies beating around in the pit of my stomach. "You're a very bad liar, Adrianna." The way he says my name almost sounds dirty and under the influence of three glasses of wine, I'm ashamed to say that my body is heating at the look in his eyes.

There's no denying that Archer Daniels is beautiful. God like in his appearance. Tall and muscular, but not too bulky, with dark brown eyes that look richer than chocolate.

He pulls me close again to the music, swaying us to the beat. "I can see the desire in your eyes, no matter how hard you try to resist."

"You are wrong," I lie.

"I'm never wrong. Haven't you figured that out yet?"

"What I have figured out is you're an arrogant asshole."

He spins me around, never once faltering from my barrage of insults. "I hear you don't have a date for the winter formal."

I narrow my eyes. "Where did you hear that?"

Coach shrugs. "Around. Is it because you are hoping to go with me, baby girl?"

I grunt in frustration. "No, I don't want to go with anyone, and the staff can't go to it, anyway. You're a chaperone, for fuck's sake."

He pulls me close again. "I am going to dance with you the night of the winter formal."

"You can't make me dance with you."

He arches a brow. "Maybe I can."

I hate this man so much and every encounter with him makes me dislike him more. It's hard to believe that someone can be so cocky in the face of constant rejection.

"Come on," he says, grabbing my hand as the music stops.

"Where are we going?" I demand, as he drags me through the crowd.

"You'll see."

I don't trust this man as far as I can throw him, and since he's probably about two hundred and twenty pounds of pure muscle, that wouldn't be very far. So I try to retrieve my hand from his grasp, but he holds it tight.

"Ouch, you are hurting me," I call out.

"Then don't try to escape."

I sigh heavily as he leads me out the back of the club toward a staircase. "Isn't this like off limits?"

He glances back at me, his eyes glimmering with mischief. "Yes, but that's never stopped me before."

We walk up the stairs and into a plush room with a wall made of glass on one side, which slides back to reveal a huge suspended pool overlooking Winby town center.

It's fancy for the town and I would have never known it was up here.

"Wow."

"Fancy a dip?"

I shake my head. "I don't have a swimsuit."

His eyes flash. "Neither do I."

I swallow hard as I realize he's talking about skinny dipping. "No way am I going in there naked."

He clears his throat. "Then your underwear will suffice, no?"

I glance at the crystal clear water, wishing it didn't look so inviting. "Surely you can get in serious trouble for this."

His eyes dance with delight. "Live a little, Vasquez."

It's a challenge if ever I've heard one, and one of my biggest flaws is I can't turn down a challenge.

"Fine," I say, struggling to unzip my dress at the back, but manging to get it down enough to wriggle out and drop it to the floor. "Last one in is a chicken." I rush toward the outside, intending to bomb into the water, when a pair of strong arms lift me off my feet.

"I'm afraid that's not fair, since I'm not even undressed yet."

My entire body sets on fire as I feel the hardness of his cock pressing against my barely clad ass. "Fine, I'll wait."

"Good girl," he purrs into my ear.

And then I hear his belt drop to the floor as he steps out of his pants. And then I assume he's taking his shirt off, but I don't look. I fear if I do, I might back out of this entirely.

Only once have I seen Coach without his top after a hot summer's day gym session when he got covered in sweat.

His body is beyond amazing and I don't want to think about that right now, not when I'm only in my bra and thong.

"Ready, on three."

My breathing turns deeper as he counts and then I rush forward on the count of three, knowing that I have speed covered. He's too muscular to get the speed up.

I bomb into the pool first, smirking in satisfaction at winning as I hear him enter the pool after.

And then his arms wrap around me before I can get up to the surface. "It's a cool night. Best to keep close and keep each other warm," he murmurs into my ear.

"Please let go of me." I hate the way my voice sounds, vulnerable and unsure.

I feel the hard press of his cock against my ass. "Why? Am I making you wet?"

"I'm already wet. I'm in a swimming pool."

He licks my earlobe. "You know what I mean."

I break free from him and swim to the other side,

unable to answer that question, because the fact is he is making me wet.

My body is reacting physically to him in a way I wish it wasn't, but there's no denying biology.

The man is beautiful and I'm a virgin who gets turned on way too easily.

Once I get to the other side and come up for air, I turn around to find him a few feet away from me.

And my entire body turns to jelly at the sight of the moonlight casting a glow over the rivulets of water cascading down his muscular chest with one large tattoo stretching across it. And my heart stutters at the sight of his hard cock tightly outlined in his wet briefs.

"Like what you see?" he asks, eyes dipping to my chest.

I glance down to see my bra is now entirely see-through so that he can see my nipples.

Quickly, I fold my arms over my chest, but he's quicker still. Before I can fully cover up, he has both my arms.

"Don't," he growls, looking almost feral now. "I want to see you. All of you."

"Coach, I—"

"Silence," he says, eyes ablaze with a desire that could melt me. And then his hands are on my hips and he's drawing my skimpily clad body against his, obliterating any common sense from my mind.

His hard, muscular chest pressed against me and his thick cock protruding against my abdomen, making my pussy ache with need, even though I don't want this man. At least, I didn't think I did, but it's almost impossible to believe that when his warm body is against mine, turning me into jelly.

He reaches up for my face and cups it almost tenderly, forcing me to meet his gaze. "You are trembling, baby girl."

I'm so far gone that the nickname doesn't even bother me. Hell, it makes me even more desperate for the man in front of me, as ashamed as I am to admit it.

"It's cold," I lie.

He smiles softly. "You are good at many things, Adrianna, but lying isn't your forte."

I beg to differ, but don't want to brag about it, since I've been lying to my family successfully for two years now. "It is cold."

His grip tightens. "Then come closer and I'll keep you warm."

I shake my head. "You are insane." However, I don't pull away when he drags me near, my body overruling my mind at that moment.

He dips his head and I still don't move away, allowing him to bring his lips to mine. At first he's tentative, just a soft brush of skin against skin, but when I don't fight, he pulls me harder against him and his tongue pushes against my lips, demanding entrance.

In my inebriated state, I let him in and instantly moan as he strokes his tongue against mine, sending a heatwave right to my core. I lace my fingers in his dark, soft hair as he devours me.

All the while, my mind repeats over and over. It's just a kiss. It means nothing. Although I doubt he will agree.

Kissing Coach will make him believe that there's a chance I'll have sex with him, and that will not happen.

Finally, that thought knocks some sense into me as I pull away, shaking my head. "What the fuck are you doing?"

He smirks. "What am I doing? You're the one that grabbed my hair, Adrianna. Don't act like you didn't enjoy it."

I grunt in frustration and dive into the water, swimming away from him toward the steps at the far end as fast as I can.

When I get to the steps, I'm glad to find that he isn't chasing me. Instead, he watches me in silence as I get out of the water and grab a towel.

The likelihood of getting dry and dressed before he gets out of the pool is slim, but I still try hard.

"You can't just run away like that," he says, closer to me than I'd like him to be.

I pull my dress on and zip it up as far as I can. "You're getting on my nerves, coach."

His hand wraps around my wrist and he yanks me into him, piercing chestnut eyes glaring at me. "Listen to me, baby girl. You can't go around kissing a man like that one minute and then turning cold the next."

I tilt my head. "A kiss means nothing."

His jaw works. "Not in my books." And then, before I can register what he's doing, his lips are on mine again. His huge, rough hands groping my ass as he pulls me tightly against him.

He's still soaking wet, making my clothes wet as his

tongue thrusts into my mouth, turning me into red-hot cinders. The passion is enough to make me explode and I wish I didn't enjoy it so much.

Forcing myself to my senses, I break away from him and turn around. "Stop this. I don't want you and never will." I rush out of the room as fast as I can, my heart pounding frantically.

Coach Daniels is insane the way he keeps pursuing me, but that kiss made me think, what the hell?

A dangerous thought indeed, as he's the last man I want to lose my virginity to. That teaches me to never go anywhere with Coach when I'm drunk.

8

ARCHER

I've been dreading this night, mainly because I know Adrianna will probably dance with other guys to piss me off.

There's no denying the chemistry between us, especially after we kissed in the pool on the rooftop of that bar. She was into it as she pulled me closer, kissing me back like her life depended on it.

And then she broke away and fled the scene as if nothing happened, leaving me with blue balls.

"Hey, are you ready?" Gav asks, clapping me on the shoulder. His eyes roam down my suit. "Looking very sharp tonight. Trying to impress someone?"

I narrow my eyes. "Don't be an asshole, Gav."

He chuckles. "Still having trouble with Vasquez?"

"I'll get her to break, believe me."

Gav's brow arches. "That's the kind of thing I'd say, not you."

I shrug. "Adrianna drives me crazy."

"Careful with girls like that. It's best to steer clear of any girl that you want that badly."

Gav sounds like he's speaking from experience, but I doubt it. In the years I've known him, he's never once had a girlfriend. At least, not that I've known of. I'm not entirely sure he's capable of having a normal relationship.

"I know what I'm doing," I say, as I turn around to grab my flask off the counter. "Hope you came prepared." I hold the flask up.

He arches a brow and then reaches into his inside jacket pocket for his. "Of course. They don't serve hard enough alcohol at this thing for me."

I nod, as all that is on offer is watered down wine and beer, as well as a very weak punch. Oak reckons allowing alcohol to be consumed actually makes the students less likely to get drunk.

"Let's go then." I clap him on the shoulder as I slip my flask into my pocket.

The other reason I've been dreading this night is that it marks the last night before winter break. Tomorrow she'll leave for Mexico, and I'll stay here, wishing I could be close to her.

No matter how much I'd love to have a break in Mexico, I don't want my brains blown out for trying to get in her pants. Her family is about as crazy as they come, which isn't hard to believe considering how tough Adrianna is.

We walk through the corridors, which are buzzing with students rushing toward the grand hall in excitement.

It's the same every year. The three older years get to go to the winter formal, and the main excitement isn't for the dance, but the after party down at the old ruins.

Oak isn't aware of it, but I am. I've been down there a few times with seniors I've been sleeping with.

This year, however, I don't have a senior to go with.

"Keep your wits about you," Gav says, as we walk into the hall. "Anyone spiking the punch will get a royal beating."

I shake my head. "I bet you can't wait for that."

He grins at me. And it's entirely evil. "No, I can't."

I roll my eyes. "Sometimes I wonder why we're even friends."

His eyes narrow. "Believe me, the feeling is entirely mutual."

"Whatever," I say, walking over to the far side where I spot Sophia. "I'm going to mingle."

Gav just grunts in response and reaches into his jacket pocket for his flask. As always, he can't keep off the alcohol.

"Hey Sophia, how's it going?" I ask.

Her cheeks blush pink as she meets my gaze. "Okay, at the moment. No incidents to report."

I nod. "No one had a fight yet, then?"

She shakes her head. "No, but it's inevitable at some point. I don't think I've chaperoned one of these dances where there hasn't been a fight."

"No, I think you might be right. Have you seen Oak around?"

Her brow furrows. "Now you mention it, no. That's odd, isn't it?"

I shrug. "He might be running a little late. After all, half the students aren't even here yet. Shall I grab us some drinks?" I notice she's not got one yet.

"That would be great, thank you."

"What's your poison?"

"I'll have a white wine."

"Okay, coming right up." I spin around and march toward the bar, determined not to sit around moping over Adrianna.

I don't know if she's coming here with a date or not, but if she is, then blood might be spilt tonight.

Adrianna belongs to me this year, even if she's resisting it at the moment.

After that kiss, I'm confident that she finds me attractive.

"Hey, Arch. What can I get you?" David, the games keeper, asks.

"One beer and one white wine, please."

He nods and pours the crappy wine and beer into paper cups. "There you go."

I take the cups. "Thanks."

As I turn around, I almost spill them when I see Adrianna step through the entrance. She's alone, thankfully, and wearing the most exquisite emerald green evening gown that makes her tanned skin look richer.

Her long dark brown hair is curled, which makes a difference from the dead straight way she normally wears it. And she's wearing subtle make-up that highlights her natural beauty. It's the second time I've ever seen Adrianna wear makeup, the first was last week at that bar.

Gav approaches. "You're staring."

I can't take my eyes off of her. "Can you blame me?"

"You look like a lovesick puppy. Pull yourself together." His serious tone breaks me out of my daze as I glance at him.

"Don't be such an asshole."

"Seriously, Arch. What's with the Vasquez girl? Why don't you pick someone else? Someone easier."

I clench my jaw and glare at him. "Are you suggesting that I normally only want easy girls?"

"No, I'm asking if she's worth all the hassle?"

The answer is certain in my mind that Vasquez is indeed worth all this hassle and so much more.

I want her so badly it's become an obsession. She is on my mind day and fucking night. And seeing her looking like this only makes my desire for her deepen.

If she is meeting a date here, then I can't be sure that I won't be the one starting the fight tonight. Adrianna belongs to me, even if she denies it. After the kiss we shared, I know she feels this connection, too.

Hernandez approaches her, the creep getting too close to her for my liking. Thankfully, he gets too close for Adrianna too as she moves away, looking uncomfortable.

"Seriously, Arch. You're being very obvious." He clears his throat. "Don't you need to deliver that wine to someone?"

I glance down, remembering that I'd gone to get a drink for Sophia. "Fuck, yeah I do." I search the crowd for her and see she's now chatting to Oak, who must have snuck in. "See you soon."

Gav grunts in response and pulls his flask out, taking a long swig. The guy is a borderline alcoholic with the amount he drinks.

Sophia is lingering on the other side of the hall with Elaine.

I approach her. "Sorry it took so long," I say, passing her the wine, which is hardly worth drinking. It's so watered down.

"Thanks," she says, smiling.

Elaine clears her throat. "I'm surprised you're even drinking the alcohol here." She gives me a point glance. "Don't you and Gavril normally bring your own?"

I pull my flask out of my pocket. "Of course."

She shakes her head. "Let me guess, whiskey?"

"What else?" I ask.

Elaine holds her paper cup toward me. "Share some?"

I grit my teeth, as I've got a feeling I'm going to need the entire contents of the flask this evening. "Fine." I pour a small amount of whiskey into her cup.

"Thank you." She holds it up and then downs my whiskey.

"You're welcome." I glance around the hall, searching for Adrianna, but don't see her. "Now, if you'll excuse me."

Sophia looks disappointed, but nods. "Of course. See you later."

I walk the perimeter of the hall, searching for that

emerald dress and the beauty in it, but can't see her. Until a swish of green catches my eye and I see her on the dance floor with Nik Kushev.

My fists clench as his hand is way too low on her back. It's almost on her ass. And no one should touch her ass but me.

The music is provocative, and rage bubbles inside of me as I make my way over to them. Adrianna notices me and tightens her grasp on Nik's hand and she whispers something into his ear.

Nik's hand dips lower and I'm about ready to murder him. When Gav steps into my path and places his hands on my shoulders. "Pull it together, Arch. We can't have you killing a student at the winter formal."

"Get out of my way, Gav."

"I won't let you act like a fucking fool. You're chaperoning this dance. Stop acting like a student."

I draw in a deep breath to calm my rage, as I don't feel like having a fist fight with Gav. We both know I'd lose. The guy is insane. "Fine." I turn around and march off the dance floor, Gav close behind.

"You've lost your mind over this girl, haven't you?" He says.

I shake my head. "No, I get pissed off when I see someone touching what is mine. Especially a weasel like Nik Kushev."

Gav gives me a stern glare. "Sort it out or I'll set Oak on you next."

My brow furrows. "Where the hell is Oak?"

"He's around somewhere. I saw him when you went to the bar."

I sigh heavily, unable to tear my eyes off of Adrianna, who is still dancing with Nik. Gav heads off in the opposite direction and I move closer to where Adrianna is dancing, ready to swoop in the moment she stops dancing with that Russian bastard.

Finally, Nik bows out and leaves her alone on the side of the dance floor, offering me the perfect opportunity to get her alone. I walk toward her from behind, knowing that if she saw me coming, she'd probably find a way to avoid me.

Once I'm a foot behind her, I place my hands on her hips and lean in to her ear. "You look beautiful, baby girl."

She stiffens the moment she hears my voice, spinning around to face me. "You shouldn't sneak up on people like that."

I step closer to her. "I'll do whatever I want, Vasquez. Now dance with me." I place my hand in front of her and she just glares at me.

"No."

"I don't enjoy hearing that word."

Her jaw clenches. "Well, get used to it because you will hear it a lot from me." She spins to walk away, but I capture her wrist and pull her back against me.

"You need to dance with at least one man who knows what the fuck he's doing."

Her nostrils flare. "I don't need to do anything." She tears her hand from my grasp and crosses the dance floor at speed, heading for the exit of the hall, which is a big mistake.

I follow her, possessive rage boiling inside of me as I chase her like a wolf starving for his next meal.

She glances over her shoulder, eyes widening when she sees I'm following her.

I smirk, as a darkness I didn't even know I harbored inside of me comes to the surface.

Adrianna escapes into the corridor and I follow her, my heart pounding erratically in my chest. It's as if her refusing me has made me primal and possessive in a way I've never been before over a woman.

Once we're in the corridor, alone, she spins on me. "Just leave me alone, Coach. How many times do I have to tell you I'm not interested?"

I don't say a word as I walk toward her, forcing her to take steps backward until she's against the wall. The moment her back hits the solid surface, her eyes widen and I can see her eyes dart to the side as she considers her escape, but I won't allow it. Instead, I cage her in with both of my hand either side of her.

I won't let her get away so easily. It's my last chance before winter break to obliterate the barrier between us.

9

ADRIANNA

*C*oach's musky scent invades my senses as he boxes me against the wall, placing his hands either side of me so that I can't get away. "Call me Archer," he finally says.

I glare at him. "No, thanks." I push his hand away and step to one side to walk around him, but he moves into my path. "Get out of my way, Coach."

Instead, he grabs my wrist and drags me out of the corridor into an empty classroom.

"What are you doing?" I ask, trying to get away from him.

"Adrianna, this hard to get act is getting tiresome," he says, making me angry.

"Are you fucking serious?" I place my hands on my hips. "It's not a hard to get act. It's simply the fact that I don't want you and never will."

"Liar," he growls, stalking toward me. Suddenly, his

palm is wrapped around my throat. "You want me as much as I want you."

Panic hits me as I struggle to draw in enough oxygen, glaring at the man who has been pursuing me the entire first term. I reach my fingers up to his and pry them away. "Get the fuck away from me."

"Never," he growls, pushing me against the wall with his hands on my hips.

"Do you not know the meaning of consent?"

He bares his teeth like an animal and then sinks them into my shoulder enough to sting. "I don't give a shit about it, to be honest," he murmurs, dragging his lips across my shoulder and up my neck. "Because I know your panties are drenched whenever I touch you, baby girl."

Again, I wish I hadn't drunk a single alcoholic drink tonight, as I feel that heat spread from my core through my veins. "That's not true."

He smirks a cruel, vindictive smile that sets my nerves on edge. "I think I'll just verify that for myself." His hand moves under the hem of my dress and I stiffen, shocked that he would go this far.

"Don't you dare," I say, remaining still as his fingers get closer to my panties.

Coach doesn't stop as his hands inch ever closer and then dip beneath the fabric.

I draw in a sharp breath as his fingers thrusts into my soaking wet core.

"Just as I thought. You're soaking wet and desperate for my cock to fill you up." He pushes his finger deeper, and I can hardly think past the desire coursing through my veins. No man has ever touched me like this, and I hate how good it feels.

"Get off of me," I say, but it's halfhearted at best.

Instead, he pushes his fingers deeper inside of me before thrusting them in and out of me. "You don't really want me to stop."

I clench my fists by my side. "If I tell you to stop, then that's what I want." Rage overwhelms desire as I bring my fist up and slam it into his chest, forcing him backward. His fingers also forced out of me.

"There's no need for violence." He appears undeterred as he steps closer again. "Do as you are told or I'll have to give you a month's detention."

"Fuck you," I say.

"Two months, then."

I narrow my eyes. "Detention for what? Not fucking you?"

"Yes," he says, grabbing my hips again, pulling me against his hard, muscular body.

I have to crane my neck to look up at him.

"I want you," he says, eyes alight with a fire that threatens to burn me. "And I always get what I want."

"Well, I'm as stubborn as a mule, so good luck." I hold his gaze, even though I know he expects me to cower. "I don't want you and I never do anything I don't want to do."

Instead of backing away, he brings his lips a mere inch from mine. My breath hitches in my throat and the memories of that kiss at the bar in town floods me with heat. My lips part despite myself, and I shudder in anticipation. "I don't believe you," he murmurs, delight flashing in his eyes. "I think you want this as badly as I do."

I can't speak as I stare at him, waiting for him to kiss me, despite telling myself that's not what I want. Deep down, I do want him to kiss me again.

His fingers slide into my hair and he powerfully yanks my lips to his, kissing me passionately. His tongue searching my mouth with a desperation I can hardly understand.

Why does he want me so badly?

The girl that doesn't fit his type in any way whatsoever. I'm tough and smart and he always goes for blonde idiots who will throw themselves at him.

I moan as the kiss deepens, feeling the hard length of him against my stomach. And I can't help myself as I lace my fingers in his hair and draw him closer. He tightens his grasp on me, and I know that despite wanting to hate him, right now all I feel if desire so acute it threatens to tear me apart.

How many times do I have to refuse him for him to get the hint?

I fear that there's no number. He will keep going for as long as it takes. Archer Daniels wants my virginity and he won't stop until he has it. That thought makes me tense as I try to pull away, but he won't let go of me, clawing into my hips and deepening the kiss like a desperate drug addict.

I nip his lip hard enough to draw blood, finally breaking free.

"Fuck." He brings his finger to his lip. "What was that for?"

"I told you no." I place my hands on my hips.

He steps closer and then he wraps his hand around my throat, pushing me against the wall behind. "Were you telling me no when you grabbed my hair and pulled me closer?"

Heat travels all through my body, making me certain I'm blushing. "A momentary blip."

"You are lying to me and yourself." His fingers flex around my throat harder, making my heart pound erratically in my chest. "No woman kisses a man like that if she doesn't want him. Our chemistry is undeniable and in the end, the need will become too impossible to ignore." He kisses my neck while keeping his palm against my throat. "I'll wear you down until you are begging me to fuck you. Until you are begging me to make you come over and over again."

"It will never happen," I say, but for the first time, I'm less certain about what I'm saying.

He kisses lower, his lips brushing over my collarbone and sending a shiver down my spine. "We will see," he murmurs.

I gasp as his lips press against my cleavage, kissing me in such an intimate place. And then he pulls the top of my dress down forcefully, making me regret picking an off the shoulder design, as I'm not wearing a bra. My breasts are completely bare and on display to him.

"What the fuck?" I try to pull it up, but he releases my

throat and grabs each of my wrists in a hand, pinning them against the wall.

"No fighting," he murmurs, before dipping his head and sucking one of my nipples before dragging his tongue around it teasingly.

"Fuck," I breathe, unable to think straight.

"What was that?" He chuckles. "Are you enjoying yourself?"

I glare at him. "No."

He moves over to the other nipple, staring at me as he clasps his lips around it and sucks hard.

I can't hold his gaze as I shut my eyes, a zap of desire racing between my thighs as I clasp them together. "Oh God," I breathe.

He takes his time as he licks and sucks at my sensitive nipples. The first man to touch them. And all that embarrassment of being so exposed is gone as he turns me into a mess of desire.

Suddenly, he thrusts fingers inside of me. I didn't even notice he had let go of one of my hands, as he groans. My pussy tightens around them as it becomes almost too much to bear. It feels so damn good, even though I try to tell myself I don't want this.

"So fucking wet, baby girl," he says, dark eyes looking up at me in awe.

I wish I had a come back, but I don't. Instead, I let my head fall back against the wall as he fingers me. If I thought it couldn't get any better, suddenly his lips close around my clit.

My eyes widen as I look down to see his head between

my thighs, and realize he's no longer holding either of my wrists. Instead of pulling away, I lace my hands in his hair and let him drive me higher.

"Fuck, Coach," I groan.

He stops and smiles up at me, looking utterly beautiful with my arousal glistening around his mouth. "Call me Archer." And then he's back between my thighs, licking and sucking me.

"I've never felt like this," I stutter, my body shuddering from the intensity of what he's doing to me.

He doesn't say a word, just continues to watch me from his knees as he devours me like a starving animal.

I can hardly support my own weight as I feel myself getting closer and closer to the edge.

He continues to lavish his attention on my clit and then thrusts three fingers inside of me, the sensation unlike anything I've ever felt.

"Oh my God," I cry out, tightening my grasp in his hair.

He growls against my center, sending a vibration through my entire body. "You taste so fucking sweet, baby girl." His eyes are dilated as he stares at me, his fingers slamming in and out of me in the most perfect rhythm, playing me like an instrument.

"Coach, I'm going to come," I warn, unable to believe that he's about to finger me to climax in a classroom just down the hall from the winter formal. All of this is insane, and mostly because I told myself I wouldn't give in to him.

Shifting a little so I can see him better, I notice that he

has his cock out and is stroking himself. My entire body grows hotter than I believed possible the moment I see his huge, hard cock jutting out between his thighs.

"Fuck, Adrianna. I wish you were about to come all over my cock," he groans, fisting himself harder. "I'm going to come for you too, baby."

I moan, unable to control anything anymore as I fall into his trap, watching his cock as if mesmerized by it. In my state of heightened arousal, the thought of this man fucking me makes my orgasm hit me harder and faster.

"Oh, God, yes!" I cry out, clamping my eyes shut as the sensation is too intense and overwhelming. Every muscle in my body quivers as I struggle to keep myself upright, my knees buckling.

Archer supports me, holding me up. "Look at me. I want you to watch while I come for you."

Despite everything, I open my eyes, because deep down I want to watch. Hell, I think I want him to fuck me, even though I know how many girls he's been with.

"Good girl," he praises.

I should hate hearing that, but it only heightens the pleasure. My eyes remain fixed on his cock as I watch him stroke it with force.

"This should have been buried deep in your pretty little cunt," he grunts, and then he releases rope after rope of thick, white cum all over the floor.

For one insane second, the idea of him coming inside of me drives me wild with need, even though I've just climaxed.

"I want to fuck you so bad," he groans, still stroking himself until every drop is released.

The proclamation snaps me back to reality as I clench my jaw. "Well, that's never going to happen." I manage to escape from him, lifting the hem of my skirt down and pulling my dress back over my breasts.

A deep growl comes from behind me and I turn to find him standing, his huge cock jutting out of his pants. He doesn't even bother to hide it. "You can't come like that for me and then say you don't want me. It's bullshit and we both know it."

I narrow my eyes. "You forced me against a wall and basically did all of that against my will." This guy is unbelievable for thinking that I wanted what happened between us.

He tilts his head. "Adrianna, you and I both know that if you really wanted to get out of my hold, you could have."

I stare at him, realizing that he's right. If I'd wanted to get out of his hold, I could have. Hell, I've done it a hundred times in combat class. And that's when the horror dawns. That perhaps deep down, I wanted what just happened.

He smirks. "You have nothing to say, do you?" The smug bastard walks over to me and kisses me softly. "See you in two weeks," he says.

I glare at him. "This changes nothing. I mean it, Coach."

He kisses me again and I taste my arousal on his lips, hating that it only turns me on again. "I told you to call me Archer." With that, he walks out of the classroom, leaving me feeling aroused and ashamed at the same time.

I think it's the first time that I've been thankful to be going home. Tomorrow can't come quick enough.

10

ARCHER

I sit in my apartment with my head in my hands, unable to believe what I just did. Killed someone.

Despite my past being linked to crime, I've never murdered anyone. Instinct took over, and I had to save Oak. He's my closest friend and I couldn't watch him be brought down by the very person who fucked him over all those years ago.

"Whiskey?" Oak asks, walking toward me with a tumbler in his hand.

I take it gratefully and down the contents. "I might need an entire bottle."

Oak sets a hand on my shoulder. "You'll be okay."

I look him in the eye. "I killed a woman."

"Yes, but she was about to kill me and tear Eva away." His jaw clenches. "I'll owe you forever. There's nothing I could do to repay you."

I arch a brow. "You owe me? I don't fucking think so. I'd be dead if you hadn't taken me in."

"Not sure that's true," Oak says, running a hand across the back of his neck. "You have a way of surviving. I think you'd have found a way."

When Oak recruited me, I was on the run from my family from Dublin who knew I'd fled to America. Oak gave me a place off the radar where I could lay low, and since then there's been no word of my family getting close to finding me. I'd always been talented with accents and quickly adopted an American lilt, which has become second nature by now, and changed my second name from Monroe to Daniels.

"How is Eva?" I still can't quite believe that Oak has fallen for the girl he planned to ruin. It's ironic really. And the shit will hit the fan when people return the start of next week and Oak announces that he's married a student, but he doesn't seem worried.

"She's shaken, but doing better than you'd expect." He runs a hand through his hair. "It might not surprise you, but she was never close with her mother."

I nod in response. Until a couple of hours ago, all I could think about is the start of next week in four days and Adrianna's return to school, but now my mind is a mess. All I can think about is the way Eva Carmichael's mother's eyes went wide as the bullet went right through her forehead and then the blood... There was so much blood.

"Try not to think about it," Oak says, reading my mind.

"Easier said than done."

"Do you want to come over to the cottage for dinner?"

I swallow hard. "I can't face going in there right now."

Oak nods. "Right. How about we go out for dinner? You, me, and Eva."

I shake my head. "It's your wedding night. I'm fine here." I stand and nod toward the door. "Go to your wife."

Oak looks skeptical, but relents. "Fine, but if you need anything you call me, alright?"

"Of course." As if I'd call my best friend on his wedding night. I'm more likely to call anyone else. Gav should be returning tomorrow, as he's been away for the winter break, God knows where. He rarely disappears for the breaks, but every now and then he does, but won't say where he goes.

Oak leaves and I grab my bottle of scotch off the dresser in my living room and drink it from the bottle. I grab my cell phone and bring up Adrianna's number, which I've refrained from using the first week and a half of winter break. My finger hovers over her name and I wonder whether to call her.

I bite the bullet and hit the button, my heart pounding erratically in my chest. The dial tone sounds and I hold my breath, wondering if she'll pick up from an unknown number.

"Hello," Adrianna says on the other end.

The sound of her voice soothes me. "Hey, baby girl."

A whoosh of air escapes her lungs and I hear it down the phone. "How the fuck did you get my number?"

"School records," I say.

"Right. Why the hell are you calling me?"

I hate how vulnerable I feel right now and wonder the same thing. "I had a pretty shitty day and wanted to talk to you."

There's a few moments of silence on the other end. "What happened?"

I bite my lip. "I can't actually tell you, not yet anyway." I sigh. "You'll learn more when you return from winter beak in a few days' time."

Adrianna is silent for a few beats more. "So, what do you want to talk about?" Her voice is calm and there's no animosity in it right now.

"I don't know. Can you distract me?"

"Distract you with what?" she asks.

"What have you been doing over winter break?" I ask.

She releases a deep exhale. "Not a lot. As always, I hate being home."

"Really?" It's hard to believe that Adrianna could hate being in Mexico. "I thought it would be nice to get some warmth and sun after freezing for months here in Maine."

"Right, the sun and warmth are good, but my family aren't."

I nod in response. "I know all about difficult families."

"You do?" she asks, sounding surprised.

I swallow hard, knowing that no matter who Adrianna is, I can't tell her about my past. No one knows who I'm running from or my real last name, which is Monroe. The Monroe clan run Dublin and after what I did, they've had a price on my head for years. It doesn't matter how long I am gone, they'll never stop looking.

"Yeah, but I can't get into that."

Adrianna makes an exasperated sound. "Is there anything you can get into?"

"Your panties," I joke.

She makes a frustrated sound. "Don't be an asshole or I'll just hang up."

"Be honest, how often have you thought about our little session in that classroom?" I ask, my cock hardening as I remember how well she came for me.

There's a few moments of silence. "I may have thought about it a few times, but that's because you are the first man to touch me like that. No other reason."

I chuckle. "What are you wearing right now?" I ask.

Adrianna is silent. "Pajamas. I am having an early night."

"Any underwear?" I rub a hand over my increasingly hard cock.

"No," she says.

"Good." I slide my hand into my joggers and pull my cock out, tugging on it. "Touch yourself for me."

"Are you insane?" She asks.

"No, my cock is hard right now and I'm stroking it for you. Do you want to see?"

Silence follows for a few painfully long seconds before she breathes the word I want to hear, "Yes."

I put her on loud speaker and take a photo of my cock, which is now as hard as steel. And then I send it to her.

I hear the beeps on the other end and then the gasp as she opens up the file, followed by a soft moan. "Do you like that, baby?"

I hear her swallow. "Yes," she says, her breathing laboring.

"Are you touching yourself like a good girl?"

"Yes, and it feels so good."

I groan and tighten my grasp on my shaft. "Send me a picture."

Adrianna hesitates for a second. "Okay, one moment."

I can hear her fumbling around on the phone, and then the snap of her camera. My cock is throbbing in anticipation as I wait for her photo. It appears that getting her into that classroom and making her come has increased her willingness to play this game with me. Which means once she's back on campus, I'm going to take her virginity.

"Sent," she says, sounding almost embarrassed.

My phone dings and I open the video message, my cock pulsing at the sight of Adrianna completely fucking naked. She's taken the photo so that I can see her beautiful breasts, stomach and her fingers thrusting into her tight little cunt.

"Oh fuck," I groan, quickening my thrusts. "I wish my cock was between those perfect fucking thighs of yours.

She moans.

"I'd fuck you all damn night and make you come so many times you wouldn't even remember your own name."

"That's not going to happen still, just so you know."

I smirk, as it's going to happen one way or another. Adrianna has more in common with me than she might think. She's betrayed her family and I know it. I had a PI follow her in Mexico, and he found out some rather damning information about her. If she won't get into my bed willingly, she will to keep this information buried.

"You can tell yourself that, baby, but you are already addicted to this." I send another photo, but this time with my shirt pulled up so she can see my abs.

Her moan tells me all I need to know.

"You like that, don't you?"

She groans. "Maybe."

"Tell me how wet you are right now," I demand.

"Soaking wet," she says.

"Show me. Take a photo of your fingers."

She fumbles again and then I hear the snap before my phone beeps.

I almost shoot my load at the sight of her fingers glistening with arousal. "Fuck, you are soaking wet."

"I told you I was," she says, her voice breathless.

Perhaps she feels less touchable over the phone, but she's being infinitely more willing than she's been before I made her come. Hopefully, I won't have to use the information I have against her if this is anything to go by.

"I want you to make your pretty little cunt come for me, baby girl," I say, fisting myself harder. "Imagine how good it would feel if I was buried deep inside of you right now, fucking you hard and fast and quenching that ache that you feel right now."

"Who says I feel an ache?" she asks, sounding a little defiant again.

"I know you do. I know you are gagging for my cock."

She moans again and I can hear her fingers making a wet sound as they plunge in and out of her pussy.

"Fuck, I can hear how wet you are." My release is rushing at me fast. "I want you to come for me. Can you do that, baby girl?"

"Fuck, yes." Her breathing becomes more rapid, warning me she's close. "Oh God, Archer."

Hearing her say my name like that drives me crazy. "That's right, baby girl. Come for me. I want you to soak your bedsheets for me while I shoot every drop of my cum over my abs."

She screams then, but it's muffled by something. Perhaps a pillow, as she doesn't want people to hear.

"Such a good girl," I praise as my release hits me, and I come over my abs. My cock still throbbing. "I want you to send me a photo of the mess you've made."

The sound of her taking a photo follows and then it dings, and I open it up, groaning at the wet patch on her bedsheets. "Fuck, you are so perfect, Adrianna."

I take a photo of my cum splattered abs and send it to her. "I should have bred that perfect little cunt with my seed."

She moans again at my dirty talk. "You are filthy, Coach."

"And you love it."

"I meant what I said. This changes nothing. I won't be having sex with you."

I chuckle. "Believe me, you will."

She grunts in frustration. "No."

"See you in four days, Vasquez." I end the call, but quickly the elation of having her so willing for me eases and reality comes rushing back in.

I killed Angela Carmichael, the wife of a fucking mafia leader. It's insane, and it's impossible to wipe those bloody images from my mind. Desperately, I try to cling onto the conversation with Adrianna, but I know it's not enough.

Instead, I take a long swig of whiskey, knowing that I'll finish the bottle and it still won't be enough to erase the images from my mind. Only time will do that.

11

ADRIANNA

*M*y plane touches down on American soil one day early. Eva asked me, Nat, and Camilla to come back a day early from winter break, as she has some important news to tell us.

Stupidly, I've been sexting Coach ever since our phone sex three days ago. It might have given him the wrong idea, but I've been bored as hell at home, locked in my castle. Not to mention, my family drive me insane.

Father has been listing off people he's considering marrying me to at the end of the year, all of them complete and utter psychopaths from South American organizations.

He even mentioned Inácio Matos, the leader of the largest crime syndicate in Rio de Janeiro. The guy makes my father look like a puppy. He's that insane.

Yet again, more proof that my family value me no more than cattle to be sent to the slaughter. It only affirms my decision to betray them as a way out. Come graduation day, I'm going to disappear and they'll never find me.

I turn my phone back on and as soon as it connects to the network, it dings. Archer's name appears on the screen.

Archer: I hear you are coming back early. You should pay my apartment a visit tonight.

Fuck.

He thinks that because I've been so into the sexting; I want to have sex with him. The thing is, it's fun messing about, but losing my virginity to a man that has had more students than I can count on two hands would be gross. I respect myself too much for that.

I type a response to him.

Me: It was fun messing around on the phone, but nothing has changed. I won't become another conquest of yours.

I send it, dreading the smarmy response I'll get back. Archer is too cocky for his own good. He may be gorgeous and completely ripped, but he's also a man whore.

I get up as the doors to the jet open, grabbing my handbag and descending the steps onto the runway.

"Shall I take your bag, miss?" The driver, Kevin, asks.

I shake my head. "No, it's fine, thanks."

My cell phone beeps as I'm getting into the back of the armored Jeep. I get settled in and then search for my cell, dreading the response.

Archer: We will see about that.

It's a rather brief and almost threatening response. I swallow hard and tuck the phone back into my bag, resting my head back against the headrest. It's going to be a long two semesters if Coach insists on pursuing me, especially since I can't stop thinking about how good it felt when he made me come in that classroom, or his dirty words while we were on the phone.

There's no doubt he knows what he's doing, but I need to remind myself of the reason, because he can't keep it in his pants.

The journey from the private airstrip is about forty-five minutes, but it feels like forever. Finally, I see the gates to SA and the driver turns in, driving up the long, sweeping driveway to the imposing building. Normally, I can't wait to get back here after being home, but right now, I feel torn.

I text our group chat to let them know I'm here.

Me: Just pulling up. See you guys in a minute.

Kevin stops the car in front of the entrance and gets out, opening my door. "I'll take your bags to your dorm for you. Is there anything else you need?" he asks.

I shake my head. "No, that's all. Thanks Kevin."

He nods. "Don't mention it."

My phone dings.

Eva: Come to my room. You are first here.

Eva has responded and I groan as although I do like Eva, I don't really like being on my own with her. I don't know why. It seems compared to Nat and Camilla, we just don't click the same.

Dragging my heels, I head toward the dorms and Eva's room. I pause for a few moments outside her door, reconsidering going in there. And then the door opens before I do.

"I thought I heard you. Why are you lingering in the corridor?"

I shrug. "Sorry, I'm a bit tired and was considering going to have a nap first." I twirl a strand of my hair around my finger. "What's this news?"

Eva purses her lips. "I can't really say until the others get here. Do you know what time they're supposed to arrive?"

I glance at my watch. "Camilla said about midday, so soon. Nat said she'd try to be here mid-afternoon, I think."

Eva nods. "Okay, what do you want to do in the meantime?"

"How about a movie in my room? I'm tired and that doesn't take much energy."

"Sounds good. I'll get some snacks together and come over in a minute."

I return to my room, where Kevin has left my bags. My brow furrows as I see a gift on the top of them. Walking over to it, I check the card.

A little aid for our texting sessions x

I swallow hard and open the box, gasping when I see the large dildo inside and some other sex toy that I can't identify. It's flared at the base. My stomach churns as Archer is insane if he thinks I'm keeping sexting him while I'm here at the academy.

The distance made it feel less real, but I won't be doing it while I'll be seeing him on almost a daily basis.

Quickly, I take the gift into my closet and hide it at the back, as there's no way I want anyone seeing what Coach sent me.

Eva knocks on the door and I rush to open it, to find it's not Eva. Archer is standing there in the doorway.

"What the fuck are you doing here?"

He smirks. "I saw your car drive up and thought I'd come and say hi." He glances past me. "Did you get your gift?"

"Archer, fuck off. Eva is going to be here any minute."

He tilts his head. "That's no way to speak to your coach, is it?"

I clench my jaw. "Seriously. Get out of here."

"Not until I get a kiss."

I grind my teeth together, knowing that this is partially my fault. Leading him on with the texting was foolish and now I'm dealing with the consequences. "No. I told you that I'm not interested."

Just like in the classroom the night of winter formal, he doesn't listen. Instead, he lunges forward and grabs me by the throat, pulling my lips against his in a harsh, violent kiss that steals the air from my lungs.

Archer is just like all the men I've been around all my life. He takes what he wants. Consequences be damned, even if I don't want it.

I bite his lip, which results in a grunt from him.

"You can bite me all you want, baby girl. I'm not going to stop," he murmurs, kissing me quickly again before turning around and walking down the corridor.

My heart is hammering at a thousand miles an hour as

I watch him walk away, thankful that he left before Eva made it over. That would have been highly awkward, as the last thing I want is my friends to know that I let that creep get to me the way he has.

The door at the other end of the corridor swings open and Eva comes marching through with bags of snacks, brow furrowing when she sees me standing half in the corridor.

"Everything alright?" she asks as she approaches.

I nod. "Yeah, just had my bag dropped off," I lie, nodding to the bags just past the doorway.

"Fair enough. I've got snacks." She holds the bags up. "I think there's enough to feed your immense appetite."

I laugh at that, some of the tension easing. "Possibly," I say, looking at the bags, which are stuffed full of chips and candy. "Although if Camilla arrives soon, we'll be in trouble." I nod at the door. "Come on in."

I slump down on the sofa, and Eva makes herself at home next to me.

"So no clue as to why we've come back a day early?"

Eva purses her lips. "I just really want to tell you all together."

I nod. "Fair enough. I can wait, but don't expect Camilla to be so understanding. She'll badger you constantly until Nat gets here."

Eva sighs. "I can imagine she will."

"What movie do you want to watch?" I ask.

"Whatever, I'm not bothered."

My brow furrows. "How come you never pitch in on what you want to watch? You must have a preference?"

Eva sits up a little straighter, her cheeks flushing a bit. "If I'm honest, the kind of movies you guys watch aren't really my thing."

"Chick flicks?" I confirm.

She nods.

"Thank God, because they're not mine either. What movies do you like?"

"I generally love a good thriller. Something with lots of suspense."

"Have you watched Gone Girl?" I ask.

She shakes her head. "No, but I've heard it's good. I want to see it."

"It's amazing. That's what we are watching," I say.

"Sounds good to me."

I select the film on the TV and play it, settling in with a bag of potato chips. And suddenly I feel a little more at ease with Eva. It turns out we have one thing in common, our love for a good thriller. I've got nothing against chick flicks now and again, but they don't exactly have much substance.

After half an hour of the movie, my phone dings and I check it.

"Camilla is here. Shall I tell her we're in my room?"

Eva purses her lips. "She's going to ruin the movie, isn't she?"

I laugh. "Yeah, but we can watch the rest another time?"

She looks disappointed, but nods. "I guess. I'm already really into it."

"I promise, we'll find some time to watch the rest when we won't get disturbed."

Within minutes, there's a rap at the door. I get up and open it to find Camilla standing there with wide eyes. "Where is she? What's the news?"

I sigh heavily. "She's not telling us until we're all here."

Camilla pushes inside. "Eva, you can't do that. I'm dying to find out here. Have you won the lottery or something?"

Eva laughs. "No, patience. Nat will be here soon, I hope."

Camilla sits on the armchair, brow furrowed. "That's not fair. She'll be at least a couple of hours." Her attention moves to the screen where Eva has paused the movie. "What are you watching?"

"Gone Girl," I reply.

"Oh my God, I love that film." She settles in. "Well, don't pause it on my account. At least it will be something to keep my mind off of whatever you're going to tell us." She glares at Eva. "It's very unfair to tell someone you've got huge news and then not spill it immediately."

"Why? Is that some rule?" Eva replies.

"No, but it should be." Camilla notices the bag of food. "Pass me some snacks."

I throw the bag at her and she selects a few before tossing it onto the coffee table in the middle.

"Let's get this movie started," Camilla says.

"It's part way through," I warn.

Camilla waves her hand dismissively. "I've already seen it about three times. I know what's going on."

We all settle in and start the movie, watching in silence. It's surprising that Camilla is into this, as I always thought it was her that only liked chick flicks. I try my best to keep my mind off of Coach, his visit and the gift he gave me, but it's almost impossible.

12

ARCHER

*W*e've been back at the academy for a week and I still don't feel myself because of what happened over winter break.

I killed a student's mother to save Oak's life during winter break, an act that I'm still trying to process. It's meant I've been unfocused, particularly on my quest to get Adrianna into my bed. Our sexting has stopped entirely since she got back, despite my attempts to reignite it.

Senior gym class is about to start and there's no sign of my beautiful cartel princess. After winter break and one week of a PI following her, I have some rather juicy information that I'm sure she won't want leaked. If I'm right, it will mean that Adrianna will finally submit to me, if that's what it takes. However, I'd rather try to wear her down the good old-fashioned way with persistence rather than blackmail. It's my last resort.

"Anita, can you stand up here for the demonstration?"

Anita glances around as if looking for someone else

called Anita. To be fair, I rarely use anyone but Adrianna for demos, because she's the only one who can match me.

The door to the gymnasium opens, and Camilla and Adrianna stroll in with their arms hooked together. I narrow my eyes. "Adrianna, you are late. Which means you get to help me with my demonstration."

I wave Anita away, who looks thankful.

Adrianna leans toward Camilla and whispers something before untangling theirs arms and walking to stand in front of me. She looks as beautiful as ever, with her dark hair tied in a bun and her bright green eyes glimmering with that arousing defiance I love so much.

"Today we're going to learn how to disable your opponent without doing damage." I pause a moment, watching her. "All you need to do is stand there and look pretty, Miss Vasquez."

Her nostrils flare.

"And let me do the work."

A few students chuckle, but Adrianna finds it far from amusing, crossing her arms over her chest.

"Arms up as if you are anticipating an attack," I order.

Rage is swirling in those green depths of hers as she watches me, anticipating my attack.

I move toward her at speed and grab her shoulder with force, flipping her onto the safety mat under our feet with little effort. Placing my foot on her ribcage, I smirk down at her. "It's as simple as that." I glance at the rest of the class. "Get a solid grasp of the shoulder and use your weight to flip your opponent to the ground. It does minimal damage but ensures your opponent is entirely subdued."

Out of nowhere, Adrianna grabs my foot and twists it expertly enough to force me to lose my balance and tumble onto the mat beside her. "Are you sure it entirely subdues your opponent, coach?" she asks, looking immensely pleased with herself.

"Well played, but I was distracted at the time." I climb to my feet and offer her my hand, which she ignores.

Instead, she gets to her feet herself.

I can't help myself as I grab her hips and pull her toward me, lowering my lips to her ear. "Careful, Vasquez, or I might just fall on top of you next time and finally give you my cock. I'm sure the class would love a demonstration in a good fucking."

Adrianna turns crimson as she steps away from me, glaring at me, but deep down I know she's aching for it. My cock is steel and throbbing in my pants as I turn my attention to the rest of the class. "Now get into pairs and practice," he barks.

Adrianna is quick to pair up with Camilla, no doubt attempting to get away from me. They start chattering, which irritates me to no end, even though all the other students are talking.

I approach them. "Enough chit chat. Get to work ladies, or I'll have you in detention after class with me." I take in Adrianna's beautiful figure slowly and purposefully to piss her off. "Perhaps that's exactly what you want, Miss. Vasquez." He winks.

She doesn't respond, merely glares at me and gets into

position in front of Camilla. Knowing that I have to focus on the entire class and not just Adrianna, I move along, giving Elias and Rizzo some pointers on their stance.

Once I circle back around, Camilla and Adrianna are at it again, chattering rather than doing what they've been told.

"What did I tell you both about chatting?" I bark, making Camilla jump, but Adrianna seemed to be aware of my presence.

Camilla gets into position this time and I watch as Adrianna carries out the move with little effort, flipping Morrone onto her back.

"Good work, Adrianna," I say, before moving onto the next pair. Rosa and Anita are paired up and both struggling with the move.

"Rosa, you need to be looser in your stance." I glance at Anita. "Both of you are too tense. Try to relax a little."

Anita scoffs. "It's difficult to relax when you are about to be flipped over."

"Try it," I instruct.

She sighs and they both try to loosen their stance. Rosa flips Anita over, but it's a little clumsy.

"Better," I say.

My eyes dart toward Camilla and Adrianna, who are still chin-wagging. I move toward them. "Quiet, both of you. I won't ask you to keep your mouth shut again."

Camilla spins toward me, eyes blazing with an uncontained rage. "Maybe I'll keep my mouth shut when you stop sexually harassing my friend and trying to get her to suck your cock."

Adrianna looks shocked, and the entire gymnasium turns quiet. I can't deny that I'm taken aback by Camilla's brazen attitude and speaking out of turn. Anger bubbles inside of me as I march toward her and set my hands on my hips. "That's it, Morrone. Go to Nitkin now. I won't stand for you talking to me like that."

Camilla's throat bobs as swallows. "Sir, I'm sorry, I just—"

"Now, Morrone. No getting out of it." I won't allow her to speak to me like that, not in front of the entire class. Camilla turns around and walks out of there, heading for Nitkin's office, and I turn my attention to Adrianna.

"Looks like it's me and you for the rest of the class."

She shakes her head. "Why don't you just send me to Nitkin, too?"

"Because." I move closer to her and lower my voice so only she can hear. "I'm going to punish you myself in detention after this class."

Her jaw works. "Detention for what, exactly?"

I grab her hand and yank her toward me. "For being a naughty girl," I murmur in her ear.

She shudders and moves away from me, reclaiming her hand. "Come on then, let's see what you've got."

It's a challenge if ever I've heard one and that only inflames the desire inside of me. Positioning myself in front of her, I launch forward and reach for her right shoulder. However, she reads the move and doesn't stay put, dodging to the side so that I miss her entirely.

And then she grabs my shoulder from behind and flips

me onto my back, leering over me. "Is that the best you can do?"

Jumping to my feet, I stand in front of her and beckon for Adrianna to attack me. She narrows her eyes and then moves toward me with admirable grace. I've always admired the effortlessness in the way she fights.

However, she is predictable as her eyes shift at the last minute to the left, and I dodge out of the way, grabbing her arm and pinning it behind her back. "Is that the best you can do, baby?" I murmur into her ear, keeping her pulled tight against me.

Every muscle in her body is tense, but I intend to change that after this class. She'll be screaming my name while I make her climax harder than ever before.

She breaks out of the hold and knees me in the groin, making me grunt in pain. And then she flips our positions, so that she has my arms in a hold. "No, I can keep at this all fucking day."

I smirk. "So can I, but I'd much rather have you on your back with your legs spread."

She releases me then, shoving me forward and putting distance between us. "You make me sick."

The five minute warning bell in the gym chimes at that moment, the sound of which only ignites the excitement inside of me. The bell in the gym is early to ensure students can change for their next class. "Time for detention, Vasquez."

I turn to the rest of the class. "That's it for today. Get your asses dressed and go to your next class."

The students slowly move into the changing room

until there's only me and Adrianna left. Only then do I turn to face her again, my heart pounding frantically in my chest. "So, you think it's okay to chat and laugh in my class?"

Adrianna places her hands on her hips. "Camilla was right. Everyone was chatting and laughing and you singled us out."

I stalk toward her. "Perhaps that's because the only girl I pay attention to in this class is you."

"Well, turn your attention to someone else. Someone who wants it."

Once I'm within a foot of her, I wrap the palm of my hand around her slender throat, enjoying the way her pulse quickens at my touch.

"We both know that's not really what you want, don't we, Adrianna?" I tilt my head to the side. "What you really want is for me to eat your cunt again and make you come."

She visibly shudders at my words, holding my gaze instead of denying it, which is a good enough answer for me.

"I thought so." I release her throat and turn away from her to lock the gym door, as I don't want any disturbances. When I turn around, she's watching me with flushed cheeks and desire in her beautiful dark eyes.

"Go and lie down on the front bleacher," I say, nodding at it.

Adrianna's throat bobs as she swallows and I wonder if she's going to disobey me, but then she turns and walks over to it, surprising me with her sudden willingness to do as she's told.

I walk over to her, unzipping my pants and pulling my cock out. "Good girl." I grab her knees and pull them apart, groaning when I see the wet patch on her bright red panties. "Wet already for me, baby girl?" I ask.

She doesn't say a word, just stares at me in anticipation. I slide my hands slowly up her thighs and then hook my fingers into the waistband of her lace panties.

She holds her breath, waiting for me to make a move. I pull them down and my cock turns to steel as I stare at her soaking wet virgin pussy, wanting nothing more than to tear her virginity away with one hard thrust.

Instead, I drop to my knees at the end of the bleacher and pull her closer to the edge, so her thighs are either side of my face, and then I suck her sensitive clit into my mouth.

She moans, a sound I've longed to hear again since our phone call during winter break. And her pussy gets even wetter, which I hardly believed possible.

I move between her clit and her entrance, lapping up every drop of her sweet nectar. Slowly, I drag out the pleasure, playing with her like she's an instrument. All the while she's gasping and moaning, proving that the incident in the classroom wasn't a one off. She wants me as badly as I want her. She's just too stubborn to admit it because of my past record with students.

As I devour her, I stroke myself, knowing that Camilla's words are still lingering in my mind. I want Adrianna to suck my cock right now. Instead of chasing my own desires, I make sure I turn her into a mess before me, and then when she's about to come apart, I won't let her until she's swallowed every drop of my cum.

One way or another, Adrianna will be in my bed before Spring Break, that I'm certain of.

13

ADRIANNA

*C*oach looms over me, staring at me with those dark eyes burning with a desire that threatens to destroy me. My arousal glistening from his mouth and making heat spread through my veins.

It's becoming clear that he's never going to let this go, and a part of me doesn't want him to. A part of me wants him to keep pursuing me, as it makes me feel wanted for the first time in my life. Yet the mere thought of giving him my virginity makes me sick to the stomach.

He's teasing me and playing with me until I'm so desperate I'm begging him, but I won't be that girl. I may want to come more than anything right now, but there's no way in hell I'm begging him.

"Such a good girl," He praises, watching me intently.

I squirm on the bleacher, waiting for him to return between my thighs. It's not unusual that I have a man on his knees for me. It's just that normally I'm the one who has brought him to his knees with my combat skills.

"What are you waiting for?"

He narrows his eyes. "I'm taking in this moment, having you on your back, looking at me like that."

I hold his gaze. "Just shut up and make me come."

Archer wraps his palm around my throat, something he's done several times, but oddly, I don't mind it anymore. Every time he does it, it makes me weak at the knees. "I don't appreciate your tone, baby girl." He blocks my airways for a few seconds. "I'm in charge."

Butterflies come to life in my stomach, making me feel a little nauseous. Coach releases my throat slightly.

"Whatever," I say.

His grasp tightens again, making it difficult to breathe. "I think I've been too lenient with you. Perhaps you need a good spanking."

The idea of being bent over and spanked by Coach is arousing and disturbing all at the same time. "I don't think so."

"On your hands and knees, Adrianna."

The way he says my name almost sounds dirty.

"I said no."

He growls like an animal, "Do as you're told." He releases my throat and grabs my hips instead, lifting me off the bleacher. And roughly forces me onto my hands and knees on the gym mat, making heat prickle over every inch of my body. As I feel so exposed.

"Fuck, you look so damn good on all fours for me." He releases my hips and then his hand comes down on my bare ass hard, making me jump in shock.

"What the hell?" I say, glancing over my shoulder at him.

"Watch your mouth or I'll fuck the bad language right out of you," he says, glaring at me like a man possessed.

I swallow hard, but I keep my mouth shut. The idea of being fucked by him right now isn't as repulsive as it normally is, but I won't call his bluff, as I don't doubt he'd make good on that promise.

"After all, this is detention and you've been very naughty," he says, his voice an octave lower as he spanks me again. The impact isn't hard, but it's firm, sending a prickling heat over every inch of exposed skin. "If I were to have to call it, I'd say you are fucking loving your punishment a bit too much." Suddenly, he thrusts two fingers inside of me. "Because you are soaking wet and ready to be fucked."

I'm on the edge of climaxing from that alone, but I resist. The last thing I want is to answer that statement with my fucking orgasm, as that would be worse than admitting I want him to fuck me.

"You are barely holding on, Adrianna." He adds another finger and pushes deeper, hitting the spot inside of me that lights my world on fire.

I scream, unable to resist the urge that pulls me over the edge. "Oh fuck!" I cry out, my body shattering into a million pieces as he continues to finger me through it.

"That's right, baby. Come for me," he says, eyes alight with a dark desire. His cock is still hard and jutting out of his pants. "And now it's my turn."

Before I can say a word, he's standing in front of me

with his hard cock mere inches away from my mouth, a bead of precum dripping off the tip. I purse my lips together, horror mixing with shame.

He grabs my arms and forces me upright on my knees, placing my hands on his thighs. "Open your mouth," he orders.

The scent of him is overwhelming and I tingle all over at the thought of tasting him, but once I do, I feel like there's no going back. He will believe that I'm into this and then there will be trouble.

I shake my head in defiance. "No."

Rage flares to life in his dark eyes as he grabs a fistful of my hair and pulls my lips to the tip of his cock. "Open. Your. Mouth."

I glare at him, a shudder running through my entire body. Resistance is pointless, as I know he's going to get what he wants. Slowly, I open my mouth and the head of his cock slips inside.

I moan around him as the salty, manly taste of him hits my tongue. The first man I've ever tasted, and I can't deny that he's delicious. At first, I explore his cock, slowly teasing him with my tongue, but I sense Coach's impatience as he glares down at me. Unhinging my jaw wider, I let him slip in further, sucking on his thick, veiny length.

He groans, eyes clamping shut as I try to ignore how self-conscious I feel.

How do I know if I'm doing it right?

"Your mouth is heaven, baby girl."

I guess that answers my question, as suddenly he pulls his cock out of my mouth and angles my face up toward him. "Brace yourself, as I'm going to fuck your throat as if it is your tight virgin cunt." And then he thrusts the head of his cock back into my mouth, but far deeper, making me gag on him.

"Open your throat and breathe through your nose," he orders.

I glare at him, but instinct kicks in as I do as he says. And suddenly, he's rocking in and out of my throat just like he said, as if he's fucking my pussy. My eyes flood with tears as saliva spills down my chin.

He's ruthless and takes what he wants, thrusting in and out of my throat brutally. I'm sure I'm about to throw up, considering how deep he's going.

"Oh fuck, I won't be able to last long in your tight little throat." He tightens his grasp in my hair and pulls me more forcefully toward him so that it feels like he's trying to choke me. "I'm going to come down your perfect little throat and I want you to swallow every drop."

My heart skips a beat as suddenly his cock gets even harder in my mouth, and then a stream of liquid hits the back of my throat, making me gag again.

"Swallow it. I don't want you wasting a fucking drop."

I swallow, but some of it spills out of the corner of my mouth as there's too much. His still hard cock slips out of my mouth and I lick my lips, wishing he didn't taste so good.

He steps away and pushes his still semi-hard cock back into his pants, watching me with a sickening look on his face. A look that tells me he thinks he's won, even though that's not the case.

Shame floods me as I realize what I just did validates Coach's perverse pursuit of my virginity. And it will make him even more relentless.

Sitting up, I pull down my skirt and pull my panties on. Archer watches me with an oddly serious expression. An expression that scares me. I grab my rucksack off the bleacher without another glance in his direction, before rushing toward the door out of the gym and unlock it.

"I hope you learned your lesson, baby girl," he says from behind me, his voice seductive.

It sends a shiver down my back as I rush out of the gym and into the female changing room. My heart pounding at a thousand miles an hour as I lock the door to ensure he doesn't follow me.

It was a mistake to be so willing, but I couldn't help it. He makes me crazy with hate and desire, which is a confusing combination.

14

ARCHER

*T*he staff room is empty, which isn't usual early morning before class. I pull my cell phone out, wondering if I've missed a memo about a meeting or something.

There's nothing from Oak, so I message Gav to find out where he is.

Me: It's a ghost town in the staff room. What's going on?

Bubbles appear instantly as he types back.

Gav: There's a meeting in the grand hall.

I clench my jaw as it's the first I'm hearing of it. Sighing heavily, I head out of the staff room toward the hall, intending to take my frustration out on Oak for not telling me about it.

When I walk into the room, he's standing at the front talking about mathematics. I know he fired Jameson for being an asshole about his marriage to Eva. I don't think she was the only one that thought it was wrong; she was the only one that had the balls to tell him to his face.

I can't say anything because I've had far more students in my bed than he has. Gav is near the front, but I take a seat nearer the back not to disturb whatever speech he's giving.

"So, do we have any volunteers to take over Professor Jameson's classes temporarily?"

The silence that resounds around the room is deafening. There's no way I can offer any help, as I'm shit academically, and always have been. Jameson taught Math, and that is my weakest subject of them all.

"Come on, people. I need a couple of you to pitch in. Who has the most free periods?"

There's some whispering between the staff, and then finally Gav stands up. "I can take the classes, but I doubt I have the skill to mark assignments."

Oak looks relieved his friend swooped in to save him. "Okay, can anyone mark the assignments temporarily?"

Sophia stands. "I'll mark them. I just don't think my workload would suit taking the classes."

Gav has fewer classes to teach than most of us, as all of them are optional and not open to every year. The younger years don't take torture or anatomy, for example. However, there are a couple of staff members who have a lower workload than him, like Janice Irwin, who takes the Money Laundering and assassination class. She would have been an ideal math teacher, since she's already into math, anyway, but she's always been lazy. Never wants to participate with the staff in an active way and keeps to herself. Same goes for Jeremiah Kane, who takes merchandise and profit class, as well as chemistry, which basically involves making your own drugs. Alice Love, who takes corporate planning and bribery classes.

All three of them are odd and don't hang out in the staff room. And now that Jameson is gone, we're left with just Sophia and Elaine, who actually go in the staff room.

And then there's the maintenance and office staff, who hang out in their offices instead of the staff room. Although Melissa, Oak's secretary, sometimes makes an appearance.

"Perfect, that's settled, then. If there's anyone who has ideas for potential candidates for the role, please come to me after the meeting." He clears his throat. "I must ask if there are any other matters we need to discuss."

Jeremiah puts his hand up. "Yes, the senior hunting trip is supposed to take place in three days and you haven't assigned any members of staff for it."

I sit up straighter at the mention of the hunting trip. All the seniors go to the woods not far from here to hunt game, which means Adrianna will be on it. "I volunteer to lead it," I say.

Oak's brow arches as he notices me in the back. "That's very kind of you, Archer, but are you really the best choice?"

"What's that supposed to mean?"

A muscle in his jaw moves. "It means you don't normally take the hunting excursions."

I tilt my head. "Surely I'm the best for the job, being that my classes are the most active and physical."

131

Oak nods. "Fine, you and Jeremiah can take the students."

Perfect. I get to take the trip with that weirdo.

"Are there any other matters that need to be addressed?"

Alice Love stands. "Yes, I think that we need more real-life experiences for my classes." I zone out then as she starts to prattle on about taking her students to New York to try to bribe a businessman on a field trip, which is completely insane.

Some of the staff have questionable ideas. I sit in the back, stewing over why exactly I didn't receive an invitation to the meeting. Once it's finally adjourned, I stand and walk over to Oak, fists clenched. "Why the hell didn't you tell me about the meeting?"

Oak shrugs. "You don't normally have any interest in them or take part."

"It's because you knew the matter of the senior hunting excursion would come up, isn't it?"

He sighs heavily. "Look, Arch. You don't have a good track record with girls in the senior class. Ideally, you wouldn't be my first pick."

I narrow my eyes at him. "So that's why you didn't send me a memo?"

He nods. "Yes."

Gav walks over to us. "What's going on?"

I glare at him. "Oak excluded me from this meeting as he didn't want me taking the seniors hunting."

"Makes sense. You can't keep your dick in your pants at the best of times. Let alone in the woods with whatever young student you have decided to prey on." His eyes narrow. "Although this year may be different, since Vasquez is very resistant to your charms, unless you've given up on her."

"Never," I growl.

He chuckles. "Someone's a bit on edge."

I can tell he's enjoying it being me for a change, as I'm normally the one teasing him about his foul moods.

"Shut up." I run a hand across the back of my neck. "What are you up to tonight?"

Gav shrugs. "Nothing. What do you have in mind?"

"Food and drink at the diner?"

His brow furrows. "We've already been to the diner this week."

"Is there a rule you can only go once a week that I don't know about?"

Gav shakes his head. "No, I just expected you to suggest some sleazy bar."

"I don't always want to go to sleazy bars, you know?"

Gav chuckles. "Could have fooled me."

"I guess it's a stupid question, but do you want to tag along?" I ask Oak.

He shakes his head. "Not tonight, sorry."

"He's totally whipped," I say.

Gav nods. "Seems that way."

Oak growls. "I'm not whipped, but we go out once a week anyway and I've got a wife to get home to."

The bell rings, warning us we have a couple of minutes to get to our classes. "Right, I've got junior gym to take this morning. I'll see you in the staff room after classes finish tonight."

Gav nods. "See you then."

I walk out of the grand hall and toward the gym, a spring in my step as it's only a few days until I'll be alone in the woods with my baby girl. Something tells me I'll be hunting for her rather than animals.

GAV and I walk into the diner, and instantly I groan. My intention for coming here was to get some space from students, and yet there's a huge group of seniors in the diner.

"What are students doing here in the week?"

Gav shrugs. "Maybe Oak gave them permission for a birthday or something."

It happens, but he could have mentioned it earlier when we decided to come here. "Great."

"What is up with you?" Gav asks as he sits down at our normal table. "Students being at the same place never bugs you normally."

I shake my head. "Nothing."

"Is it because you can't get Vasquez to fuck you?"

I growl at that and open my menu. "No. It has nothing to do with her."

Gav nods. "That's lucky, as she's here tonight."

I freeze when he says that Adrianna is here, at this diner. My brow furrows as I scan the group of kids, none of whom are her usual friends she hangs out with. And he's right, she's sitting facing our way, chatting to Rosa Cabello.

"What the fuck is she doing here?"

"I think it's Rosa's birthday today. Maybe she was invited to celebrate." He runs a hand through his dark hair. "After all, their families work together."

Adrianna glances up and our eyes meet. A wave of electricity shoots through my veins as I meet her gaze. Anger ignites every time she sees me, but she looks away quickly, her cheeks flushed pink.

Jenny comes over. "Fancy seeing the two of you again. Twice in one week!"

Gav gives her a tight smile. "Can't keep away. The ribs are too good."

"So, what can I get you?"

I look at her and she smiles widely. "A full rack of ribs and a beer."

She jots down the order.

"Make that two of the same," Gav says, passing the menus to her.

"Sure." She places her hand on my arm. "It's good to see you again."

As always, Jenny is flirting with me, and while I'd usually flirt back, I can't right now. I glance over at Adrianna to find she's looking at me, her eyes darting between the waitress and me. And if I didn't know any better, I'd say the look in her eyes is jealously.

So I make a snap decision to flirt with Jenny, grabbing her wrist gently and yanking her toward me. "I also wanted to see you again."

Her cheeks heat as she looks at me with wide eyes. "Oh, that's very sweet of you, Archer."

The girl is your typical small-town girl who gets easily embarrassed by a man's attention. There's no way she could handle me. Even though before I was obsessed with Adrianna, I would have fucked her if it didn't mean it risked being able to come here every week.

She scurries off to get our drinks, and I glance at Adrianna, who is glaring at me.

I smirk at her, which only makes her more angry.

"What the fuck was the flirting all about, Arch?" Gav asks.

His eyes shift to where Adrianna is sitting, and he shakes his head. "For fuck's sake. Get a grip."

"What?"

"You are making a fucking fool of yourself with this girl."

I clench my fists on the table. "How?"

"Because you look desperate."

I straighten at that, wondering if Gav is right. Objectivity isn't exactly my strong suit when it comes to Adrianna Vasquez because she's driving me insane.

Jenny returns with our beers. "Here you go." She winks at me as she sets mine down in front of me. "Is there anything else I can get you?"

"No, thanks." I keep my tone short, as I don't enjoy being told by I'm being desperate.

Jenny frowns, no doubt confused by the hot and cold treatment I'm giving her, but right now, Adrianna Vasquez is under my skin. I can't help how I'm acting, as this is what she does to me.

Chugging my beer, I glare across the table at Gav. "Let's eat and get the hell out of here." So much for escaping the academy to clear my head about Adrianna. Her appearance here is beyond frustrating. Especially as all I can think about is her pouty lips wrapped around my cock.

15

ADRIANNA

he bus stops in a clearing at the center of the woods where we're going hunting. It's the first time we've been on an excursion like this, and I'm a little surprised that they think it's a good idea. Getting together a bunch of mafia heirs and arming them seems like a recipe for disaster.

Unfortunately, Coach is the one leading this trip, and he won't stop looking at me in a way that sends a shiver down my spine.

He stands, eyes lingering on me as he clears his throat.

"The rules are simple. I'm going to pair each of you off and you will walk the woods together." His eyes narrow. "No one will split up under any circumstances. You will return here in three hours with whatever kills you make. And under no circumstances do you shoot your classmates."

"No fun," Nik says.

Coach glares at him, shaking his head. "If you've got a

problem with the rules, Kushev, I'll send you back to the academy on your own."

Nik falls silent.

"Here are the pairs," he says, and I hold my breath, knowing that we've got an odd number on the trip, and hoping he doesn't pair me with him.

"Camilla and Rizzo, Eva and Nik." He continues on and Nat groans when he pairs her with Elias, which is terrible luck.

"Great," she murmurs.

I glance at her. "Maybe you should ask to swap? I don't think you should be alone in the woods with him when he's armed. The guy is crazy."

Nat shakes her head. "I can handle myself."

I know she can handle herself, but he's stabbed her before. The boy has spent years trying to torment her. It just seems dangerous.

Coach continues calling names until there's only three of us left. "Rosa and Jax."

He smirks at me. "And that just leaves me and Adrianna."

I frown at him. "Can't I go with Rosa and Jax?"

He shakes his head. "It's pairs only. Now, everyone get off of the bus and into your pairs. And grab a rifle on your way."

As everyone gets off the bus, I want to go back to the academy. Three hours alone in the woods with this man will be pure torture. "I think you should swap me with Elias, as he might kill Nat in the woods."

He shakes his head. "Nice try, Vasquez, but you are with me whether or not you like it."

I grunt in frustration and shoulder my rifle. "Whatever. Let's get this over with." The rest of the students are already heading into the woods, so I march after them, knowing he'll follow.

I can hear his boots crunching on the frosty ground behind me as I try to keep close to the other pairs, knowing that if he gets me alone, he'll try something. And the shameful thing is I'm not sure I can resist his advances, not considering how good he makes me feel when he touches me.

I hate how much I enjoy it.

"Adrianna, wait," he calls.

I come to a stop and glare at him over my shoulder. "What? Can't you keep up?"

"Don't be an idiot." He nods to the ground. "We're on the wrong trail. There are fresh tracks leading that way."

I hate that he's right, but the tracks are clear and definitely fresh. They are leading away from everyone else. "Great," I murmur.

"What was that?" he asks.

"Okay, you lead the way."

He nods and walks in front of me, following the tracks. My heart pounds erratically in my chest the moment we're entirely alone. The drone of other students chatting is no longer audible, but to my surprise, Coach just follows the tracks without a single glance back at me.

He wouldn't even know if I slipped off in the opposite

direction. It's like a light bulb goes off in my mind at that moment. Turning around, I head back the way we came.

"Where the fuck do you think you are going, baby girl?"

I freeze, wondering how he knew I turned around. "Away from you," I reply.

Suddenly, his hard, warm body presses against my back while his hands slide onto my hips. "First rule of hunting, never split up from your partner," he murmurs into my ear, warm breath teasing my earlobe. "Do you want to learn the second rule?"

I swallow hard. "Not really."

"A partner who breaks the first rule needs punishing." His hand teases over my backside, making me thankful I'm wearing pants. "You have such a beautiful ass." I swallow hard, hating the way I dampen between my thighs the moment his hands are on me.

"Let go of me, Coach."

He nips my earlobe. "No chance. I have you all alone in the woods. I intend to make the most of it."

"Fuck you," I say, knowing that I have no power here. I can't resist, because my body just reacts to him on a primal level.

He chuckles, a deep and unfriendly sound. "I'm going to fuck your pretty little mouth right here in the woods, and I want you to swallow every single drop of my seed. Do you understand?"

My knees shake at the prospect of being forced to my knees for him in the woods like a fucking whore. "No."

He spins me around and places his hand around my throat, squeezing. "What do you mean, no?"

I grind my teeth together as I know that my resistance is futile in the end. "I mean, no."

He pushes me to the floor with his hand still wrapped around my throat, blocking my airways. "You will do as you are told, baby girl."

I glare at him, hatred and lust merging in a confusing, tangled web, as he unzips his pants and frees his hard cock. The tip coated in pre-cum. It's sickening that the sight of him like this opens a deep gaping hole inside of me that longs to be filled by him. And before he even orders me to, I open my jaw and slide his cock into my mouth, groaning as the masculine taste of him over-whelms my senses.

"Good girl," he praises, looking down at me with a passionate light in his eyes.

I squeeze my thighs together, and in that moment, I wish I wasn't wearing pants. The need to touch myself clawing at me. Any moment one of my classmates could catch me sucking Coach's cock, and that thought only arouses me more.

He slides into my throat like he did in the gym. Only this time he hasn't brought me to my climax and turned me into a desperate slut. This time, I'm doing it almost willingly and it's a sickening prospect.

"That's it, baby. Take it to the back of your throat." His fingers slide into my hair and yank hard, forcing his cock even deeper. "Your throat is so fucking good, but I bet it's not half as amazing as your cunt."

My entire body shakes with need as I feel a pressure building inside of me, even without touching myself. Every part of my body is sensitive, and my nipples are hard peaks longing to be sucked.

I pull off of his cock. "Please, Coach. I need you to touch me."

He smirks down at me, looking a little evil. "Are you begging me, Vasquez?"

The question brings me back to my senses as I lean back on my haunches. "No."

He kneels down in front of me and then pushes me so that I fall back onto the cold, hard ground. "I'll give you what you want, baby girl." He unzips my pants and pulls them down roughly, the cold air hitting my skin and making me gasp.

Suddenly, he's mounting me so that his cock is pressed against my lips. "Open wide. I want you to suck me while I devour you, and you won't come until I tell you to."

Opening my mouth, I suck on the tip of his cock at first and explore it with my tongue, but he shifts position so that his cock slips into the back of my throat, making me gag.

"Good girl, I want you to suck me while I lick your delicious pussy," he says, and then he's devouring me.

All other thoughts obliterate as I suck eagerly on his cock, saliva spilling down my chin as he moves his hips, fucking my throat. It's a wonder I don't throw up all over it, but then I've never had a strong gag reflex.

He groans as he sucks on my clit and then stops.

"Fuck, baby. When I come, I want you to swallow every drop. Do you understand?"

I hum around his cock in response.

"Such a good girl," he praises and then his lips are on me again, driving me insane.

My whole body shudders, and he stops. "Remember, no coming until I tell you."

I groan around the thick girth of him, wishing I could speak back, but his cock is gagging me from speaking.

He spanks my ass and then continues to lick and suck me, always noticing when I'm getting close and backing off. It feels like any moment I'll die of desperation. Shifting slightly, I slide his cock out of my mouth. "Please, I need to come," I beg.

He growls. "Cock back in your mouth, or I won't let you come at all."

Grinding my teeth, I get back into position and slide his cock back into my throat. After what feels like forever of torturous pleasure, he stops when I'm so close. "I want you to come so I can lap up every drop of you." he orders, spanking my ass at the same time. "Come for me." And then he grazes his teeth over my sensitive clit and that's all it takes.

I hate how responsive my body is to him as instantly I fall over the cliff edge. Every bone in my body becomes liquid and I shudder violently, screaming around his cock. Archer roars as he comes apart too, both of us finding our release at the same time. Somehow it only makes it more intense as I swallow, trying to keep up and not let any go to waste as he instructed, but there's too much. I choke a little, shifting back so I can pull his cock out of my throat and breathe.

"Good girl," he praises, shifting from on top of me. He stands and helps me to my feet, pulling me against him and yanking my pants and panties back up, zipping them for me, even though I could do it myself. "Such a good girl," he murmurs, and then he kisses me, the taste of my arousal on his tongue.

It's intoxicating as I kiss him back, even while I scold myself for it.

"We've got some hunting to do." He shoulders his rifle and shoves his cock back into his pants, zipping them up. "Come on." He walks off, leaving me full of shame as I grab my rifle and rush after him.

I should have fought harder, but deep down, I enjoyed every second.

Two WEEKS GO by without incident after our session in the woods, as I try my best to stay away from Coach and he keeps making suggestive comments, but no attempt to take me against my will again.

I tap my feet impatiently on the tile floor as I sit, freezing my ass off on poolside, waiting for Camilla to arrive. One thing I hate more than anything is tardiness, and she knows it, too.

We agreed to meet here at four o'clock. It's now ten minutes past and my patience is wearing thin. I hear the door to the pool. "Finally!"

Camilla looks flustered as she dashes toward me. "Sorry, I was in detention with Nitkin."

It's one thing after another with her lately. "Not again. What did you do this time?"

Her cheeks are more flushed than usual. "I was doing my anatomy assignment in law class."

"Does that mean you're too sore to swim?" I ask, looking at her through narrowed eyes.

"No, he gave me an essay to write."

Camilla is practically the color of a beetroot now and I wonder if something is going on between her and Nitkin. However, that would be ridiculous. Nitkin is a sadistic son of a bitch and Camilla doesn't strike me as the kind of girl to be into that.

"Thank fuck for that." I clench my jaw as I want to get in and swim now. "Get dressed." I nod toward the changing room.

Almost the moment Camilla walks into the changing room, the door to the pool opens and Coach strides in, setting me on edge. He watches me from the other side of the pool. "Imagine seeing you here," he says, tilting his head.

"You know I always swim every weekday after school ends." I cross my arms over my chest. "What do you want?"

Those dark amber eyes darken as he strides toward me. A shiver racing down my spine at the darkness swirling around the usually calm and collected man.

"I want you," he growls, grabbing my hips as if he has the right to touch me.

I swat at him, trying to push him away, but he uses one huge hand to capture them and hold me captive. "I don't want you."

"What happened to the good girl I was speaking to on the phone during winter break? Or the dirty little vixen who came with my cock in her mouth in the woods?"

Her eyes narrow. "I told you that changes nothing. My virginity isn't up for grabs by you, or anyone."

"Listen to me, Vasquez. You can play hard to get all you fucking like, but I have some information you won't want out."

It feels like my entire body turns numb, as the only thing I don't want out is the fact that I've been betraying my family for years.

"Are you about to blackmail me into fucking you?" I ask, glaring at him.

His jaw clenches. "If that's what it takes." Sliding a hand into his inside jacket pocket, he pulls out some polaroids and places them in my hand.

It feels like all the blood drains from my body as I stare down at the images of me and Hernandez Estrada, my family's biggest rival, meeting last week two towns over last week. "Where the fuck did you get these?"

He yanks them off of me and slides them back into his inside jacket pocket. "I hired a PI to follow you when I learned you leave the academy every Tuesday. He followed you over winter break and mentioned you met with some men of a rival cartel, so I asked him to follow you out of the academy last Tuesday."

"You are a desperate and pathetic man." I shake my head. "So what happens if I don't fuck you?"

His smirk widens. "If you don't obey me, baby girl. I'll expose your treachery to your entire fucking family."

My nostrils flare as I glare at him, wishing I could dunk him in the pool and drown him. No doubt he'd out power me, but perhaps with the air of surprise I'd come out on top. I value my life a little too much to try it out.

He pulls me even closer so that I can feel the warmth of his breath falling against my face. "Tell me, baby, tell me who owns you."

I grit my teeth. "Fuck you."

"No, Adrianna." He spins me around and pulls my back against his chest, making me feel the hard length of his cock throbbing against my ass. "I'm going to fuck you, and when I do, you will wish you'd got into my bed the first time I asked."

"Over my dead body."

He chuckles into my ear. "That's likely what would happen if your father knew you've been going behind his back and feeding information to his enemy."

I swallow hard, knowing that what I did was wrong, even if I have no respect for my family. My decision to betray them was difficult, as I've always thrived in the criminal world, but I won't be sold off like an asset. It's not like they've ever made me feel cared for in my eighteen years of life. It was my only option if I want to break free of the Vasquez Cartel for good once I graduate.

Hernandez Estrada has been paying me hundreds of thousands of dollars to feed him information for the past three years. I have a few million stashed in an untraceable bank account that my family can't touch. It's my only way to escape their clutches.

"What do you want from me?" I ask.

His lips skate over the skin at my neck, making goose-bumps erupt over my entire body. "I want you to admit that you want me as badly as I want you."

I grit my teeth. "So you want me to lie?"

His jaw works as he steps closer to me. "Are you going to force me to rat you out, Adrianna? As I will."

I long for Camilla to walk back in here, but I know that even changing into a swimsuit takes her an age.

I narrow my eyes and glare at him. "I've never met a man so pig-headed he won't accept when a girl doesn't want to fuck him."

His nostrils flare and he closes in on me. "If you don't stop fighting this, then everyone will know your little secret, not just your family. The academy doesn't take kindly to traitors."

My stomach churns as I wonder what he's talking about. "So you are blackmailing me into having sex with you?" I'm almost shocked, but not quite, as Coach is that fucked up.

A sinister smirk twists onto his ungodly, beautiful lips. "Perhaps."

"Hey, leave her alone," Camilla calls, rushing toward us. Thank God she's back, but I would have liked her to be here five minutes earlier.

Coach's dark eyes move to her. "Morrone, didn't Nitkin teach you a lesson? Or do I need to?"

I glance at Camilla as she swallows hard. Instantly, I can tell she's thinking about giving him shit, so I shake my head to tell her to back off.

Camilla nods. "Fine, I'm getting into the pool."

At this moment, I'm wondering why I bothered waiting for Camilla before getting into the pool. I could have warmed up without her and then this asshole wouldn't have gotten to me.

I wish she wouldn't leave me alone with him, even though I told her to back off. "Coach, please——"

His hand slams around my throat, and I struggle to draw in oxygen. "Listen to me, Adrianna. You'll do as you're told from here on in or daddy finds out how naughty his little traitor of a daughter is."

"He'd kill me, coach, please——"

His fingers flex harder around my throat. "Call me Archer from now on when we're alone."

I struggle to draw in oxygen, clawing at his hand.

"And I don't give a shit what he'll do. You know how to avoid your father and everyone else you know and love ever finding out about your treachery."

I feel sick to the stomach that this man is blackmailing me into giving him my virginity as if it's some trophy to be won. "You make me sick," I spit.

He releases my throat, but before I can pull away, he grabs a fistful of my hair and angles my face up. "Such a liar, Adrianna. I know your pussy is wet from thinking about my cock." His grip tightens. "You will meet Oak, Gav, and I in town tonight with your friends, or the truth is out. I will text you the details."

With that, he releases my hair and storms out of the swimming pool, slamming the door behind him. I want to scream, but all I can do is clench my fists and blow out a frustrated breath, as I need to avoid awkward questions from Camilla.

I'm shaking from either shock or pure anger as I walk toward the pool, putting my bathing cap on as I do. And then I put on my goggles, knowing that all I need right now is the cold water to encase me and cool me off, as I'm beyond pissed.

Diving in at the deep end, I take my rage out on the water, thrashing through it harder and faster than ever. Wishing the crystal blue surface was Coach's face as I punch my hands through is viciously.

He's an asshole, and if I want to beat him at this game, I'm going to have to play dirty, too.

16

ARCHER

"*W*hat are you waiting for, Gav?" I ask as I clap him on the shoulder.

Gav moves away. "Keep your hands to yourself."

"Sorry, forgot how touchy you are." I wink at him. "Come on, let's have fun." I stride into the bar toward the table where Oak and the three girls are already sitting. Adrianna has her back to me.

"Good evening, ladies," I say as I sit my ass down next to Adrianna and smirking at her. "How are you tonight?"

My question is directed at Adrianna, but it's Eva who replies. "We're all great."

I clench my jaw and stare at Adrianna, making her shuffle uncomfortably next to me. After the conversation we had earlier that afternoon, she's no doubt stewing over the revelation that she's indeed going to sleep with me if she doesn't want people to find out she's a traitor to the Vasquez cartel. Grabbing a glass from the center and the bottle of scotch, I pour myself some.

153

"You two are both late," Oak says, glaring at Gav, as he expects it from me.

Gav shrugs. "Sorry, got held up."

"This is nice, isn't it, Adrianna?" I ask, moving closer to her.

She looks at me like she wants to kill me and it's arousing. "Not particularly."

"When are you going to stop harassing Adrianna, Archer?" Eva asks.

I smirk, not at all intimidated by Oak's little plaything. "I'll stop once she gives me what is mine."

Eva glares at me. "And what is that?"

I smirk as I lift my glass to my lips. "Adrianna knows." I take a sip, enjoying the burn of the liquid.

"I don't owe you shit," Adrianna says, clearly forgetting our conversation earlier this afternoon.

I move closer to her. "You know that's not true, unless you've decided you don't care about your family leaning the truth," I whisper into her ear. "And let's be honest. If the other day after gym class is anything to go on, you want this as badly as I do."

"Archer," Oak snaps. "Leave the girl alone."

My nostrils flare as I glance up at Oak, who is clearly reacting to Eva's wishes.

"What?" I say, grabbing my glass and taking another swig. "I'm having fun."

Eva snorts. "That's a lie if ever I heard one. You're a fucking predator."

I glare at her. "And what does that make your husband?"

Her cheeks heat. "I wanted Oak. That's entirely different. I think Adrianna has made it clear she's not interested time and time again."

Grabbing Adrianna's leg under the table, I squeeze forcefully. "Is that true, Adrianna?"

She swallows hard. "Just leave it alone, Eva."

Eva's brow furrows, but she does as Adrianna says. "Fair enough. Let's talk about something else." She tilts her head. "How about why Natalya still isn't back?" Her attention moves to Oak accusingly.

"As I stated, it's classified and not down to me to tell you."

She grunts in frustration. "I'm your wife. You should tell me everything."

As they descend into a martial spat, I glance at Adrianna, who is trying her hardest to focus on anything but me. "So baby girl, how are you feeling about our arrangement?"

Her nostrils flare. "What arrangement?"

"The one where you sleep with me so that I keep my mouth shut."

Her jaw clenches. "You are disgusting. Did you know that?"

I shrug. "You won't think that once I'm making you come over and over again with my cock buried inside of you."

"That's never going to happen."

My fingers dig into her thigh, making her gasp. "Then are you telling me to go and tell your family and everyone at the academy the truth?"

She glares at me with a hatred so deep it surprises me. "No."

"Then you'll be coming on my cock."

She shakes her head. "I won't enjoy it, that's for sure."

"What are you two talking about?" Oak asks.

Suddenly Camilla gets up. "Excuse me a moment," she says, and then she races away from the table as if she's trying to escape. No doubt Gav freaked her out.

Thankfully, her sudden departure took Oak's attention off of me and Adrianna. I run my hand up and down her leg, making her shudder.

"So, Adrianna, how was your winter break?" Oak asks.

Her brow furrows. "As terrible as always."

Eva sighs. "I would have loved to spend two weeks in the sun."

Oak takes her hand and squeezes. "Maybe we'll go somewhere warm for our honeymoon."

She smiles at him, but I know Oak and I think she does too. He's not the kind of guy who likes sitting on a beach for a couple of weeks getting a sun tan. "I know that's not really your thing."

Adrianna clears her throat. "Maybe we can have a girls' weekend in Mexico one weekend this semester, preferably one when my family is out of town."

Eva beams. "Sounds good."

Oak growls. "Like hell, you're not going on a trip without me to Mexico."

It's amusing seeing Oak's possessive side, as it's something I've never witnessed before from him. "How about a girls and guys weekend?"

Adrianna's brow furrows. "There's no way in hell you are coming to Mexico. Oak, fine. You, no."

I tighten my grasp on her leg. "That's rather rude."

Adrianna takes a long swig of her drink and glances across the table at the two empty chairs where Camilla and Gavril had been sitting. "Where did Camilla go? She's been gone quite a while."

Eva's brow furrows. "Not sure. When did Gavril leave?"

The guy is like a fucking ghost. As I must admit, I didn't see him leave the table. "Probably to get more alcohol knowing him."

Adrianna stands suddenly. "I'll go and find Camilla." She marches away before I can tell her to sit back down.

"And then there were three." I sip my whiskey. "Not going to lie. I feel like a third wheel right now."

Eva leans forward. "Please, can you stop tormenting Adrianna? All you're doing is making her cranky."

I meet Eva's gaze, knowing I have to be diplomatic in my response, considering Oak is sitting next to her and married her. Otherwise I'd tell her to keep her nose out of my business, but I can't deny that after killing her mother, whenever I see her, I'm wracked with guilt too.

"I'm sorry, Eva, but I can't do that."

She shakes her head. "Why not? You have a student or multiple every year. Why not move onto the next one and be done with it?"

My throat constricts a little at being asked and I take a

long drink before answering. "Because I like a challenge," I say simply, even though it's a lie.

Adrianna Vasquez is nothing like the girls I've fucked before. There isn't going to be a next one after her. She's it for me, at least. That's how I feel at the moment, even if she won't put out.

I've never felt this way about anyone before. Never wanted anyone on such a visceral level that it almost feels like she's a part of me.

I wait impatiently for her return, and when she does return, she's empty handed. "No luck?" I ask.

"She not in the bathroom or out front." Her brow furrows. "I don't get it."

Less than a minute later, Camilla appears looking flushed pink and sits down on the other side of Adrianna. "Where were you?"

Camilla turns even redder. "I went to the bathroom and then went to the bar, but the queue was so big I gave up."

Oak has disappeared now, so it seems like there's never all of us there at the table. I notice he's standing at the bar with Gav having what looks like a stern conversation.

"So, how are you girls enjoying your night out on the town?"

Adrianna replies, "I'd be enjoying it much more if we weren't out with our professors."

Oak and Gav return with their drinks, and Gav sits down next to Camilla, giving her an odd look.

"We need to liven up this party right away. How about a beer drinking contest?" I suggest.

158

Adrianna straightens. "If you want to lose, sure."

"I've never met someone as competitive as me before I met you, Miss Vasquez."

Adrianna grabs my beer and chugs it in two in front of my eyes, which I must admit is fast.

I clench my jaw. "You owe me a beer now."

She smirks. "First to finish doesn't pay."

I nod. "Okay, but I'll wipe the floor with you."

"Quit now, Daniels. No one can beat me at drinking games."

"It's true," Eva says, leaning forward slightly. "She beats all the guys at beer chugging."

I frown at the two of them, knowing I'll never live it down if she does best for me. "Challenge accepted." I signal for the waitress, noticing and ignoring the looks Oak gives me. "Two large beers, please."

She nods in response, clearly rushed off her feet and heads to the bar to get the drinks.

"How are you even a professor when you act like a fucking child?" Gav asks.

He's always such an asshole. "How are you a professor when you're such a sadistic son of a bitch?"

Oak clears his throat. "I never thought I'd be sitting in a bar with my two adult friends and find that the more mature guests are students. Stop being idiots."

I ignore the glare that Gav gives me as he drinks his whiskey. He's quickly distracted by Camilla and if I didn't know my friend better, I'd say he was into her, but Gav never goes for students.

"Seriously, when are you going to grow up though, Arch?" Oak asks.

"Are you suggesting I'm immature?"

Oak tilts his head. "Don't even pretend you aren't. You're about to participate in a drinking game with an eighteen-year-old."

"And your point is?"

He sighs in defeat and turns his attention to his drink. Meanwhile, Adrianna turns to me. "What beer did you order? I hope it was Budweiser."

I shake my head. "I just ordered beer and was pretty sure they only serve Heineken here."

"Heineken is shit."

I tilt my head. "Does it really matter when you are chugging it? I prefer it to Budweiser, to be honest."

"Principal Byrne, what do you think? Heineken or Budweiser," Adrianna asks.

Oak wrinkles his nose. "Neither."

Adrianna sighs, glancing at Eva, who shakes her head. "Don't ask me."

"What do you think, Camilla?"

Camilla looks like someone shot her. "About what?"

"What beer is better, Budweiser or Heineken?"

"You know I don't drink beer."

At that moment, the waitress returns with the two large Heineken. "Thanks," I say, passing one to Adrianna, who takes it begrudgingly.

"Rules are simple. First to finish the beer wins," Oak says.

"Yeah, that's generally how this works," I say, sarcastically, which results in a scolding look from my boss.

"Shall I count you in?" Eva asks.

I glance at Adrianna. "Are you ready?"

"Always."

I nod and tighten my grasp on my beer. "Yeah, count us in."

"On three okay?"

We both nod, watching each other intently.

"One. Two. Three!"

I bring the beer to my mouth and chug it as fast as physically possible for me, but somehow Adrianna slams the glass down a good few seconds before me.

"Have that!"

"Motherfucker," I growl, hating that I got beat by her.

"I'm afraid Adrianna is the winner," Oak announces, smirking at me, which only makes me more angry.

I'm ready to claim Adrianna right here in front of everyone, humiliate her the way she humiliated me.

Adrianna smirks at me, but she won't be smiling later when I force her to open her legs for my cock. "I told you no one can beat me."

"You're particularly cocky tonight, Adrianna."

Oak chuckles. "She beat you. She has a reason to be cocky, doesn't she?

"Whatever."

Gav stands suddenly. "I'm getting another drink. Anyone need one?"

"Get a round in on my tab," Oak says.

The rest of the night is kind of uneventful until the question of leaving comes up. I lean toward Adrianna.

"You won't be leaving with Oak, do you understand? Tell them you'll stay with me and Gav."

Her nostrils flare. "Or what?"

"It's a silly question, you know what?"

She sighs heavily.

"Adrianna, are you ready to go?" Camilla asks.

Adrianna shakes her head. "No, I think I'll stay a bit longer. You guys go ahead and I'll get a cab back with Professor Nitkin and Coach.

Eva looks confused by Adrianna's refusal to head back to the academy. "Are you sure?"

She nods. "Yeah, I'll finish up my drink and head back with these guys."

"Okay, see you tomorrow then?" Camilla says.

"Yeah, see you tomorrow."

Oak, Eva, and Camilla leave. Gavril looks a little irritated being left here with me and Adrianna as he watches the other three leave.

A tense silence falls between us. After a few minutes, Gav stands. "Well, this is thrilling," he says, "But I've got to admit I've had enough fun for one night."

Adrianna tips the contents of her drink back. "I think I'll go back with you."

I grab her wrist and yank her back down. "No, we'll go back together in a moment."

Gav gets the hint. "Right, I've got some unfinished business to attend to in town before I head back, anyway." He leaves us alone in the bar.

Adrianna glares at me hatefully. "You're a real asshole, you know?"

"If you think I'm an asshole now, wait until later." I glance at my watch. "Shall I order the Uber, or do you want to?"

Adrianna looks beyond frustrated. "I don't care. I want to get back to the dorms."

I pull out my phone and book the Uber for ten minute time. "That's not happening tonight."

Her body stiffens with tension. "What do you mean?"

"I mean, you're coming back to mine and it's non-negotiable."

"But, I—"

I press my lips to hers, silencing whatever bullshit excuse she was about to come up with.

Tonight is the night I intend to tear away Adrianna's so called innocence. She'll be screaming my name all night long, and I don't care what I have to do to make it happen.

My phone dings, informing me the driver is outside. "That was quick." I grab her wrist, yanking her to her feet. "Come on, our ride is here."

Keeping hold of her wrist, I lead her out onto the side-walk. The driver is parked right out front, so I open the back door for her to get in.

She stares at the back of the cab for a while, hesitating.

"Come on, we haven't got all night."

Adrianna relents and gets into the back of the cab, and I slide in next to her, placing my hand on her thigh. Anticipation sending tingles down my spine as the car moves toward the academy.

17

ADRIANNA

*a*rcher is sitting close to me in the back of the Uber, his hand firmly planted on my bare thigh.

Right now I'm so angry at him. He's going to force me into something I don't want and take my virginity like a trophy for his shelf.

"Why are you doing this?" I ask, hoping for one last chance to get him to change his mind. To force him to realize that blackmailing someone into sleeping with him is wrong on so many levels.

"I told you. I want you."

I grind my teeth. "And it doesn't matter that I don't want you?"

His smirk is condescending. "We both know that's a lie. Especially after you so enthusiastically swallowed my cum in detention and then again in the woods. You want me, and it's only a matter of time until you finally admit it to yourself."

I've ever felt so much hatred toward someone before in my life. "You make me want to puke."

"Keep telling yourself that, baby girl. It doesn't make it any less of a lie."

I grunt in frustration and cross my arms over my chest, looking out of the window of the Uber to avoid talking and looking at the bastard next to me.

The moment the academy's gates come into view, I feel sick to the stomach. This is happening and unless I want my family to know the way I've betrayed them, then I've got no choice but to sleep with this man.

The car pulls up and Archer walks around to open my door. He offers me his hand, which I ignore and get out of the car by myself, shoving my shoulder into him to get past.

"Now that was very rude. It's almost as if you want a good spanking tonight."

I try to walk away, but he grabs my wrist.

"Where do you think you are going?"

I glare at him. "To my dorm room."

He yanks me against him, his hands settling on my hips. "I already made it clear. You're coming to my apartment tonight. No negotiation unless you want your family to know the truth."

None of this makes sense.

Archer can have any girl he wants, or any other girl than me. Which begs the question, why's he resorting to blackmail to get me into his bed?

I let him grab my hand and drag me in the opposite direction to the main entrance. There's an apartment at the top of the library building. Rumor is that it has a beautiful view over the grounds and forest behind, but I don't want to find out, because that means I'm going to have to have sex with Archer.

"Are you sure you want to do this now?" I ask, trying to think of a reason Coach might listen to.

He squeezes my hand tighter. "There's no time like the present. I'm not sure why I'd wait when you've been driving me fucking crazy for an entire semester."

The closer we get to the building, the more my breathing labors. There's this pulse of adrenaline as the fight or flight instinct kicks in, and I know I have to get away. Yanking my hand free, I spin around fast and burst into a sprint across the courtyard toward the main door to the building where our dorms are.

"Adrianna!" He calls my name.

I keep running until I get to the door and every hope I had escapes me the moment I yank at it, finding it's locked.

Of course it's fucking locked. It's well past midnight now.

Archer grabs me around the waist and lifts me away from the door.

I thrash out in an attempt to break free. "Put me down!"

"No, you're being irrational." He carries me across the courtyard to a door next to the library entrance. Archer places me down on my feet, but keeps a good grasp on me as he unlocks the door and pushes it open. "In. Now." There's anger in his tone and it makes me shiver.

I step forward, knowing that fighting is stupid, as it doesn't stop him from telling my family the truth. And I step into the entrance, my head pounding hard in my chest as I gaze up the stairs.

"What are you waiting for, baby girl?" he asks, his hands on my hips.

I swallow hard and take my first step as his hands fall from my hips. A part of me wants to look back and check if he's following, but I don't. Instead, I keep walking until I make it into his apartment, which isn't what I expected.

I thought it would be modern and have bachelor pad vibes, but it's old-fashioned.

"I've changed nothing since the previous occupant. It suits the building, this style."

I glance at him. "Yeah, but not sure it suits you."

He shrugs and loosens his tie. "I'm not fussy."

I walk around the living room, which is decorated in a colonial style with brown furnishings and dark beige walls. The curtains are also dark.

"A drink?" Archer asks, holding two glasses of clear liquid.

"What is it?" I eye the glass warily, as I wouldn't put it past this man to drug me.

His jaw clenches. "Vodka. If you think I've drugged it, take mine."

I arch a brow. "What if that was your plan all along and you actually drugged yours?"

He sighs heavily and then downs both glasses. "Do you want to pour your own?" He shakes his head. "I may be blackmailing you to sleep with me, but I want you to be aware during. Drugging you wouldn't satisfy me at all."

I watch him as he moves closer.

"I want to hear you moaning my name while I fuck you, baby girl." He grabs my throat and pulls me toward him. "You'll be making noise all night long."

I hate the way my body tingles at the prospect. Even though I'm dreading what's about to happen, a part of me wants it. The horny, virgin side of me who can't keep her hormones in check.

"And I'm going to fill your pretty little cunt up with so much cum it'll be dripping out of you for days."

I shudder and take a step back, anticipating his next move.

"Tell me that doesn't turn you on."

I purse my lips together. "If I tell you that, you'll just tell me I'm lying."

His smile is beyond beautiful as he grabs hold of me and pulls me against him. "Right. You should admit that you want this."

I'm about to open my mouth to tell him that's not true, but he kisses me before I can. The moment he kisses me, any rational thought I have floats away like a helium balloon.

I claw at his hair and pull him closer, allowing him to swipe his tongue around my mouth frantically.

Archer lifts me off my feet, and I wrap my legs around him. He carries me as if I weigh nothing through the living room and into a lavish bedroom with a ridiculously large four-poster bed.

Dropping me onto the bed, he pulls my dress down my arms until it's around my waist, and then he climbs over me. Eyes alight with a fire that makes me so hot it feels like it's burning me. "What are you—"

He places his finger against my lip. "No questions. It's one of the rules."

"What are the others?"

"I will get to that soon." He kisses my neck and lower, trailing them over my cleavage. "Put your hands over your head like this." He grabs my wrists and forces them above my head together. "And don't move them."

"Is that another rule?"

Instead of answering, he continues to kiss me lower until the dress is in his way. And then he grabs hold of the fabric of my dress and tears it apart.

"Hey, I liked that dress."

He pulls my panties down and smirks up at me. "You'll like this more." And then his lips are on me, sucking my clit so hard it feels like I might combust there and then. My eyes are fixed on him as he devours me, watching me at the same time. Those dark brown eyes are full of passion.

I try to tell myself that I hate it, but it's a lie. What he's doing to me is the best sensation I've ever felt. It's addictive, even more addictive than working out or eating pizza.

His large hand rests on my stomach, holding me down. "You taste like fucking heaven," he murmurs, gazing at me with a look that makes me feel warm inside. "I can't wait to fuck you."

I lick my lips, honestly unable to believe that I can't wait either.

And then he sucks my clit into his mouth again, making me jolt against him. My body shudders for him as he thrusts his fingers deep inside of me at the same time, turning me into a white hot mess within seconds.

I moan loudly. It's shameful how good this man is making me feel, a man who literally got me into this bed because he's blackmailing me, and yet all of that doesn't matter right now.

His fingers thrust in and out of my pussy, making sounds as he does because I'm so wet. The man is a god, even if he's an asshole.

Maybe it feels so good because I hate him so much. That passionate hatred only makes the flames of desire more ravenous and all-consuming.

I can tell from the look in his eyes he's playing with me. He's not in a rush and he'll keep going until I'm so desperate I'm begging him.

"Please, coach," I moan, arching my back in an attempt to get his mouth back where I want it. "Let me come."

He smirks. "No chance in hell, baby. You won't come until my cock is inside of you." And then he sits up on his haunches, pulling his tie all the way off and tying it around my wrists above my head.

I watch him as he unbuttons his shirt and throws it to one side, before unbuttoning his pants and shifting position so he can get them off. My mouth waters at the unbelievably beautiful sight in front of me. His muscular yet lean body is completely on display and the outline of his huge cock is visible in his tight briefs.

"Do you like what you see?" he asks, rubbing a hand over his straining erection.

I swallow hard, knowing that my answer shouldn't be spoken, so I nod instead.

"Good girl," he praises, and that praise in itself is enough to set an inferno blazing deep in the pit of my stomach.

How can I dislike someone so much and want them on a physical level?

And then he pulls his cock out of his briefs and discards them. "I'm so hard for you." He fists his cock and my mouth waters, memories of tasting him rushing to the front of my mind. "I'm so ready to fuck your tight virgin cunt and make you mine."

I moan, unable to hold it in any longer. His words are like petrol on a bonfire and there's nothing I can do to stave off the hunger building inside of me.

He looms over me, stroking his erection with slow, forceful strokes. And then he moves closer so that he's between my thighs, his cock dripping precum onto my pussy. Slowly, he slides the tip through my entrance, coating himself with my arousal.

"Wait, I'm not on the pill." I place my hand on his chest, trying to stop him from moving forward.

He just looks me dead in the eye and then pushes forward, burying his cock inside of me with no protection. The rational part of my brain is screaming for him to stop, but the other, less rational part thinks the opposite.

And the pain tearing through my body is enough to render me mute, anyway.

"Fuck, that hurts," I groan, forgetting entirely about the fact we're fucking with no protection.

I've never felt so full before, so stretched. It's satisfying and painful at the same time.

"Oh fuck, you're so tight." Archer nips my lip with his teeth. "Relax, and it won't hurt so much."

I glare at him. "Easy for you to say. You're not the one being broken in half by a giant pole."

"Are you saying I have a giant cock?" he asks in that cocky, irritating manner.

"Shut up." I hit him.

That brings his focus back as his expression darkens. "Are you going to make me gag you?" And then his palm closes around my throat, squeezing hard enough to block the oxygen. "Or should I just choke you while we fuck, as I sense you'd get a kick out of it? Every single time I touch your throat, your heart rate quickens. Galloping faster with each second that ticks past."

I can feel his cock throbbing and pulsing inside of me as he holds still. "No. Just fuck me."

He growls then and presses his lips to mine, kissing me frantically. "I'm going to fuck you so damn hard and deep, baby girl. You won't know where I end and you begin."

"Archer," I gasp his name, longing to feel him move inside of me. "What are you waiting for?"

"Waiting for you to admit that you love this. I want to hear you tell me how badly you want me to fuck you."

I bite my lip, my stubbornness still waging war against my desire for this man.

"Tell me," he orders.

Swallowing hard, I nod in defeat. "I want you to fuck me so badly."

His eyes light up with victory as he moves slowly at first, pulling his thick cock almost all the way out of me. So only the tip is still inside. He takes so long I'm about to scream at him to get on with it, when he thrusts into me with a violent and deep stroke, tearing a scream from my lips for another reason entirely. The pain. It feels like I'm being clawed apart by him.

Archer kisses my neck and collarbone, before dragging his tongue lower to my nipples and circling each one. "It won't hurt for much longer." He moves with torturously slow strokes, somehow getting deeper with each one.

"You feel so damn good," he groans, eyes clamping shut as he looks like he's struggling to remain in control. And I feel surprisingly powerful in that moment, even though I'm beneath him.

I arch my back and he sinks even deeper inside of me than I believed possible. The ache he had ignited being quenched by his cock, but the stinging pain of being stretched open is there, even if it's diminishing with each stroke.

"Archer," I moan his name, unable to help myself.

He groans. "Fuck, your virgin cunt is so damn tight."

I bite my lip as his eyes open and they burn a hole through me. "Fuck me harder."

Archer is no longer being cocky or irritating as his eyes darken. "As you wish."

He quickens his pace, slamming into me with hard and forceful strokes.

My body bending to his will as he pounds into me with all his force. The pain is almost non-existent now as pure, unadulterated pleasure overtakes everything else.

"Oh fuck," I say, wriggling my arms in an attempt to free them.

Archer notices and puts his hand forcefully on my wrists. "No. I want you bound for me."

I grunt in frustration as he trails his finger down the center of my chest slowly, his cock still inside of me. And then he circles my clit with the lightest of touches and I combust.

"Oh my God!" My entire body shudders with the intensity of an orgasm unlike any I've ever experienced. "Archer!" I scream his name as my muscles clamp down around him.

He growls as he continues to fuck me through it, eyes flashing with a determination that tells me he's not done with me yet. Archer grabs my bound wrists and pulls them down to my chest and then flips me over, so that I'm on top, his cock still embedded deep inside of me.

"Ride my cock and make me come," he orders.

It's a challenge, but one that makes me feel unbelievably self-conscious.

"I want you to come again." He spanks my ass, the sensation only adding to the pleasure still coursing through my veins.

I bite my lip and then move my hips, never one to back down from a challenge, especially not from Coach.

He watches me as I move up and down, grinding my hips in a way that pushes him so deep inside of me it feels like he's going to tear me in half. "That's right, baby girl, fuck yourself on me." He spanks my ass, and it only adds to the intoxicating desire I feel right now, spurring me on like a horse being spurred into a gallop.

My hands remain bound in front of me and rested on his muscular abs as I use them to push myself up and down.

"You're so beautiful like this, Adrianna," he murmurs, watching me with an admiration that makes butterflies come to life in the pit of my stomach. "So fucking beautiful."

His words shouldn't make me feel the way they do, as no doubt he's said that to enough girls in his time here as the gym coach, but the way he looks at me makes me feel like the only fucking girl in the world. With that thought in my mind, I ride him harder, my hips finding a perfect rhythm as I chase my orgasm harder.

Archer's finger nails dig into my hips as he helps me, pushing me up and down his cock with force. And then I feel him hit a spot inside of me that sends me over the edge for the second time, and this time is even more intense. All of my muscles tense as I come apart, my body shaking with the force of my climax.

Archer growls. "Fuck, baby girl. Your cunt is like a vise." And then I feel his cock grow impossibly harder before he shoots his cum deep inside of me. The sensation is an odd feeling and yet it only makes my orgasm more powerful. "Take my cum like the good girl you are," he groans, fingertips digging hard into my hips.

When he finally stops rutting into me, I collapse by the side of him, my hands still bound. And slowly, as we lie in silence, apart from our labored breathing, reality creeps in and shame hits me hard. I just fucked Archer Daniels, and I enjoyed every minute, despite all that he's done.

What the hell is wrong with me?

It's time for me to beat him at his own game. He may think he's won, but I'm in it for the long haul. Taking my virginity may be the start, but what happens when he gets in too deep and wants more? I'll break his heart, and he'll wish he never went near me.

18

ARCHER

J can't help but walk with a spring in my step as I enter the academy the next morning. The frustration that had been plaguing me finally eased.

Adrianna gave in to the inevitable and we fucked like animals all damn night. The first time, afterward she was reluctant to go again, but I soon convinced her and by the time the fourth time came around she was the one begging for more. It was the best sex I've ever had, and I've had a lot, which isn't necessarily something to be proud of.

Once she let go of her inhibitions, she was a fucking goddess. It's hard to get the image of her riding my cock out of my mind.

I open the door to the staff room to find Gav, sitting in his usual chair, looking a little frustrated. "Morning," I say.

Gav's brow furrows as he looks up at me, as if in his

own word. "Morning," he grunts, and goes back to staring into space.

"Everything alright?"

"Great."

I detect a hint of sarcasm in his tone. "What's up?"

"Nothing. My workload is just getting to me this semester."

"You have math first period, don't you?" He's been grumpier than ever since he volunteered to cover math.

"Yes," he says simply.

Gav is difficult company on the best of days, but when he's like this, he's practically impossible to speak to. So, instead of persisting, I head to the coffee machine and pour myself a cup.

"Coffee?" I ask.

He just shakes his head in response.

Our moods couldn't be anymore opposite. "You seem chipper this morning. What happened between you and Adrianna?" Gav asks, glancing in my direction.

I clench my jaw. "That's for me to know and you to wonder."

Gav shakes his head in frustration and goes back to staring into nothing.

The guy may be my friend, but I can't deny that sometimes he scares me.

These moods he gets into differ from someone sulking. He's cloaked in a darkness I could never understand. Oak saved him, much like he saved me from my family, but they won't ever talk about the details. All I know it involved a double homicide and Gav going to jail for a very long time.

Gav did something he couldn't have come back from and Oak gave him a way out. "I'm going to head to class," I say, watching him carefully. "You coming?"

Gav shakes his head. "Go ahead. I've still got five minutes."

I pity any student that gets sent to him today, as he's truly in a bad mood.

"Okay, see you later." I walk out with my cup of coffee and head toward the gym.

Adrianna isn't in any of my classes today, unfortunately. Ever since she left my apartment in the early hours of the morning, insisting she didn't want to sleep in my bed until we had to get up, all I can think about is her. Hell, I even dreamed about Adrianna.

She's taken my mind captive and I'm not sure whether I like it. As I walk down the corridor, I'm in my own world. Until I knock right into the girl I was fucking daydreaming about. My hands instinctively land on her hips to steady her.

She looks a little dazed too as she glances up. "Sorry, I —" When she realizes it's me, her cheeks flush a beautiful crimson color. "Oh."

"Hey, baby girl," I murmur, tightening my grasp on her. "How are you feeling this morning?"

Her jaw clenches. "Tired and sore."

I smirk at that, as it's not surprising she's sore. We fucked four times, and she's never had sex before. I'm surprised she can even walk. "Good."

"I'm going to be late for class," she says, trying to wriggle out of my grasp.

"Me too, but I'm not sure I want to let you go." I glance around, noticing there's fewer and fewer students by the moment as everyone heads into their classes.

"It doesn't matter what you want." Her eyes flash as she manages to slip out of my grasp. "I'm going." She heads in the opposite direction, but I won't let her walk away from me like that.

I chase after her and grab the back of her neck, jerking her to a stop and swiftly forcing her to face me. "Listen to me, Adrianna. You may have fucked me last night, but that's not where this ends. You'll be in my bed every damn night until you graduate. Do you understand?"

Her nostrils flare. "That's ridiculous."

"I have information on you, so it's my choice if I want to use it to have you in my bed as much as I want." I lean close to her and drag my lips against her earlobe, making her shudder. "And after the amazing sex we had last night, I want you in my bed as often as possible."

"I can't explain that to my friends."

I move back and look into her beautiful, dark eyes. "Explain what, exactly? You'll come to my apartment late when your friends are asleep. Simple."

Her jaw clenches. "I've got to get to class. I have math with Professor Nitkin."

"I didn't hear you agree to my terms." I tighten my grasp on the back of her neck, ignoring the slightly odd looks we receive from students passing by. I've never been discreet about my relationships with students before, but I guess this is the first resistant one, so I don't normally have a student by the back of the neck in the corridor.

"What terms?" she says, impatience in her tone.

I sigh heavily. "You'll come to my apartment once your friends have retired to their rooms," I demand.

She glares at me. "And if I don't?"

"I'll be in touch if you don't turn up like a good girl."

Her nostrils flare and rage ignites in her eyes. "Whatever."

My grasp tightens on the back of her neck. "I don't appreciate the attitude, baby girl."

She licks her bottom lip, drawing my attention to it. And then I kiss her, not even checking if there are students around, as I don't care. Instead, I thrust my tongue into her mouth and kiss her deeply, taking what I want from her. It's amusing the way she bends to my will, moaning softly into my mouth the moment my lips are on hers.

After a too short a period, we break apart.

"I'm going to be late for math," she says, glancing at her watch with a worried look in her eyes.

"I'd run," I say, looking at the clock on the wall behind us. "He's in a foul mood this morning." I release her neck at that moment.

"Great," she says, dodging around me and rushing down the corridor.

"I'll see you later, Adrianna."

She doesn't reply or look back as she rushes toward Gav's classroom.

I ignore that doubt clawing at the back of my mind

about continuing this with Adrianna, as it feels different to any other relationship I've had with a student or woman in my past.

The all-consuming need to have her close constantly threatens to drown me. I can feel it eating away at me. Today is going to be a long and torturous day, but I can't wait until Adrianna is in my bed tonight, sitting on my cock where she belongs.

THE CLOCK HAND moves to quarter past eleven, and I pace up and down faster, rage coiling through me as I wonder if Adrianna is defying a direct order. All the girls have to be in their rooms by ten thirty, which means she should be here by now.

I pull my cell phone out and type a text.

Me: Where are you? Don't make me come to your dorm and drag you here.

If she doesn't reply or isn't here within thirty minutes, I'll be at her dorm. I don't care what kind of scene I make. Adrianna belongs to me for this year, and that's the only way the information I found gets buried.

Adrianna: I'm busy finishing an assignment.

Adrianna is testing my patience. Clenching my fists, I consider my options. The desperate need to see her right now is threatening to tear away any self-control I have.

Me: You have made a big mistake.

I grab my coat and head down the stairs of my apartment and out into the courtyard, unlocking the door into the main building. My cell phone dings.

Adrianna: I can't help it if I have work to do.

This conversation is over. Adrianna isn't taking my threats seriously, so perhaps it's time I make her. I have her father's email address and with one click of a button, I could send him the photos of his daughter meeting with his arch nemesis. It would be that simple, so I need to show her how easy it would be, even though I don't intend to tell her family or anyone for that matter.

I key in the code to get into the girls' dorms and march into the empty corridors. As I expected, there's no one out at this time of night. Adrianna's room is one of the biggest rooms because her father paid for it. I navigate to it and stop in front of her door, trying to ease some of the rage inside.

Bringing my fist to the door, I beat on it hard.

There are soft footsteps on the other side. "Who is it?"

"Don't play games with me, Vasquez," I say in hushed tones, not wanting to draw unwanted attention to my presence in the girls' dorms.

"I'm not playing games. I have a torture assignment due tomorrow morning."

"Open the damn door before I break it down."

I rarely lose my temper, but Adrianna is driving me to aggression. Even though I know this door is impossible to break down. It weighs about 200lbs and is bulletproof.

She fumbles with the lock and then opens the door with the chain across, peering out at me. "What do you want?"

"You know the deal, Adrianna, so why are you defying me?"

Her throat moves as she swallows. "When am I supposed to do my assignments?"

"You had all fucking night to do them." I slam my hand against the door. "If you don't take that chain off right this minute, I'll snap it off."

She sighs heavily and pushes the door shut enough to unlatch the chain and then opens it to me.

I move fast, driven by adrenaline, as I step into her room and slam the door behind me. My breathing is labored as she backs away from me, a glint of fear in her eyes.

"What are you going to do?"

I pull my cell phone out of my jacket pocket and go into my draft emails. "I think maybe we have our wires crossed or something." I move toward her, phone facing her. "I addressed this email to your father. The moment I decide you aren't going to co-operate, I hit the send button and it's all over for you."

Adrianna glances at the email, the blood from her cheeks draining as she turns a pale white color. "I am co-operating, but you're asking me to get in to trouble with Professor Nitkin because you are too impatient to wait." She sets her hands on her hips.

"Listen, Adrianna." I place the phone down on the desk with the email still up and ready to be sent. "Tonight we settle this. Either you do exactly as I tell you from this moment until the end of the year, or I send the email to your father. It's your choice."

She glares at me hatefully. "You're a fucking bastard."

"I don't care what you think of me. You need to make a decision and stick to it. What's it going to be?" I grab my phone. "Shall I send it?"

She launches at it and grabs the phone out of my hand. "No. I'll do whatever you want." She deletes the draft, which is a bold move. "I promise. No more defiance." For the first time, I believe her.

"Fine." I snatch my phone out of her hand. "Lie on the bed."

Her cheeks flush a dark red. "Surely not here. People will hear."

I grab her hips and drag her against me. "You should have thought about that before you defied my orders." My cock is harder than stone as I tighten my grasp on her hips, pushing her back toward the bed against the far wall. "Lie down."

As always, there's that defiant light in her eyes, but she sighs heavily and does as she's told, lying down on her bed. I pull my shirt off and then my pants until I'm only in my briefs.

Adrianna's attention dips to the outline of my hard cock and I rub it.

"Are you ready for it, baby girl?"

She glares up at me. "No."

I grab her knees and spread her thighs wide apart roughly. "Well, it doesn't matter, because I'm fucking this pretty little cunt, no matter what you say."

I lower myself over her and kiss her lips forcefully,

pushing my tongue through them as I kiss her like my life depends on it. Right now, it feels that way. Adrianna will wish she hadn't defied me by the time the night is through. I'm going to show her how powerless she is.

19

ADRIANNA

*A*rcher is a beast.

There's a difference tonight, as he's being more aggressive and assertive. I can't work out if it's because I pissed him off by not turning up at his apartment tonight or if he was being gentle last night.

He bites my collarbone, and the pain is thrilling. As he uses his teeth and tongue to tease every part of my body slowly and roughly. Every touch is rough as he grabs hold of my wrists and forces them above my head. And then his teeth sink into my left breast, making me yelp.

I'm entirely at his mercy, as it feels like his presence zaps all the oxygen from the room. A darkness that wasn't there before seems to surround him as he nips and sucks at my body, turning me into a desperate slut for him. A mix of both fear and desire, making for an addictive combination. It shocks me to find that I actually enjoy the sensation, being scared.

Let's face it, I hardly know Archer and what he's

capable of. All I know is he's the gym coach at this academy and he's ridiculously stubborn. Slowly, he explores my body with his tongue and teeth, driving me crazy with the mix of pleasure and pain in the perfect quantities.

I moan, unable to control my reaction to his ministrations. Even here in my dorm room, where I should be fucking quiet.

"I'm going to fucking devour you until there's nothing left," he growls into my ear and then nips my earlobe. "You'll enjoy every second."

Slowly, he stands and pulls down his briefs, freeing his thick, veiny length. "I'm going to fuck your ass, baby girl."

I freeze, the idea sending terror right into my heart. "No."

He tilts his head. "What did I tell you earlier?"

I swallow hard, realizing that I have no power. If I don't want that email to be sent to my dad, then I have to do as he says. After losing my virginity last night, there's no way I expected to graduate to anal sex today. "There's no way you'll fit that in my ass."

"I think you underestimate my persistence." There's an evil glint in his eyes as he grabs my hips and flips me over to my front. "Now be a good girl and do as you're told."

He doesn't say another word, just slams forward and buries himself in my sore pussy.

I scream, the pain unexpected.

He reaches around and places his hand on my mouth,

muffling the screams that try to break free. And then he fucks me like a madman. His cock thrusting in and out in hard, violent thrusts, as his heavy cock fills a hole that I didn't know I needed filling until that moment. "Fuck," I grunt into his mouth.

He pulls his hand away. "I want to hear you moan while I tear you apart, baby girl."

I moan out loud and it's a sound so foreign to my ears it makes me cringe. And then suddenly he spanks my ass hard, the impact a surprise but so damn good. Instead of crying out, as you'd expect from being hit, I moan louder.

"If I didn't know any better, I'd say you're a masochist."

I wouldn't have pegged myself as one until now.

"You're so wet. Even wetter than last night. Is it because you are excited to get your little ass stretched?"

I shudder at his words. "No, please don't——"

He spanks me again, this time even harder.

I bite my lip to stop myself from making any more shameful noises. He's right, though, as I can feel my arousal dripping down my legs as I get wetter. I try not to give away how turned on I'm as I clench my comforter.

The sickening thing is that I like how dominant and forceful he's being. Not giving me a choice or caring if I consent to what he's doing. He's a crazed beast taking what he wants no matter the consequences, and I hate to say that I love it.

Archer tightens his grip on my hips and uses his muscular arms to pull me toward him with each thrust of his hips, burying himself so deep it feels like he's trying to break me.

Suddenly, he stops moving and I groan in frustration, trying to back onto his cock, but he holds me firm. And then I feel his finger probing at my asshole and I'm brought right back to reality.

"What are you——"

"No questions," he growls. And then I feel him gathering my arousal onto his fingers and smearing it over my asshole.

I feel shame as the sensation of his touch makes me melt, despite what he's about to do to me.

"Such a tight hole," he muses, and then slides a finger through the muscles. "Do you like that?"

I groan, the sensation unlike anything I've ever felt. There's no way I can answer him right now. My mind is a mess of jumbled thoughts.

Archer's hand wraps around the back of my neck and he yanks me upright. "I asked you a question, baby."

I grind my teeth together. "No," I answer, as I won't give him the satisfaction.

"Naughty little liar." He spanks me hard, and the impact steals the breath from my lungs.

"I'm not lying."

He thrusts another finger inside of my ass and my whole body feels like it sets on fire. My pussy soaking wet as he plays with my ass. The feeling is better than anything I've felt before, but that's just his fingers. There's no way it will feel that good if he sticks his cock in there. It's too thick.

"You're lying because I've never seen a woman get this wet ever, and it's because I'm fingering your ass."

And then he spanks my pussy and my whole word shatters. The impact of his hand on such a sensitive area of my body ruins me. I scream, hating that I can't even keep quiet in my dorm room with this man, because he has turned me into a quivering mess and shattered all rational thought.

"Fuck, Adrianna," he groans, his voice laced with awe. "Did you just come for me, baby girl?" He pulls his cock out of my pussy. "You've got me nice and wet and ready for your ass."

I shudder, trying not to give in to what this man is doing to me.

He pulls his fingers out of my ass next and then I feel the hot, hard length of him against my hole. "I bet deep down you are craving this dick in your ass, aren't you?"

I shake my head.

"More lies." He adjusts himself so the tip is pressing against my tight ring of muscles.

"It's going to hurt. Don't you need lube?" I ask, frantic to get him to stop.

"You're making more than enough lube." He pushes forward with force and I scream into the pillow below me at the excruciating sensation of being stretched open so wide. "And by the time I'm through with you, you'll be begging for more." His fingertips dig into my skin as he grasps me harder, spearing me with his immense length. My clit is throbbing for friction and I try to move one hand between thighs to satisfy the need, but Archer spanks my ass.

"No, you don't get to touch yourself. Only I get to touch you."

I growl in frustration, glancing over my shoulder at him. "You're being an asshole."

He smirks, but it's not friendly, it's vindictive. "No, you've got that wrong. I'm fucking your asshole, baby. And I don't appreciate being called names while I do."

I jolt as his large hand comes down on my backside again, making my nipples ache. I'm thinking that there's more than first appears when it comes to Archer. The darkness he harbors inside set free as he pushes forward slowly, stretching my tiny hole with his cock.

I groan into the pillow beneath me, wanting nothing more than to scream at the top of my lungs. And then the pain eases as I feel his balls against my clit.

"You've taken every inch of me inside, baby." Archer licks the back of my neck. "I'm going to make you climax again while I fuck this tight virgin ass." A shiver starts at the top of my head and races down my spine, making me prickle with anticipation as he holds still, the pain of being stretched only adding to the sickening desire I have for him.

I wait with bated breath for him to begin the fucking. It feels like excruciating minutes pass by as I wait in silence.

"What's going—"

"What did I tell you, Adrianna?"

I swallow hard. "No questions, but you aren't moving."

"I'm biding my time and enjoying this moment," he says, amusement in his tone. "Are you saying you want me to fuck you in the ass?"

"I'm saying fuck me or don't. Stop lingering in no-man's-land."

He reaches around and grabs hold of my throat with both hands, squeezing. "You don't tell me what to do, Adrianna, not in this situation." He removes one hand and spanks my ass again, making me sure he'll leave bruises on my skin. "Now be a good girl and tell me what you want me to do."

I bite my lip so hard I draw blood because my stubbornness is at war with my desire. "Fuck me," I mumble.

"Sorry, what was that?" he says, smugness dripping from his tone.

"I said fuck me, for God's sake."

He chuckles. "Ask nicely, baby."

"Fuck me, please," I grit out.

"Good girl," he growls, and then he fucks me.

His cock slides in and out of me with slow and painful thrusts. While he'd been still, the pain had subsided, but the moment he moves the intense pain returns.

"Fuck, your ass feels so good."

I bite my lip so hard it bleeds. "It hurts," I complain.

He places his rough hand against my back and drags it gently down my spine, making me shiver. "Relax, baby girl. If you relax, it'll feel good."

"Easy for you to say," I grit out.

He doesn't say another word, brushing his hand against my back and moving his cock in and out, slowly but forcefully. Our bodies melding together in the dirtiest way as he plows into me faster with each thrust, building the pleasure and decreasing the pain with every movement.

I never thought I'd submit so easily, but it feels so good. Archer is in the driving seat and all I have to do is feel. Every sensation he'd coaxing from me building with each thrust of his cock.

"Oh fuck," I moan, knowing that before long I will come. "It feels good," I say, almost shocked.

The pressure between my thighs is unbearable as I long to touch my clit, but resist since Archer won't allow it. "Please, Archer," I beg, forgetting that either side of these walls are other students.

Coach hasn't been very subtle about his pursuit to get me into bed with him. And it will be pretty humiliating if people know that he's fucking me. The last thing I want is for my friends to find out after I was adamant that I won't have sex with him.

"What do you want, baby?" he asks, his voice deep and laced with lust.

"I need to come," I cry, tears gathering in my eyes as the sensation becomes impossible to bear. Every single nerve in my body is on fire, making my thighs shake as I'm so close to climaxing.

Archer's hand runs down my back slowly, and then he spanks my ass.

"Oh fuck, yes!" It's all it takes to send me over the

edge as I scream so loud I'm sure the entire fucking academy can hear me.

"That's it, baby girl. Come with my cock in your ass," he growls, pumping harder and faster. And then suddenly he bends over and presses his lips to my shoulder, roaring into my skin as he comes too. Filling my ass with his seed as we both ride the wave of ecstasy. Our uneven breathing fills the room, which suddenly feels too small.

Archer doesn't move for a long time, keeping me pressed against the mattress as his cock pulses inside of me. I can hardly believe what just happened.

Archer finally moves off of me and his cock slides out of my abused hole, leaving me feeling so empty. And then he stands up and dresses, sliding on his shirt first and then his briefs and pants. Once he's dressed, he glances at me. "See you tomorrow night at my apartment."

He walks out of my dorm room without another word, as if he didn't just turn into a fucking animal and fuck my ass. I sit upright, wincing at the pain radiating through my abused hole. Archer Daniels is a monster and I'm wondering if being ratted out to my family might be a better option, even if they'll kill me.

20

ARCHER

*T*wo weeks ago, I lost control while I was with Adrianna because her defiance makes me insane. And ever since, it's like she's obeying me, but there's always an undercurrent of defiance.

It's both infuriating and intoxicating, and it drives me crazy. That's only way I can explain my vicious actions that night when I forced my way into Adrianna's dorm room and stole her anal virginity. There's been no mention of it since, but I know she resents me for being so forceful, as Adrianna isn't naturally submissive. I've forced her into submission and while usually that's Gav's kind of thing, it's odd how much I enjoy it.

My favorite trail through the woods helps me blow off steam as I jog up the hill toward the old ruins, getting close to the academy. I've hardly even broken a sweat and consider doing another couple of miles when something catches my eye, or should I say someone.

Adrianna is sitting on a large boulder by the stream,

her legs hugged against her chest as she rocks slightly back and forth. The position is vulnerable, and it surprises me, but there's no way I can jog past her without acknowledging her.

Instead, I slow to a walk and approach her.

She appears to be in her own world, as even branches snapping underfoot don't alert her to my presence.

"Hey, baby girl," I say softly once I'm a few feet from her.

She stiffens at the sound of my voice. "I'm really not in the mood right now, Archer."

I smile as it's taken a lot of persuading, but she's finally calling me Archer and not Coach. "Okay, mind if I sit with you?"

She glares at me. "I do, as that's why I'm here. To get away from people."

"People?" I ask.

"Yeah, I needed some space to clear my head."

I nod. "I can understand that. Anyone in particular?"

"You," she says, but then a whisper of a smirk twists onto her lips. "No, I'm pissed at my dad. He's sent me a summons to go to Mexico a week before Spring Break to meet a potential suitor."

I clench my fist. "A what?"

She raises a brow. "He intends to marry me off as soon as I finish here at the academy. Isn't that what happens to practically every female student?"

She's right. It is. But I never imagined that Adrianna would accept that fate. Even though she said she doesn't want me to sit, I sit down on the rock next to her, which is terribly uncomfortable.

"Do you never listen?"

"Rarely," I say, smiling at her. "So, who is this suitor?"

"No idea. You'd have to ask my father."

I tilt my head. "I don't think he'd tell me, do you?"

She grinds her teeth, which I notice she does when she's stressed. "No," she says simply, turning her attention back to the water.

"Do you come down here often?"

Adrianna shakes her head. "Only when I need to think, and that's not too often when I'm here at the academy."

"And when you're home?" I realize that her home-life must not be the best, and as someone who also betrayed his family in a different way, I get a sense I may understand more about Adrianna than she would expect.

"I don't see it as home, not really."

I understand more than she can know, as I felt exactly the same about my home. "You feel like an imposter?"

Her eyes widen. "Yeah, how did you—"

"Let's say I had a difficult family, too."

She smiles, and it's a smile that warms my heart. A worrying sensation, considering normally I feel nothing when I'm having an intimate relationship with a student, but Adrianna is different. Special.

"It's why I betrayed my family, you know?"

"Why?" I ask.

She looks at me then and it feels like she sees past all

the bullshit right to my soul. "Because I want to escape their clutches."

"I could give you some tips."

Her eyes narrow. "Are you saying you ran from your family, too?"

I clench my jaw as I rarely talk to anyone about my past. Oak knows the full story, but no one else does. "Yes, some shit went down, and I had to flee."

"What kind of shit?"

I shake my head. "It's not important."

Her brow furrows. "Did you betray your family?"

I guess I betrayed them, but not in the way that Adrianna did. "Kind of." I run a hand across the back of my neck. "I don't like to talk about it."

Adrianna doesn't question me, turning her attention back to the running water. "I know what I'm doing is bad and it will hurt my family in the long run, but they don't care about my future. My father wants to marry me to some thug with no regard as to the life I'll live after marriage."

It's unfair what the females of this school go through, like stepping back in time to an era when women didn't have rights, but that's the way of the criminal system. There are a handful of female leaders, but they're a minority.

"It's a disgrace what the women of mafia organizations are subjected to," I say.

Adrianna's eyes widen. "Few men would admit that out loud."

I shrug. "I've always thought it. You're stronger than

most of the boys and yet you have to submit to some chump who you could probably beat up."

Adrianna shudders. "That's why it won't happen."

"You honestly think you can escape your family? They're pretty powerful."

Her expression turns pensive as she gazes over the water again. "Money is the key to everything. If I have enough money, I can hide."

It is the key to everything, whether it's in the criminal world or outside of it, but I don't believe it can hide her forever. Adrianna is recognizable and her father, Damien, would put a reward out for her. If anyone saw her, she'd quickly find herself pursued. "You father has more money, though."

She tilts her head. "What does that matter?"

"What kind of ransom will he offer for your return?"

Her throat bobs as she swallows. "I don't want to think about it."

She knows that any ransom he offers will be so high that she couldn't contend with the manpower that comes after her.

"It's important to think of every eventuality if you're going to succeed."

"Are you going to coach me on how to evade my family?"

"I could do, or..." I lean forward and kiss her neck softly. "I could teach you something more exciting."

Adrianna sucks in a deep, shuddering breath. "Archer, not here."

I tilt my head. "Why not, baby girl?"

"Because this is my safe place. When I have something to think about, this is where I come." She looks me dead in the eye. "I need it to remain that way. Untainted."

"Are you saying that having sex with me would taint it?"

Her jaw works. "Yes."

I realize it's true. When I was still at home, I had a place I escaped to that was all my own. The old tree house in the woods that a distant relative had built years before I was born. It was my escape, and no one bothered me there. "Fair enough."

Adrianna's eyes widen. "I thought you were going to push me."

I shake my head. "I know what you mean about having a safe place." I stand and hold my hand out to her. "Shall we take this to my apartment?"

"It's the middle of the day."

"What's your point? It's a Sunday, which means we're both free."

She crosses her arms over her chest. "My point is there's no way I'm walking into your apartment without being seen by many students. I don't want anyone to know that I gave in to your pursuit of me."

"No?" I ask, pulling her against me and wrapping my arms around her waist. "We should go to the gym instead."

Her nostrils flare, but I see the fire of desire ignite. "Fine."

It's amusing how over time her defiance has diminished and her willingness to submit to me only increases with every passing day. "I'll go first and you meet me there in five minutes. Okay?"

She nods in response.

I turn and walk up the incline, following the path toward the academy. It was difficult to walk away from her rather than fucking her against a tree like an animal, but if I want her to forgive me for the blackmail, then destroying her safe place probably isn't the best way to go about it.

The walk to the gym feels like it takes forever and then waiting for her to arrive feels like an age, too. Finally, the door to the gym swings open and she strides in confidently. Even when obeying my rules, she's always so feisty.

Adrianna walks straight up to me, eyes fixed on mine, and then she grabs my shirt and yanks me toward her, our lips melding.

She groans the moment I rock against her, my cock hard and trying to break free from the confines of my sweatpants. "Fuck, baby," I murmur against her lips. "What are you doing?"

"Quiet before I change my mind." She drops to her knees before me and pulls my cock out of my pants, making me grunt the moment her soft hand wraps around my girth.

And then she slips my cock through those beautiful lips of hers and stares up at me as she teases the head with her tongue. It's fucking heaven.

My fingers are tingling to wrap around her hair and force the length down her throat, but I let her have the control for now. Allowing her to set the pace as she teases me with her tongue and lips, never taking me deep enough into her throat.

"Stop teasing me, baby girl."

Her eyes narrow at the use of the nickname she still hasn't grown accustomed to, but she keeps doing what she's doing, teasing me. And the way she looks at me, it's as if she's goading me to take control.

It's because no matter how much Adrianna puts on a show that she doesn't enjoy being dominated, it's clear she loves it. So, I give her what she wants and wrap her hair around my palm.

And I slam every inch down her throat, making her eyes bulge at the force. I've never been a forceful lover, but Adrianna makes me this way.

She gags, saliva spilling down her face as tears gather in her eyes. It's a beautiful sight to behold. I wish I could keep this picture as vivid as a painting in my mind, as she is on her knees of her own free will right now.

And she relaxes as I fuck her throat. I'd go as far to say that she's enjoying it. Right here in the gym where anyone could walk in and catch us, since Adrianna didn't lock the door behind her. It's thrilling as I slide into the back of her throat harder, and more saliva spills from her mouth.

"Fuck baby, you suck my cock so well," I groan, letting my head fall back as I slide in and out of her throat as if it were her pussy.

She grumbles something, but I can't hear her.

"So fucking perfect," I say, as I gaze down at the beauty before me.

It's the truth. So many men praise their women,

calling them beautiful or perfect, but with Adrianna, it's the goddamn truth. I haven't found one weakness in her. She's strong, independent and more beautiful than any girl I've ever laid eyes on.

"I'm going to come down that throat," I growl, forcing it even deeper so she gags more forcefully. My cock swells in her mouth. "And I want you to swallow every drop for me, baby girl."

My climax hits me like a tonne of bricks as I'm flooded with pleasure.

She readily accepts my cum, swallowing fast enough to keep up as if she's hungry for it.

"I want you on your hands and knees over there." I point to the gym mat and she saunters over to it, giving me a flirtatious look.

This girl is going to be the death of me, and I wouldn't have it any other way.

21

ADRIANNA

I glance at my clock, noticing it's just turned ten.

Archer insists I head over to his apartment at ten o'clock on the dot each night. It's irritating as hell and I still have work to do on a torture assignment, but I've got a free period in the morning. There's no doubt that the sex with Archer is good.

For two weeks, I've slept in his bed every single night. After the first time we had sex, I went straight to Nurse Jasper and asked her to give me the contraceptive pill, as clearly I'm the only responsible one in this relationship.

Archer doesn't take unwanted pregnancy seriously for a man who's fucking a student. There's no way in hell I want to be the kid that gets knocked up the last year of the academy by her fucking gym coach.

I won't lie and say I don't enjoy our time together. He's a fucking God in bed, but it's time I set my plan in motion. It's time I get some payback for him forcing me to give up my virginity to him.

He'll wish he never got into bed with me. As always, I'm wearing no panties, as per his request, as I grab an overnight bag and sling it over my shoulder, creeping out into the corridor.

"Where are you going, Vasquez?" Anita asks, making me jump.

I swallow hard and turn to face her. "It's none of your business."

Her eyes narrow as she moves toward me. "You are going to see Coach, aren't you?"

Heat prickles over my skin at the prospect that one of my enemies knows I'm sleeping with Archer. "No chance in hell. Why do you say that?"

"The two of you went at it a couple of weeks ago." Her lips twist into a smirk. "The walls aren't made of soundproof material, you know." She pokes her finger into my shoulder. "You shouldn't act like you're above being a slut and then secretly sneak around with him. It's dishonest."

"I don't know what you think you heard, Anita, but it wasn't me and Coach."

"Please, Archer," she mimics in a begging voice. "Don't tell me that there's another Archer here I don't know of. I know what I heard."

"What do you want?" I ask, getting fed up with being threatened by everyone around me.

She taps her chin. "I want you to let me have him."

I arch a brow. "Let you have him?"

"Yeah, leave Coach alone."

"Believe me, I've tried, but he won't leave me alone." I

run a hand through my hair. "Do you think I want this?"

"Who the hell wouldn't? He's gorgeous."

I roll my eyes at Anita's pathetic argument why I'd want to sleep with Coach. "He's a cocky bastard who blackmailed me into sleeping with him."

"Then you won't mind stopping."

I clench my jaw. "He won't let me, because he's black-mailing me."

"Well, so am I, so get out of being his this year."

"What do you have on me?"

"You're sleeping with Coach."

"And where exactly is your proof?"

Anita frowns. "What do you mean?"

"It's your word against mine. No proof, which means you can't blackmail me." I shake my head at how dumb she is. "Now if you would excuse me—"

She yanks my hair as I try to move around her and so I grab her wrist and bend it at an unnatural angle, cracking the bones. Anita screams at the top of her lungs, and then swings at me with her right hand, landing a punch over my right eye.

I retaliate and grab her other wrist, twisting it until I hear a crack and then forcing her face first against the wall. "You're an idiot to take me on in combat."

She growls and tries to kick me, but I grab her ankle and twist it, which puts her off balance and she falls, screaming as she breaks it with her injured wrists.

"What's the meaning of this?" Professor Davidson's voice echoes down the hall.

I turn to face her. "Anita wouldn't get out of my way

and yanked my hair, so I retaliated," I say simply.

Professor Davidson shakes her head as she looks at my eye, which is no doubt already bruising. "You can get that looked at at the infirmary."

I nod and turn around, leaving her to sort out Anita, who's clearly an idiot for challenging me. Archer is going to get angry when I don't turn up on time, so to avoid him banging down my dorm room door, I grab my cell phone and text him.

Me: Had a fight with Anita. Been sent to the infirmary.

I slip my cell phone back into my pocket and continue walking toward the infirmary. Not that I need to get my eye looked at. It's just bruise. Professor Davidson is probably the weakest of the professors.

My cell phone dings and I check it.

Archer: I'll come and see you.

I swallow hard, as I don't want him to come to the infirmary.

Me: Not much point. I will be out soon.

I text him, but deep down I know he'll probably come, regardless. Nurse Jasper's waiting by the entrance when arrive, her eyes narrow. "I hear you caused quite a few injuries to your fellow pupil."

"As I told Professor Davidson, Anita started it, and I wouldn't roll over and take it."

She narrows her eyes before nodding. "Fine, let me look at that eye before Anita arrives."

Nurse leads me into a room and gets a flashlight. "Try to keep your eye open. I need to check for any damage."

I laugh. "I can tell you that there's no damage. Anita hits like a pussy."

She makes a tutting sound before checking my eye and then nodding. "Fine, ice it for twenty minutes and then you can go." She nods to a bucket of ice on the counter. "Unfortunately, your classmate won't be so lucky from what I gather." And then she walks out.

I grab some ice and wrap it in cloth, wincing as I place it against my bruised face.

Within five minutes Archer walks into the infirmary, and straight into my room. "I hear you got yourself into a bit of trouble." He approaches me and stops within a foot, brushing a hand across the bruised skin around my eye.

"You should see Anita."

He winces. "I'd rather not. I heard you broke a few of her bones."

I shrug. "She started it."

"Come on, I've been told to escort you back to your dorm room since Elaine says you don't need to stay."

I swallow hard. "Okay."

"We both know you're not going back to that dorm room."

Archer places a hand on my back and steers me out of the infirmary and towards the courtyard. My heart pounds erratically, as all I want is to break free from the constraints of this stupid agreement. Anita may well tell my friends, and I don't know how to explain why I'd slept with a man I professed to hate.

I can't imagine telling Nat and Camilla in particular that I've betrayed my family to the Estrada Cartel. They wouldn't approve, as they're both big on family and loyalty. Archer opens the door to his apartment and allows me to go first. It feels strange that I've spent so much time here in the last two weeks.

I walk into the kitchen followed closely by Archer. It may be his apartment, but I make myself at home when I'm here. I pull open the fridge door and retrieve a carton of milk, helping myself to a glass. "Milk?" I ask, noticing Archer is watching me with an odd look on his face.

He shakes his head. "No, but I'd like to see you in this kitchen more often."

I narrow my eyes at him. "Why? I can't cook."

Archer licks his lips. "I've got other ideas for you in here."

I sigh heavily and drink the milk. As it always has to be sexual with him. He doesn't have an off button and it can get tiring.

He tilts his head, looking at me oddly.

"What?"

"Are you going to tell me why you ended up in a fist-fight with Anita?"

"Wasn't planning on it."

He stands and walks toward me. "Tell me, Adrianna."

"She wants you and told me to back off." I notice the way his eyes light up. "And before you get too cocky, I wasn't fighting her because I want this to continue between us. I was fighting her because I told her I had no way out and she still tried to stop me."

He moves toward me, eyes alight with fire. "Deep down, you don't want this to end. Admit it, baby."

I roll my eyes. "I would happily walk out of this apartment and never return if you allowed me to."

He grabs my hand and pulls me toward him. "I've told you many times before, you're not a talented liar."

"It's not a lie." And although the sex is good, it's true. If Archer confirmed he'd never tell my family right now, I'd walk out of that door and never come back. He's an asshole and not the man I want to be wasting my time with.

"How about I make you some pancakes?" he asks.

"Sure, I could eat."

He smiles. "Can't you always eat?"

I narrow my eyes, wondering how he knows that. "Perhaps."

He releases my hand and gets to work making pancakes. It's strange watching him in the kitchen, as I never would have imagined him cooking anything, even if it is something as simple as pancakes.

"I've got to admit I'm proud of your handiwork, but don't tell anyone else."

"What handiwork?"

He glances over his shoulder. "Anita. You really put your combat training into practice."

I feel heat radiate around my body at the way he's looking at me. "Of course. I'm not about to let her walk all over me." My brow furrows. "I think she's stupid for even trying to start a fight with me, considering."

"Yeah, it surprised me to hear she started it."

I sit up straighter. "Why the hell would I start a fight?"

He shrugs. "You can be hot tempered, baby girl."

I clench my jaw. "Only with you."

He chuckles as he plates up a stack of pancakes and puts them in front of me. And then he grabs the maple syrup and some blueberries out of the fridge. "Buon Appetite." He winks.

Although I'm annoyed at him for thinking I would start a fight with Anita, my greed wins out.

I dig into the pancakes, moaning. "These are delicious. Are you alway this good at cooking?"

He shrugs. "I have hidden talents. You should try my homemade marinara sauce. It's pretty good."

"I might take you up on that. I love food."

He smirks. "Well, you might fall in love with me once you try it," Archer teases, but there's a hint of seriousness in his tone.

I glare at him. "There's more chance that pigs will fly than me ever feeling anything other than contempt for you."

A flash of hurt enters his dark eyes. "I doubt that's true."

"Believe me, it is. I feel nothing for you beyond enjoying the sex." It's surprising that I seem to be under his skin already. "And if you cook good food, then that's a bonus, I guess." The look on his face tells me that my words hurt, but they're true.

How can he expect me to feel anything for him after the way he's treated me?

An awkward silence falls between us as we both eat our pancakes. Maybe my plan is working a little too well already.

22

ARCHER

"In a line, all of you. I want you to pick your partners for basketball."

I narrow my eyes as I glance at Adrianna, hoping she doesn't get selected so that I get to go with her. Normally, I'd just pick her, but even if I'm obvious most of the time, I can't pick her every single class.

"Nik, you go first."

He steps forward. "I'll go with Adrianna."

Rage slams into me as he gives her an objectifying glance, clearly checking her out. No doubt trying to make his ex-girlfriend, Rosa, jealous.

Adrianna smiles flirtatiously at him as she joins him, setting a hand on his biceps and squeezing. "Thanks for picking me," she says.

Nik nods. "You're welcome, beautiful."

I'm about to knock his lights out when Elias clears his throat. "I'll pick Nat."

Natalya moves toward him and hooks arms with him. "Thanks."

It's hard to believe that Natalya Gurin and Elias Morales are now engaged, considering I've witnessed the torment Elias put her through over the years.

The rest of the class pair up and the only person without a partner is Jeanie. She's always been flirtatious with me, so that's not ideal. Not to mention she started a fight with Adrianna over me, but perhaps I can use it to my advantage to make my girl jealous.

The most irritating thing is that basketball requires touching. If it was tennis, there's more distance between Nik and Adrianna. I watch as he chats to her, making her laugh at whatever he's saying.

"Okay, start practicing moves with your partner. After twenty minutes, you'll all play a game." I keep close to Adrianna and make sure we practice close by.

Jeanie smiles at me. "Show me your moves, Coach."

Adrianna catches my eye as she glances over at us, an odd expression on her face. And then she notices me looking and places a hand on Nik's shoulder and gives him a flirtatious smile.

A soft growl rises in my throat. Anita doesn't seem to notice as I bounce the ball and dribble it easily around her.

"Jeanie, you need to match my footwork and not lose me or you'll never succeed."

Jeanie looks a little flustered. "Sorry, I'll try harder."

I glance over to see Nik holding himself against Adrianna as she dribbles the ball, trying to get around him.

The contact between them ignites a possessive rage like none other.

"One moment, Jeanie."

I walk over to them. "Nik," I bark his name, making him jump.

"Yeah, Coach?"

"Basketball isn't a fucking dance. You need to keep a distance between you and your opponent."

Adrianna shakes her head. "Neither of us had fouled."

I clench my jaw. "Are you saying I don't know the rules, Miss Vasquez?"

"I don't know, but I wouldn't call Nik's move a foul." There's a challenge in her eyes, as she knows watching him get so close to her is pissing me off.

I glare at Nik. "Keep your distance."

Nik holds his hands up in surrender. "Sure."

I return to my practice with Anita, who won't stop giving me flirtatious looks. As she dribbles the ball, she tries to rub up against me. A part of me wants to use the opportunity to make Adrianna jealous, if that's even possible. It's like she's made of fucking stone.

"Jeanie, that's a foul," I bark.

She looks disappointed at my lack of reciprocation as my eyes continue to dart toward Adrianna and Nik, who are still getting too close to each other for my liking.

I have to force myself not to look in their direction, focusing on Jeanie as she passes me the ball. "Focus on your footwork if you want to keep up with me."

She twirls a strand of blonde hair around her finger and smiles. "Sure thing, Coach." There's a flirtatious tone to her voice. The ironic thing is Jeanie is exactly the kind of girl I'd normally be after any other year, and she'd be a lot less trouble than Adrianna.

Is it because she doesn't want me that I want her so much?

All my life I've been a ladies' man, never settling for one girl. And yet, ever since I started this dance with Adrianna, I can't imagine having anyone else but her.

After twenty minutes of excruciating practice, being forced to watch Nik rub up against Adrianna way too many times, I blow my whistle to get everyone's attention.

"Right, time to put your skills to the test. Each pair will play first to three goals." I meet Adrianna's eyes, wishing I were the one playing with her. "Nik and Adrianna, you go first."

Adrianna grabs the basketball out of my hand without a word and walks onto the court, standing in front of Nik. As expected, she literally runs circles around him. It's the fastest game I've seen, as within a couple of minutes she's scored three goals to zero.

"Well done. Elias and Nat, you go next."

Nik and Adrianna walk off the court. I'm so surprised Nik picked Adrianna as people rarely beat her, and he's the kind of guy who likes to win.

"Do you want to go to the game tonight?" Adrianna asks.

Nik looks surprised. "The hockey game in town?"

I give her a warning glare as she knows the deal. She belongs to me for the year and that means no dating.

She ignores the look I give her. "Yeah, thought it might be fun for a group of us to go."

Hearing the word group makes me feel a little less angry, but I don't like the way this kid checks her out.

"Sure, sounds good, as long as you can clear it with Principal Byrne."

"That won't be a problem. Eva will run it by him."

Nik nods. "Cool, it must be a perk having a friend married to the principal."

"Yeah, I guess it is."

"Stop blabbing both of you," I snap, nodding toward the court. "You should watch your fellow pupils play."

Adrianna looks irritated, but they both fall silent and watch as Natalya and Elias play their game. And I am thankful they've shut up. If she's going to the game tonight, then so am I. I need to get Gav to go with me, which may be a bit of a challenge. He's not that into Hockey, and Oak won't go unless Eva does. But, I'm nothing if not determined.

After class, I head to the staff room and Gav's already there. And instantly I know he's in a bad mood, which means breaking the ice will be difficult. He slams shut the fridge so hard it rattles against the wall.

"What the fuck is wrong with you today, Gav?"

"Nothing," he says, cracking open a coke can and drinking it.

The likelihood of getting him to agree to do anything when he's like this is slim to none.

"You've been off for weeks now. What is it?" I ask.

Gav glares at me, as he hates me asking him questions when he's like this. "Mind your own fucking business.

Since when have I been into sharing and caring, you fucking fag?"

I chuckle, as he is in a terrible mood. "Okay, there's definitely something up with you." I hold my hands up as he glares at me even more. "Keep it to yourself. I don't give a shit."

The door to the staff room opens and Oak strides in, brows furrowed. "What are you two bickering about? Every time I come in here, you're bickering like an old married couple."

"Archer being a fucking asshole, as usual," Gav says.

Oak laughs. "After all this time, I'd think the two of you would have got used to each other's bullshit by now."

"Any news yet on a substitute for math?" Gav asks.

I know that his workload has been bothering him, but he seems extra frustrated. It's hard to believe that taking a class could put him in this bad a mood.

"A few leads, but you might need to give me until after Spring Break," Oak says.

"That's four weeks from now, for fuck's sake," Gav replies.

I don't even want to think about how close spring break is, as it means two weeks without fucking Adrianna. The idea of not seeing her for any length of time, let alone two weeks, makes me feel sick to the stomach.

"I know. I've had trouble finding anyone who has the qualifications," Oak says.

"Fuck the qualifications." Gav spits. "We're a secret and illegal academy for mafia heirs. Find someone who knows their math."

He has a point, to be honest. Who cares whether the replacement is qualified to teach math? It's not like this place has any fucking rules, anyway.

"You have a point. I think you've given me an idea," Oak says, a glint in his eye.

"Good, well, I hope that idea means I'll be able to stop taking math class ASAP."

Oak shrugs. "Hopefully."

I clap him on the shoulder reassuringly. "It can't be that bad."

"It's impeding my time to dole out punishment. I've got less free periods and so I'm getting fewer students sent to me."

My friend truly is unhinged. "You are fucking crazy. Did you know that?"

Gav nods. "Yes, and proud of it."

"There's a hockey game on tonight at the stadium in town. Either of you up for a guy's night out?" I ask.

Oak shakes his head. "Sorry, I've got plans."

"Fucking married life is cramping your style, Oak." My eyes shift to Gav, expecting him to flat out refuse.

He nods. "Sure, I could do with a break from this place."

The easy agreement surprises me, especially from Gav. I expected him to put up some resistance to going.

"Perfect, shall I drive?" I ask.

"I'll order us an Uber," Gav says, taking a sip of his coke. "I want to drink and so do you, right?"

I think I'll need a drink tonight. "Yeah, sure."

"I'll book it for seven o'clock out front."

I wink. "See you then." I walk out of the staff room and leave my two friends, heading toward the gym, where I've got junior combat class. Tonight, I'm going to make Adrianna regret being so loud about her plans in front of me.

I sense that she did it in an attempt to make me jealous, asking Nik in the way she did. An act that can't go unpunished.

———

GAV SQUISHES his hot dog between his meaty bear paws and his cup of beer, spilling it everywhere.

"Gav, what the fuck?"

His jaw is clenched tightly, and he looks about ready to murder someone. "It looks like your hooks aren't as deep as you thought." Gav nods in front of us.

Adrianna is sitting with Nikolai Kushev's arm around her shoulders, her head rested in the crook of his neck. "Motherfucker."

A rage unlike any I've ever felt overwhelms me. Adrianna may think she's untouchable emotionally, but she won't get away with treating me like shit, not if she wants me to bury the truth about her.

Gav sits down in his seat and then leans forward to tap Camilla on the shoulder. "May I ask what you're doing here, Miss Morrone?"

Camilla's eyes go wide as she and Rizzo turn to face us. "Hey professor, we're enjoying the game. That's not against school rules, is it?"

"Yes, just enjoying the game," Camilla adds.

"And who cleared you to leave school grounds?" Gav questions her.

Adrianna has the gall to turn to face me, meeting my gaze with a cocky little smirk on those damned beautiful lips. "Principal Byrne gave us permission." She slides her hand into her pocket and pulls out the slip.

Oak knows I'm after Adrianna and yet he still gave her permission to leave the grounds with a bunch of boys. It's clear she's trying to piss me off as she leans closer to Nik, who hasn't even bothered to join in the conversation.

Gav clears his throat. "I find that hard to believe that he'd approve an outing for a student who has been constantly in detention lately."

He's talking about Camilla as she's been a real loose cannon this year, which isn't like her at all. The remark she made about me wanting Adrianna to suck my cock may not have been untrue, but she spoke out of turn. "My name is on the slip, just like everyone else's."

Gav's voice sounds deadly as he says, "Well then, enjoy the game."

Camilla nods. "Thanks, you too." And then the conversation is over. But Adrianna lets her gaze linger on me for a few beats more, taunting me with those beautiful chestnut brown eyes.

Nik is barely paying her any attention as he focuses on the game, but she's trying to get under my skin and make me jealous. I can't deny that it's working.

A dark part of me wants to murder Nik for even being

within a foot of what is mine. Gav suddenly gets up. "I'll be back shortly, just going to grab a drink."

My brow furrows. "The game is only just starting."

"If you hadn't noticed, I spilled my drink on the way in here."

I sigh, irritated by Gav leaving me so soon, sitting here like a pathetic loner behind a woman who's trying to make a fool out of me.

I dig my cell phone out of my pocket and type a text to her.

Me: Are you trying to make sure I expose you as a traitor?

Adrianna's cell phone dings, but she ignores it. No doubt fully aware that it's me texting her. Rage slams into me as I type another text, barely containing the desire to stand up and grab her by the hair, dragging her out of here for everyone to see.

Me: If you don't answer me, you'll wish I'd told your father the truth months ago.

On the second chime, she sighs and pulls out her cell phone, glancing over her shoulder at me briefly.

Adrianna: We had a deal that I give you my virginity. That's all. What's your problem?

My hands are shaking from the anger as I type the next message to her.

Me: You belong to me until I say so. No dates with other men. Now stand up and come back here before I drag you over the chair myself.

Adrianna glances over her shoulder, glaring at me as if trying to ascertain how serious I am.

"Now," I mouth.

She clears her throat and leans toward Nik, whispering in his ear. The dickhead barely looks in her direction, clearly unaware of what a treasure he has sitting by his side.

And then she stands and walks back to my aisle, shimmying her way through the crowd to sit in Gav's vacant seat.

"Seriously?" She asks.

"You're with Nik to make me jealous, aren't you?"

"Why would I give a shit if you're jealous or not?"

I tilt my head. "Because you like to piss me off and get a rise out of me. It seems to be your favorite fucking pastime." I narrow my eyes. "If I didn't know any better, I'd say you were trying to get me to punish you."

Her brow pulls together. "You're so fucking full of yourself. I didn't know you'd be here."

The only reason I'm here is because I overheard Adrianna mention she was attending the game.

I grab her thigh and squeeze. "Are you playing games with me, baby girl?"

Her jaw works. "How many times have I told you not to call me that?"

"I dont know and I don't care. I'll call you whatever the fuck I want." I place my hand on her thigh and move it higher beneath the hem of her dress.

She freezes. "Not here."

"Yes, here." I let my fingers skim the edge of her panties, which results in a soft gasp. "You're going to come

227

for me like the dirty little girl you are, right here in public," I murmur into her ear.

She shudders as my finger teases against her soaking wet entrance. "Archer." Her voice is full of longing, even though I know she's warning me not to do this. She doesn't want me to take it any further here, but I don't give a shit.

The girl brought this on herself by acting like she's on a date with this guy. When she asked him to come to the game with a group, I assumed she meant as friends, but the way he had his arm around her was not just friendly. They're on a date together and that makes me beyond angry.

I rub her clit forcefully, and she makes a high-pitched squeal. The sound of the crowd drowns out her moans, but her cheeks turn a deep red as she glances around nervously.

When she's confident that no one is looking, she grabs my wrist. "Seriously, this isn't right."

I quicken my fingers, moving softly over her sensitive nub.

She grits her teeth as her body jerks and shudders. "You are insane."

"I think you'e the one that's insane, winding me up like this when I have information that could screw your entire life up."

Her body tenses, but I continue to work her into a frenzy, plunging my fingers in and out of her wet pussy. The sound is so filthy, especially since we're in public. And she's wetter than ever, which makes my cock strain against my tight pants. It appears my baby girl likes being touched in public, but I think fucking might be a step too far.

I use my free hand to grab her hand and place it on my crotch, forcing her to squeeze. Once I remove my hand, she quickly takes it away from my cock.

"Did I tell you to let go?"

She glares at me. "We're in public, for fuck's sake."

I lean toward her ear. "I don't care. The least you can do is give me a squeeze and alleviate the pressure until later, when I'm going to fuck you so hard you can't walk in the morning."

She shudders, affected by my words more than she wants to let on. Adrianna is quickly turning into the perfect lover, even if she's resistant to begin with. Once the desire takes over she submits, and it's delectable.

23

ADRIANNA

*A*rcher is right that I made sure he heard me so that he'd see me with Nik and get jealous, but I never thought he was this insane. I'd seen the way he was looking at me during gym when Nik got too close, so I thought I'd play on his jealousy, as I need to get revenge on him for blackmailing me into fucking him.

My intention is to make him fall for me, and the way he's acting, I'd say it won't be hard. It may be a challenge to get a self-professed man whore to fall for me, but I'm determined. When he thinks he has me, I intend to break his heart. Because this man deserves pay back for black-mailing me into sleeping with him, no matter how good the sex is. And it is fucking good.

I bite my lip so hard I draw blood, my hand in his lap reluctantly as I squeeze the hard length of him. It doesn't help being forced to touch him, as it only makes the ache inside of me deepen. He's trying to tip me over the edge right here in front of an entire crowd of people, and he's so close. It's going to be impossible to stop myself at any minute, as I'm like a volcano ready to explode.

"Stop this," I hiss at him.

He just smirks in the most infuriating way. "No can do. Sorry, baby girl." His fingers quicken over my clit and I cry out, bringing my free arm up to my mouth as I bite down on my jacket. Humiliation and heat merge as one as I climax right there in a stadium full of people, thankful that it's so loud, otherwise people would hear me.

"You are a fucking bastard," I say.

He smirks. "And you love it, baby." He pulls his fingers out of me and then sucks them clean, one by one. "Delicious."

I wish it wasn't such a sexy fucking move, as the ache deepens inside of me.

"Now be a good girl and return to your seat." He stands to allow me past.

I stand and move past him, but he grabs my wrist. "And later I'll fuck that soaking wet cunt of yours."

I shudder at the deep, dark quality of his voice. And I hate that butterflies flutter to life in my stomach at the prospect. Quickly, I make my way past him and apologize as I shuffle past the rest of the people.

When I get back to my seat, Nik doesn't even notice as I sit down. At least he wasn't aware of me sitting behind him, getting fingered by Coach. It's probably a blessing that he doesn't notice, as he doesn't put his arm around my shoulders this time. Something tells me that Archer wouldn't like that at all.

I shuffle as I feel like he's watching me, and sure

enough, when I glance over my shoulder, his dark eyes are pinned on me.

He smirks at me and I feel that deep ache reignite between my thighs.

What the fuck is wrong with me?

Quickly, I turn back to face forward and resist the urge to glance back there for the final thirty minutes of the game, which is beyond boring. The hockey game was my idea and I'm really regretting it about now. I should have suggested a movie or something.

Camilla cheers the moment the game is over and then leans forward across Alek to speak to me. "Remind me to give you a stern talking to later for suggesting such a terrible outing."

I laugh as we all stand and walk out of the stadium seating and wrestle our way through the busy corridors and out into the parking lot. Humiliation still claws at my insides as I walk, feeling my thighs wet from the orgasm Archer dragged out of me. Even though no one seemed to notice what happened, I know what happened, and it makes me feel sick.

Archer is an asshole. A talented asshole, but an asshole all the same. Making me come while sitting in the middle of the stadium in front of so many people was humiliating and degrading.

"That game was boring as hell," Camilla whines.

"You don't say?"

Her brow furrows. "It was your idea to come here."

"Yeah, well, I didn't realize how much I hate hockey."

Camilla laughs. "Me neither. Let's vow to never come to one again."

Nat approaches with Elias' arm around her. I still can't wrap my head around those two.

"How did you like the game?" Elias asks.

"Hated it," I say.

He chuckles. "Not sure Nat was too fond, were you?"

Nat shakes her head. "I've told him I'm never coming to one again." Her eyes narrow as she glares at me. "Why the hell did you suggest it?"

I shrug. "Thought it would be a fun evening away from SA. Clearly, I was wrong."

"Clearly," Camilla says.

Nik walks over and places an arm around my shoulders. "What are we talking about?"

"How shit the game was," I say.

He shakes his head. "I thought it was good, but then I'm a hockey fan." His expression changes as he leans toward me. "Can I have a word in private?"

"Sure," I say.

He pulls me away and grabs my hand. "So, Adrianna. Why did you want to go to the game with me?"

I swallow hard and shrug. "Just thought it would be fun."

He smirks. "You got the hots for me, Vasquez?"

The thought makes me want to puke. "No chance."

His brow furrows, and he suddenly looks a little vulnerable. "Well, can you pretend like you do?"

"What?"

He clenches his jaw. "It's Rosa. She's playing hard to

get, and I want to make her jealous." His eyes dart toward Rosa, who is talking to the new kid, Rizzo.

I'm surprised Nik would even admit that, but it's exactly what I've been trying to do with him. Make Coach jealous. "Sure, no problem."

He smiles, pulling me close. "In that case, shall we make it convincing?"

I glance at him, his eyes dancing with amusement. "How do you propose we do that?"

He smirks. "How about a kiss?"

I can't understand why the thought of kissing Nik, even as a ruse to make Rosa and Archer jealous, makes me feel dirty. Especially since I just climaxed less than an hour ago with Archer's fingers inside of me. It makes me feel like I'm cheating on Archer or something, which makes no sense considering the way he forced me to have sex with him. Anger coils through me that I'm even thinking like that. "Okay, one kiss."

His lips curve into a smirk as he draws me against him, eyes darting briefly to Rosa, who's still chatting to Rizzo. And then he kisses me. His lips are firm against mine, but I feel nothing as his tongue dips into my mouth. It's such a conflicting contrast between when Archer kisses me.

And then suddenly Nik is being ripped away from me. It's a blur as Archer is standing there and he has his hands on Nik as he punches him in the face.

I start forward, grabbing his arm. "Stop!"

He tries to shrug me off, but I intercept him and grab hold of his fist before it hits Nik's face again.

"What the fuck, Coach?" Nik says, holding his mouth,

which is bleeding.

"Don't fucking touch her ever again. Do you hear me?"

Nik's eyes widen and he nods. "Sure."

I drag Archer away. "What the hell are you doing?"

He spins on me. "What am I doing? I told you that you can't date another guy and then I come out into the parking lot to find you kissing Nik."

"He kissed me and what's the big deal?"

His expression is scary, and I take a few steps backward.

It forces him to pursue me across the parking lot. "The big deal is you're mine, Adrianna. That's the agreement."

I place my hands on my hips. "There's no agreement that I wouldn't date. All you said was that I have to be at your apartment every night this year." It's a fact, even if I knew he'd get angry seeing me with Nik.

Ever since he's had his eyes set on me, he's been possessive and easily wound up. And it makes my plan that much easier. Archer needs to fall for me if I'm going to get my revenge on him and make him suffer for blackmailing me. I'm not the type of girl to just take this shit without some kind of retaliation.

"You're mine for the year. That's the agreement." He wraps a firm palm around my throat. "There's no need for me to tell you not to date, as it's expected when you belong to someone else," he growls.

Professor Nitkin approaches, clearing his throat. "Am I interrupting something?"

The sound of his friend's voice seems to snap him out

of his violent daze as he releases my throat. "Not at all."
It's like he changes at the flick of a switch once his friend
appears.

"Our Uber is here," Professor Nitkin says, his eyes
darting between me and Archer. "Are you ready?"

Archer's jaw flexes as he clenches it. "Sure. Just give
me one moment."

Nitkin looks reluctant about walking away, but doesn't
question him.

Archer grabs my wrist. "If I see or hear that you've
been within five fucking feet of that boy again, I'll kill him.
Do you understand?"

I shake my head. "Do you think I care what you do to
Nik Kushev?"

"No, because you were using him to get to me."

"You're so vain." I yank my hand from his grasp. "Not
everything is about you, Archer."

He's right, of course, but I can't let him know that.
Not if I want my plan to work. Archer can't know that I'm
trying to break his heart or he'll make sure it doesn't
happen.

"Be at my apartment by eleven o'clock or I'll come
and find you." He turns around and walks over to
Professor Nitkin, who's watching us intently. I watch him
as he gets into the cab and drives away, wishing I could
stand up to him.

Although my home life has always been fraught with
discipline, at the academy, I've done what I want when I
want. And Coach is taking that away from me. It makes
me hate him more.

24

ARCHER

"What are you doing for Spring Break?" I ask, while gently running my finger in circles on Adrianna's soft, tanned skin.

"I told my father I'm not coming home." Adrianna shrugs. "Eva wants me to stay here, and I agreed."

"And your father accepted that?" I find it hard to believe that Adrianna can dictate what she does, especially since she mentioned he wanted her home a week earlier to meet a potential suitor for marriage.

Adrianna shakes her head. "He didn't oppose it, so I guess."

"What happened to the suitor?" I ask.

"Oh, I think he had a falling out with the father of the guy he was going to marry me off to. My father makes enemies faster than he makes friends."

I chuckle. "I know the type." My fingers dance over her skin lightly and she shivers. "We can spend some time together, then," I say, thankful that Adrianna isn't leaving for Spring Break. The last thing I want is to spend any time away from her.

She shakes her head. "I've got plans with Eva."

"Not for the entire two weeks. Oak is only away for one of those weeks." I brush my fingers lightly over her bare breasts and her nipples harden instantly.

"Archer," she says my name in a breathless voice that drives me wild. "Not again."

I smirk. "Can't handle it?"

We've been in bed since eleven o'clock last night fucking and then sleeping. It's now almost eleven o'clock in the morning on a Saturday, and I'm still hungry for her.

She draws in a deep breath. "If I don't get out of here before lunch, my friends will get suspicious. There's no way I'd ever miss breakfast and lunch."

I arch a brow. "You still have an hour and a half until lunch is served. Or better yet, tell them you feel sick and say you're staying in bed."

"Knowing my friends, they'd be at my dorm room in a heartbeat trying to look after me. That won't work."

I nod in response. "That's because you have good friends that care about you. Do they know your plans for after graduation?"

Adrianna stiffens then. "No, I can't let anyone know."

"Except for me?" I confirm.

"You found out by following me. That's different."

I smirk, as I can't help but feel a little privileged at being the only one who knows Adrianna's deepest and darkest secret. "And will you factor me into your plan?"

Her brow furrows. "What?"

"I mean, I don't want this to end after graduation," I say, kissing her shoulder.

"There's no way this is continuing after I graduate." She shakes her head. "I won't even be in the states."

"Where will you be?"

"If I told you that, I'd have to kill you… Literally."

I roll my eyes. "Don't be so dramatic, baby girl. I'll go wherever you're going."

Her jaw clenches. "I told you, Archer, this means nothing. It's just sex."

It feels like her words are a sucker punch to the gut as I stare into her beautiful, cold brown eyes. "You don't mean that."

"I mean it." She sits up straighter. "Why wouldn't I mean it?"

As always, Adrianna shocks me with how cold and detached she is. We've been sleeping together for a while now. If she feels nothing, I don't know how. "Because this has to mean something to you."

"I'm afraid the moment you blackmailed me into sleeping with you, there was no chance I'd feel anything but anger toward you."

"Bend over," I order, knowing that the only way to keep myself from falling apart is to do what I do best. *Fuck.*

Her eyes narrow. "I told you not again. I'm starving and going to pass out from lack of sustenance."

"That's not possible. I've already made you two sandwiches since last night." I grab her thigh and force her over onto all fours. "Now be a good girl and do as you're told." I spank her ass, as this is the only way to mask my pain. I care about Adrianna, more than I've cared about any woman before. She's strong, independent and beautiful.

"Archer," she whines.

"This is happening whether or not you want it to."

She groans in response. "You're insane."

"And you love it," I say, lowering my face between her thighs and licking right through her center. "I'll never get enough of tasting you, baby girl."

Adrianna moans despite herself. Her back arching, proving to me she's ready to be fucked as much as I'm ready to fuck her. My cock is straining against the fabric of my briefs. I keep licking and sucking her while freeing myself and stroking my cock.

You'd think after a night of fucking I'd be satiated, but I'm not. It's as if I can't get enough of Adrianna Vasquez, no matter how many times I have her.

"Do you realize how damn addictive you are?" I ask, running my hand down her spine.

She shudders at my touch. "Just get on with it already."

I spank her ass again, and she cries out. "Who's in charge, baby girl?"

Her anger practically radiates from her like a separate entity. "You," she spits, rather unconvincingly.

I grab the back of her neck forcefully. "Say it like you mean it."

There's a few moments of silence before she says. "You are."

"Better," I reply, releasing her neck.

And then I slide my tongue through her increasingly wet pussy, turning her into a mess before me. Her thighs shudder as I thrust my fingers into her and suck her clit hard simultaneously, pushing her closer to orgasm.

It's amusing the way I've learned all her little tells, from the way her breathing quickens to the little mewling sounds she makes in the buildup. They get increasingly louder until she's crying out and coming apart beautifully.

And right now she's on the edge of crying, so I stop. As I won't let her come until I'm buried inside of her.

Adrianna makes a frustrated little grunt. "What the —" I flip her onto her back and then plow my cock into her cunt before she can finish her sentence. "Oh, fuck!"

Her entire body convulses with the force of her orgasm and I fuck her right through it, enjoying the sensation of her muscles spasming around my cock. "Such a perfect girl," I say, looking into her eyes. "You come so damn well." I kiss her then, drowning in the woman who's made me feel for the second time in my life.

"Archer," she moans my name.

"Yes, baby?"

She glares at me as I bury myself inside of her with slow, soft thrusts.

I know why she's moaning my name, because she wants it rough. If there's one thing I've learned about her, it's that she does nothing by halves. It's all or nothing in every single aspect of her life, and it's something I love about her.

"Fuck me harder," she orders, as if she's in command here.

I shake my head. "Who's in control, baby girl?"

"You are," she grits out, glaring at me.

"That's right." I kiss her lips, thrusting my tongue into her mouth and drawing out a deep moan. "I control the pace and the force." I wrap my palm around her slender neck. "I control whether you can breathe or when you come."

Her pussy gets wetter as I squeeze her throat enough to restrict her airways. She places her hands on my back and drags her nails down my skin. It's a painful yet thrilling sensation.

I lean down with my hand still around her throat and nip at her lip. "Hurt me all you like. I know how much you're getting off on being choked." I lick a path up the side of her face. "Your pussy is so fucking wet."

She moans then, eyes rolling back in her head. And I know I won't get anymore smart remarks from her, as she's let go of control.

I fuck her harder and give her what she wants. No more teasing. I feel that tension in her muscles building again and she moans and claws at my back even harder. "I could spend the rest of my life fucking you," I murmur into her ear.

She stiffens at that comment, no doubt because it's forward, suggesting that she would even let me fuck her for the rest of my life. It's what I want though, even if we haven't discussed what happens once she graduates.

Instead of dwelling on her reaction, I continue to fuck

her roughly. Trying to bury the feelings that are trying to rise from the dark pit of my soul. Adrianna is the first woman I've felt anything more than sexual attraction toward since the first woman I slept with, and it frightens me.

My fingers tighten around her throat and her eyes bulge a little. I know what I'm doing, though. Adrianna has to trust me as I fuck her more ferociously, pouring every ounce of energy into bringing her to the most intense orgasm she's ever experienced. My sole purpose in life is to make her feel good in every way possible. At least, that's how it feels.

She draws in a sharp breath, making her breasts jiggle as she does. I bite her collarbone and then drag my mouth lower to those perfect breasts, sucking on her hard nipples.

Her body arches at my attention as I continue to fuck her with hard, slow thrusts. "Oh my God," she cries.

I cover her lips with mine and swallow her cries, fucking her faster and harder. It feels like this woman is consuming me as she kisses me back with a passion that drives me wild. Sucking on her tongue elicits a deep, guttural moan from deep within her. A moan that makes my cock swell inside of her.

Ever since this started, I've fucked her bare, and it's heaven. I checked the medical records; After our first fuck, she went straight onto the pill. Smart girl. There's a part of me that wished she didn't, though. A part of me that wants her to get pregnant with my baby so that she can't deny that she belongs to me. That she's mine in every sense of the word, forever.

I move in and out of Adrianna with such desperation; the bed creaking beneath us as I pound into her with all my strength. Adrianna is addictive. I love the way she smells, tastes and fucks. She's become my world in such a brief space of time and the more I have her, the deeper my need for her grows. It's a never-ending cycle, as my desire only feeds more desire.

"I'm going to make you scream so loud that the entire academy will know you're being fucked by your coach, baby," I murmur into her ear.

"Archer," she moans, eyes rolling back in her head as she lifts her hips off the bed. "I'm so close."

"Good," I growl, sucking on her bottom lip. "I'm going to make you come so hard it shatters you into a million pieces."

"Yes, fuck, yes." She claws at my back as the wave of ecstasy hits her.

"That's it, come on my cock like a good girl," I instruct, before kissing her and swallowing her moans and cries as if they feed my soul. Adrianna is under my skin and deeply embedded inside of me, and nothing I do will ever remove her. She's more than a fling.

Her pussy clamps around my cock so tightly it drags me over the edge with her. And her body shudders beneath me at the intensity of her climax. My release is mind-blowing considering we've been fucking all damn night. I sink my teeth into her collarbone and growl against her skin as I fill her to the brim with my cum.

We're both panting for oxygen desperately when we finally come down from our mutual pleasure. And I pull my cock out of her and take a step back, admiring how beautiful she looks splayed out on my bed with my cum dripping out of her pussy. "You're a vision that needs to be immortalized in a painting right now."

Her cheeks redden more than they already are. "Archer," she breathes.

"I'll make you some food since you've been such a good girl," I say, turning away from her as I know if I don't walk away now, I'll never stop fucking her.

ADRIANNA

*M*y cell phone rings, and I groan when I see it's my father.

"Yes?" I answer.

"Why has my jet just taken off from the private airstrip near your academy empty?" he growls.

Unbelievable. It was a while ago now when I told him I wasn't coming back, after he canceled me coming back a week early to meet some guy. "I already told you a couple of weeks ago I'm not coming back for Spring Break."

He growls down at the phone. "Insolent girl."

"What's the problem? It's not like you're around, anyway. I sit in that house alone. At least this way I can chill out with a friend for the break at the academy."

There's a pause on the other end. "You're remaining at the academy and not leaving the premises?"

"Yes, except maybe to go shopping a couple of days or go out to the movies in the nearby town."

"Fine," he barks. "I'll call the principal to confirm that he keeps an eye on you."

I shake my head as my father is ridiculous. "At eighteen years old, I hardly need to be babysat."

"Quiet." There's some noise on the other end of the phone. "I'll call and inform him or you can get on a commercial airline flight back home tomorrow morning."

"Fine, call him," I say, shaking my head. "I have nothing to hide."

There's a few moments of silence. "I'll see you at your graduation, then?"

I shake my head. "You're going to attend my graduation?" I ask, not expecting him to say that.

"Of course."

"You didn't even attend Eric's graduation. Why would you attend my graduation?"

Eric is my eldest brother and the heir to the entire Vasquez empire, so I can't see why he's attending my graduation. In fact, my plan always hinged on him not being there.

"Because I want to see my youngest daughter graduate and I have someone I want you to meet at your graduation."

I sigh heavily, as he always has an ulterior motive for everything he does. "Don't say it's a potential husband."

"Listen, Adrianna. I know you're a very independent girl and you would like to do whatever the hell you want, but your duty to this family is to marry and strengthen our control in Mexico."

Duty to the family, my ass.

I don't owe them shit.

"Whatever, I'm sure by then you will have fallen out with that guy's father, too."

He growls. "When did you become so insolent?"

"I'm not being insolent. It's a fact."

All I hear is a frustrated sigh on the other end. "Enjoy your break, Adrianna." He ends the call.

I clench my phone so hard it's a wonder it doesn't break in half and let out a frustrated noise.

"Someone sounds like they're in a bad mood," Camilla says from behind me, approaching with all her bags.

I turn to face her and force a smile. "Father being his same old self."

"Oh, ignore him. He's an idiot for not coming here himself and bringing you home."

"Thank fuck he didn't do that."

She laughs. "So, if you get bored once Eva's husband is back, the offer stands for you to come and stay with us. We'll have loads of fun and my driver can come and pick you up."

It's strange that while her offer is inviting, something, or someone, is tempting me to remain at the academy.

Archer.

He's going to keep me company once Oak is back, and I'm kind of looking forward to it, even if I wouldn't admit it out loud. We have a lot in common, from interests to our family history. I may never forgive him for black-mailing me into sex with him, but I can't deny I'm enjoying spending time with him, not just the sex which I never expected.

It changes nothing, though. The simple fact is that Archer Daniels blackmailed me into having sex with him, and that's something I can never forgive him for.

"I'll think about it. But a week to myself sounds quite good right about now."

There's a flicker of hurt in Camilla's eyes, no doubt because she hoped I'd agree. And to be fair, it's offensive if I were declining to spend a week alone, but that's not the case. I can't tell her that, though.

"Okay, call me if you change your mind." She pulls me into a tight hug. "See you in two weeks. I'll miss you."

I return the hug. "I'll miss you too."

And then she grabs her bags and walks toward the exit. Nat already left last night, which means it's now me and Eva left here. I'm due to meet her in forty-five minutes, in the cafeteria for lunch, and then we're going to catch a movie this afternoon.

My cell phone rings and I take the call. "Hello?"

"Get your butt over to the gym right now."

I swallow hard at the sound of Archer's deep, gravelly voice on the other end of the phone. "Sorry, I've got plans."

There's an animal like growl on the other end of the phone. "I said, now." He ends the call, and I realize I can either disobey him and he'll come and find me and embarrass me in front of Eva, or I can go and find out what he wants.

Sighing, I check my watch. As long as I'm quick, I'll

still be on time to meet Eva for lunch. The gym is obviously empty when I get there, except for Archer, who's sitting on the bottom bleacher, waiting for me.

"Come here," he demands.

I purse my lips together. "I told you I have plans. What's this about?"

"Now, Adrianna." The tone of his voice sends shivers through me, even though I wish it didn't.

Who knew that after years of opposition to authority that I'd love being bossed about by a lover?

I still give him my best glare as I walk over to him. "What?"

He pats his knee, and the desire to disobey him claws at me.

"Do you think I'm like five years old or something?"

His eyes flash with irritation as he reaches out and grabs my wrist and instead of sitting me on his lap, he pushes me face first over it. His hand teasing over my ass, which is only covered by the hem of the skirt I wore today. My nipples are hard peaks against the fabric of my shirt already at the slightest of touch from him.

And then he spanks me, making me yelp.

"When I tell you to come to me, you come without question. Do you understand?"

I bite my lip, not intending to answer his question. Which results in him lifting the hem of my skirt up and slamming his hand down on my bare ass. The evidence of his erection presses incessantly into my stomach.

"I said, do you understand?"

I wriggle in his lap to break free, but he keeps a firm grip on me.

"Answer me, baby girl."

I grit my teeth together before submitting to his demand. "Yes," I murmur.

He spanks my ass hard, and I yelp at the stinging sensation. "You're being naughty," he murmurs, his fingers teasing at the sensitive flesh between my thighs. "Now be a good girl and stand up."

I stand, breaking free from his grasp. And then I turn to make my way toward the exit.

Archer grabs me by the back of the neck and forces me around to face him in one swift move.

My body tenses at the sudden force of being grabbed like that. "Don't walk away from me, Adrianna."

"Or what?" I ask, staring him out.

He pulls me closer, his lips mere inches from me. "Or I'll spank your ass red."

My thighs clench at the thought of him spanking me more than he already has. "I've got to meet Eva in thirty minutes."

"Thirty minutes is enough time."

"For what?" I ask, knowing that I'm going to regret asking.

"For me to fuck you over that pommel horse until you're begging me for release."

I glare at him. Somehow, the gym setting ignites my competitive side. "I'd like to see you try."

He smirks, and I know that we've both issued a challenge to each other. This man is going to get me to beg him to make me come, and I'm going to resist. There's no fucking way I'm going to be on time to meet Eva.

He yanks me forward, his hand still on the back of my neck. Our lips come together in a heated kiss that sets my world ablaze. I want to hate it, but I just can't. Every time we're together like this, it's pure electricity.

I drown in him, even while a part of my mind wants to hate him. It's as if the anger and dislike for him only fuels the flames of desire.

Archer grabs me roughly and lifts me off my feet, carrying me toward the pommel horse. He places me down and forces me over the horse, gripping my hips so hard it's like he's trying to leave bruises; trying to leave a mark on me that sticks.

Cold air hits my skin as he yanks the hem of my skirt up around my waist. And then I hear the sound of fabric tearing as he tears my panties apart. I shudder, knowing that if he keeps acting so forcefully I have no chance of resisting my climax.

He shoves three thick fingers inside of me and I groan, rolling my hips as the need for more drives me. And then I feel his lips tease the back of my neck. "You know that you won't be able to help it, baby girl." He bites my earlobe. "You will come so damn hard you won't remember your own name, let alone the fact you were supposed to resist."

"That's not true."

"Liar," he purrs, teasing the tip of his cock through my soaking wet entrance. And then he parts my ass cheeks and rubs the length of his cock against my puckered hole.

"Can you feel how fucking hard I am for you right now, Adrianna?"

I groan, as I can feel how hard he is. It makes me want to feel him in every part of me. He's not fucked my ass since that time in my dorm room, but deep down, I've wanted him to.

"I haven't touched this tight little ass for a while, have I?" he asks, gently touching it with his finger. "Do you wish I had?"

I shudder. "No."

He laughs. "You're very unconvincing."

And then, without a moment's warning, he slams his cock deep into my pussy.

"Fuck," I moan, arching my back as he sinks as deep as possible inside of me.

He holds himself still. "How about I get my cock nice and wet in this tight cunt and then fuck your ass?"

His dirty talk is driving me close to the edge alone, let alone his cock deep inside of me. "Archer," I say his name.

"Is that a yes?"

I groan. "Just fuck me."

He chuckles. "Dirty girl."

I claw the pommel horse as he starts to fuck me with slow, teasing strokes. The slowness is excruciating, as all I want is him to fuck me rough and hard, but I've got no control, especially not in this position.

"You are so fucking wet, baby," he growls, fucking me harder with each thrust. "I could never get bored with fucking you." He brings the flat of his palm down on my ass hard and I buck forward, groaning as the pommel horse causes friction on my clit.

"Oh fuck," I cry out, knowing that holding back my orgasm is going to be a ridiculous challenge.

"Are you almost going to climax already? I knew this would be easy." He stops fucking me and gently trails his lips over my spine. "I won't let you come until you beg."

I grind my clit into the horse, trying to chase my orgasm by myself.

Archer notices and uses his weight to pin me to it, making it impossible for me to move. "Naughty girl, that's cheating."

I groan as he grabs the back of my neck and starts to fuck me again with slow and meaningful thrusts. They don't quench that thirst and every time I think I might be getting close, he pauses.

Suddenly, he removes his cock from me and I whimper at the emptiness he leaves.

"If you won't beg me with it in your cunt, I guess I best try your ass."

I tense, as while it felt so fucking good last time, there was no denying that it hurt, especially at the start.

He teases the head of his cock against my entrance and then pushes forward, opening up the tight ring of muscles.

I scream into the pommel horse beneath me, trying to muffle the sound, as I didn't even lock the gym door behind me.

Archer doesn't give me a chance to adjust, he just

BIANCA COLE

pushes on until every inch is buried in my ass and his balls are resting against my clit.

"Oh fuck, that feels…" I trail off, unable to put it into words. It feels better than the first time, painful still but less so, and he hasn't even started fucking me yet.

"I think you were hungry for an assfucking, considering how much your pussy is dripping right now." He plays with my clit. "Such a dirty girl."

The pain is nothing compared to the euphoric pleasure. "Fuck me," I grit out, as he isn't moving.

"What was that?" Archer asks, sounding smug.

"I said fuck me."

"Are you begging me, baby girl?"

I shake my head. "No, just telling you to fuck me."

He laughs. "Sounds like begging if ever I've heard it, but what is the magic word?"

This man is as infuriating as he is arousing. "Fuck me, please," I grit out.

"It will do," he murmurs, before moving almost all the way out of my ass, only to slam back in with force.

The scream that tears from my throat is impossible to drown out. Thankfully, most of the academy students and staff should have already left by now.

Archer growls and grabs a fistful of my hair, yanking me upright at an unnatural angle that sinks his cock even deeper than I believed possible. He pounds into me so hard it feels like he's trying to shatter me to pieces. There's no more teasing now as he's as lost to the pleasure as I am. He's not controlling himself, instead he's letting go and fucking me like an animal.

It doesn't take much to push me to the edge. "Oh fuck, I'm going to come!"

"Good," he growls, spanking my ass cheek. "Come for me while I fuck that tight little ass."

I rub my clit against the pommel horse and grind back against him at the same time, driving myself right over the edge. "Fuck!" Everything in my field of vision goes hazy, and it feels like I'm no longer connected to my own body, suspended in the middle of nowhere. The intensity of my climax is unlike anything I've felt before.

Archer bites my shoulder as he comes, a growling sound comes from deep within his throat. And I feel his hot cum as he unloads it deep in my ass. My whole body shuddering from the intense orgasm he forced from me.

After we've both regained a normal breathing pattern, Archer slips out of my abused hole. "That was fucking perfect, baby girl." He forces me around and kisses my lips. "You take my cock in your ass like a pro."

I kiss him back, despite myself. And then it hits me. "What's the time?"

He pulls away and checks his watch. "Five minutes past one."

"Fuck!" I push away from him and sort out my skirt, realizing that I don't even have any panties now that he ripped them apart. His cum will be dripping out of my ass and onto my fucking skirt. "I'm late." I grab my bag and I'm about to run out of the gym when he grabs my wrist and pulls me back toward him.

"Enjoy your lunch with Eva while my cum is dripping out of your ass," he murmurs, his lips inches from mine.

"You are an asshole."

He smirks. "One that just fucked your ass after you begged for it."

I narrow my eyes. "I'd hardly say I begged."

"We'll have to agree to disagree." And then he kisses me quickly, before releasing me so that I can rush out of there.

The shame I feel as my torn panties rub against my thighs is deep. The corridors are empty, thank God, but I should go and get changed before meeting Eva. However, I'm already way too late. Instead, I go to my locker and grab my gym shorts out, slipping them on beneath my skirt.

And then I rush to the cafeteria. Eva is sitting there, drumming her fingers on the table as she stares at her phone. No doubt expecting a text from me. I didn't even check my phone to see if she had sent me a message.

I sink into the chair opposite Eva, feeling a little disheveled.

"You're late," Eva says.

I bite my bottom lip. "Sorry, completely lost track of time."

"I text you twenty minutes ago, but you didn't reply." Her brow furrows, as she knows it's unlike me to be late for anything. That's Camilla's thing. "No worries. I grabbed you everything." She nods at the food as the cafeteria closed at one o'clock for Spring Break, fifteen minutes ago.

"You know me so well." I smile and sit down, dragging

a plate of pasta over and tuck in first, ignoring the fact it's gone cold.

My body feels like it might combust at any minute, still completely high-strung by my encounter with Archer only minutes ago. It's becoming painfully clear that my plan to get Archer hooked on me and then break his heart may well sink me deeper into his clutches, too.

ARCHER

*S*pring Break is going far better than I expected now that Adrianna is staying here for it.

Oak assured her father that he'd keep an eye on her, even though he's not even going to be here for the first week. Instead, he put me in charge of watching her for the week, despite knowing how much I've wanted her all year. He doesn't realize that Adrianna finally submitted because of a bit of blackmailing on my end. If he did, he'd probably kill me.

Adrianna insists she can't see me much since she's spending time with Eva while Oak's away. Apparently Eva would get suspicious if they're not together during the week twenty-four-seven. I find it hard to believe that she won't be able to get away.

Gav's in his cabin outside, chopping wood with an axe like some cave dweller. I approach, a shudder racing down my spine at the look of him with an axe like that. He may be my friend, but I've always thought he's got murderous vibes.

"Gav!" I shout his name.

He doesn't hear me as I get closer, and that's when I realize he's got wireless in-ear headphones in.

I won't risk approaching him from behind while he's wielding an axe, so instead I walk around the front and wave my arms to get his attention.

He swings for the next chop, stopping mid-swing when he sees me and dropping the axe into the top of the log he was splitting. He reaches up and pulls out his headphones. "How long have you been standing there?"

"About two seconds. I realized you couldn't hear me and thought it wise not to approach you from behind when you have an axe in your hand."

He smirks. "Of course. You may have lost your head."

I shudder, as I'm pretty sure that's not a joke.

"What's up?"

"Nothing much." I shrug. "I wondered if you wanted to grab some food and beer at the diner for lunch?"

He tilts his head. "Bored already, Arch?"

Three days into the break, and the fact is, when I'm not with Adrianna, all I can do is think about her. And right now she's spending the day with Eva in Winby. Apparently they're getting their hair done, followed by lunch, and then an afternoon movie. "Maybe," I admit.

Going to the diner will keep my mind off of her until I can see her tonight for dinner. Apparently, Eva's going out with some people she met at the high school tonight, where she took her SATs, for some drinks. Eva invited Adrianna, but she didn't want to tag along. It leaves her free to spend the night with me, thankfully.

I can't wait for Oak to return, so that I have Adrianna all to myself for a week.

"Sure. Might as well, since I've got to go out of town in a couple of days."

My brow furrows as Gav rarely goes out of town. "What for?"

He picks the axe up and swings it against his shoulder, turning around. "Mind your own fucking business."

I shake my head and follow him into the cabin where he lives. It's bare and hardly decorated, a stark contrast to the colonial apartment I live in that adjoins the main building. But this is what Gav wanted. To be honest, it suits him. There's no way I could imagine him living in my apartment.

"Help yourself to a beer and take a seat. I need a shower."

I nod as he pulls off his plaid shirt and throws it onto the washing machine, before walking into his bedroom and slamming the door. It's weird to be hanging out with him without Oak, as we're always together, the three of us.

I grab a beer out of his fridge and sit down on the sofa, which isn't exactly comfortable. Gav's all about living with the bare minimum. If the apocalypse struck, I'd want to be with him as he's got excellent survival skills.

Within five minutes, he's showered and out in a pair of beige pants and a casual dress shirt. "Ready to go?"

I nod. "Uber?"

"Already booked it." As he says that, a car horn honks outside of the cabin.

"Perfect, let's go." I tip the rest of the beer down, chugging it and then throwing the empty bottle in the trash can where Gav puts his recycling. "I'm starving."

"Tell me something new," he grunts.

I often forget that he hates that saying. A part of me wants to confide in him about Adrianna, but it's not what we do. He doesn't talk to me about anything and I'm the same way. If I want to talk to someone, I normally talk to Oak as he's a good listener. However, this year he's been distracted by Eva from the get go.

Once we get to the diner, an awkward silence falls between us. "So, not going to tell me where you're going?" I ask.

He shakes his head. "Nope. Still fucking Adrianna Vasquez?" he asks, shaking his head. "Never pinned her as your type."

I swallow hard. "Yes, I'm still fucking her. She stayed behind for Spring Break."

There's a flash of something in Gav's eyes, but it's gone in a millisecond. "Careful that you don't get too attached. You've been obsessing over that girl since the start of the school year."

"And your point is?"

He shakes his head. "No point. It's just graduation is fast approaching."

He's right, once Spring Break is over, it's ten weeks until she graduates. That time will fly by far too fast. "Yeah, it is."

"And if you get too attached, then it'll hurt when she's gone."

I arch a brow. "That's sentimental for you, isn't it, Gav?"

His eyes narrow. "I'm warning you to keep your guard up."

Ironically, that ship sailed months ago. Hell, it might have sailed before I got her in my bed. Adrianna Vasquez is the other half to my whole. A perfect fit, even if she might not see it yet.

"Thanks for the warning."

Jenny isn't here, so another server I don't recognize approaches. "What can I get you?"

"I'll have a beer to drink. And a burger and fries, thanks." I hand her the menu.

"Sure, and you?" she asks.

Gav nods at me. "The same."

"Alright, coming up."

She walks away and I watch her, and that's when I see Adrianna enter the diner with Eva.

Fuck.

I was supposed to be here to forget about her, not be reminded of her.

Eva notices us and waves.

"Oh, great."

Gav smirks. "It's your girlfriend."

"Fuck off."

Eva approaches, and Adrianna follows her, looking utterly mortified. "Hi Gav and Arch," she says happily. "I didn't know you would be here. Oak recommended we

267

come to this place, as they do the best ribs and burgers in town."

Of course he fucking did.

"You should join us," Gav says, looking smug.

Adrianna cuts in then. "That's kind of you, but we wouldn't want to intrude."

"You wouldn't be intruding at all." Gav smirks at me.

Eva shakes her head. "I appreciate the offer, but we're here to eat and go as we've got a movie to catch."

The server returns with our beers.

"Are you two joining?" She glances over at the kitchen. "We can add your orders if you are."

"Oh what the heck," Eva says. Adrianna pales the moment she agrees. "Yes, I'll have a burger and fries, please."

"And for you?" The server asks.

"Same and a side of a half a rack of ribs."

Her eyes widen. "A side of ribs with your burger?"

"Yes," Adrianna says simply.

She nods. "Okay, I'll have your food out to you as quickly as I can."

Adrianna sits down next to Gav, much to my irritation. Gav looks amused by that as Eva takes the seat next to me.

"What brings you two into town?" Eva asks.

Gav shrugs. "Arch was bored, so we came for food."

Eva raises a brow. "Bored already? Spring Break has hardly started."

I clench my jaw, giving Gav a warning glare. "I'm easily bored." My attention moves to Adrianna, who's sitting in silence, looking like she wants to be anywhere but here right now. "What movie are you going to watch?"

"We're torn between Uncharted and The Batman," Eva replies, completely oblivious to the tension between me and Adrianna. She's the only one in the dark about us "What would you pick?"

"Uncharted for sure. I've never been a superhero fan."

Gav nods in agreement. "Yeah, same."

Eva nods. "I think that's what we'll watch then, right, Adrianna?"

"It's probably my preferred choice," she replies.

"That's settled then."

The server comes over with the food and sets it down in front of us. Adrianna isn't fazed by the amount of food on her plate, but she has an appetite like no one I've ever met, except for myself.

An awkward silence falls over the table as everyone eats, but Eva is the one to break it. "If you guys want, you can tag along for the movie."

Adrianna glares across the table at Eva, and I'm pretty sure she kicks her under it.

Gav chuckles. "Thanks for the offer, but I've got a lot of wood to split this afternoon."

"Yeah, I've got things to do too," I say, since Adrianna's coming round this evening and I intend to make her my marinara sauce and pasta.

Adrianna relaxes the moment I decline and we have a mundane conversation while finishing the rest of our food. I struggle to keep my eyes off of Adrianna and she struggles to look at me at all. I can't wait to have her alone in my apartment tonight.

I HUM to myself as I stand over a pot of my marinara sauce.

Adrianna should be here any minute, and I've cooked her dinner. One time, I joked she might fall in love with me if she tried it. I can't deny that I hope that's the case.

Lunch was awkward, but I'm thankful she sat with us. As while it didn't take my mind off of her, it satiated the desire to spend time with her until tonight.

The bell to my apartment rings. My heart pounds a little harder as I turn down the stove, descending the stairs to open the door. Adrianna is standing there wearing a little black dress that flaunts all her assets and enhances the tanned quality of her skin. "Hey, baby girl."

Her cheeks blush. "Hey." She's holding a bottle of wine. "I bought this."

I take it from her. "Perfect, we'll drink it with dinner. Come on." I lead the way into the kitchen.

"What smells so good?"

"My marinara sauce."

She licks her lips. "Looking forward to that."

I laugh. "How do you have any room after that lunch?"

"I have an enormous appetite, if you hadn't already noticed."

"Yeah, kind of gathered that over the time we've been

fucking." I tilt my head. "Although that order at lunch was impressive. And no leftovers."

"I don't leave food. It's wasteful."

"Couldn't agree more." I tap my chin. "You better eat a lot of pasta and sauce as I've made tonnes."

"As long as it tastes good, I'll eat the lot."

"Believe me, it tastes good." I get two wineglasses out of the cabinet, placing them on the island in my kitchen. "How was the movie?"

She groans. "How awkward was that? It felt so weird having to sit and eat with you two."

I remove the cork from the bottle and pour us each a glass. "It's nothing we haven't done before over drinks."

"That was before we started sleeping together."

I pass her a glass. "True, but it wasn't for a lack of trying on my end."

Her eyes narrow as she brings the glass up to her lips and takes a sip. She hums in appreciation. "It's not bad. I didn't know what to buy."

"How did you buy wine? You're underage."

"Why? Are you going to arrest me?"

I raise a brow and move to the other side of the island, closing the distance between us. "Don't tempt me. I'd love to cuff you to my bed."

She licks her lips in a way that tells me if she isn't careful, she won't be tasting my marinara sauce at all.

"Don't look at me like that."

"Like what?" Adrianna asks, innocently taking a sip of her wine.

"Like you want me to cuff you to my bed?"

She smiles. "Maybe I do."

I growl. "I slaved away at this sauce all afternoon. So behave. I want you to get around to tasting it before I cuff you to my bed for the rest of the night."

She stands and saunters over to the pot on the stove and dips her finger in, glancing at me as she places her finger in her mouth and sucks. Her eyes widen slightly. "Delicious."

I walk over to her, grabbing her wrists and pinning them behind her back. "Careful, baby girl. You're tempting the wrong fucking man. If you push me, no dinner for you tonight."

She shudders. "Can I not eat dinner right now so we can get to handcuffing?"

"We won't make it through dinner if you carry on like that." I press my erection into her backside and she moans.

"Cuff me first and then dinner?"

I bite her shoulder, the need to fuck her driving me near on insane. "You asked for it." I pull open a drawer and grab some string, tying her wrist together behind her back. "The handcuffs are too far away." And then I hike the hem of her dress up and bend her over a stool. "Just how I like it, no panties," I muse.

Her pussy is glistening wet between her thighs. An invitation if ever I've seen one. I spank her firm, tanned ass first, groaning at the way her skin reddens.

"So fucking beautiful, and all mine."

Her back arches as I hold her over the stool with her tied arms.

"What do you want, baby girl? Tell me."

"I want your cock," she gasps, clearly as desperate right now as I am.

"Good girl," I purr, pulling down the zipper of my pants and freeing my straining erection.

And without a word, I slide into her with a slow yet forceful thrust, savoring the way she wraps around me like a glove. Her tight pussy squeezing around me as if her muscles never want me to leave, and damn, I never want to. I belong inside of this woman, that I'm sure of.

Adrianna moans loudly. I love that when we're in my apartment, she's so free and loud. As if no one can hear us here, but that's not strictly true. My apartment is above the library, which is always open, so it's likely people have heard us on countless occasions.

"You feel so good." I spank her ass again. "So tight." I grab her hair and yank her more upright. "Do you like having my cock deep inside of you?" I drag my lips over the shell of her ear, which results in the most cock-hardening mewling sound I've ever fucking heard.

"I love it," she moans, clearly forgetting about her desire to make me believe she doesn't enjoy what's happening between us

I fuck her hard, not holding back at all as the sound of my skin clashing with hers echoes around the room, adjoined with her fucking ball tightening moans, and I'm almost ready to climax within minutes.

Clenching my jaw, I hold out. This is the first time a woman has tested my control. Adrianna gets even wetter the more I fuck her, and it only makes it harder to hold out as I see her skin glistening with arousal. "You're so wet for me, baby."

She moans louder. "Choke me," she pleads.

I pause a moment, shocked by the request. And then I wrap one hand around her throat while the other stabilizes her, holding her wrists. She's got no control as I choke her just enough to inhibit the flow of oxygen.

Within seconds, her whole body shudders in the weirdest way. I thought I had been too hard with my hand around her throat. But then she screams, "Archer! Fuck! Oh! Fuck!" And I realize she's coming as her muscles clamp tight around my cock, so tight it feels like my cock is in a vise.

I feel my release come a moment later as I explode deep inside of her, breeding her tight little cunt. "That's it, baby. Take every drop of cum," I growl.

She's breathless and panting when I release her throat. But I don't remove my cock from her, not yet. I'm not ready. Tonight is going to be very long. I'm doubtful whether we'll ever get around to dinner at this rate.

27

ADRIANNA

*E*va spins around in the dress she tried on. "What do you think?"

I smile. "I think you've changed a lot since we met."

She pauses then, brow furrowing. "Is it a good or a bad change?"

"Good. You've loosened up." I arch a brow. "Perhaps that has something to do with fucking your hot husband."

Her cheeks turn red, and she flings a shoe in my direction. "Don't be an idiot."

I can't deny that Eva has grown on me a lot since she first started here. When Nat invited her to join us, it felt like we were replacing Giorgia, but now I realize she'll never replace her. They're both so different and it's amazing how well she's integrated into our group. I'm pretty sure it would have been the same if Giorgia were still here.

"Sorry." I hold my hands up. "How's married life, anyway?"

She looks thoughtful. "It's weird, to be honest. Good, but weird that I'm married so young. You know?"

I nod. "Yeah, I can understand that."

"But I love Oak so much I couldn't imagine life any different."

"What happens when you finish at the academy?"

"What do you mean?"

I shrug. "Do you want to attend college or get a job?"

Her expression turns a little serious. "We haven't really discussed it yet."

"Is it bothering you?"

She shakes her head. "I want to attend veterinary school in the fall. It's what I've been working for and there's one not too far from here." Her throat bobs as she swallows. "As long as I get in."

"You will, as you're the smartest person I know when it comes to normal subjects." She really is a brain box with school, as in traditional school subjects, rather than the unconventional subjects we take at SA. "Does that mean you're going to sit your SATs?"

She nods. "Of course. I've booked my slot already."

"A true planner. I wish I knew what the fuck I was doing after graduation."

She comes to sit next to me. "You don't have any idea?"

"My father wants to marry me off. I don't want that."

"So tell him."

I shake my head. "It's not that simple."

Eva nods. "Believe me, I understand that more than you know." She draws in a deep breath. "My family were

276

exactly the same. They wouldn't listen to me." Her brow furrows. "My mom even tried to kill me for doing what I wanted."

I swallow hard, as the Carmichael family is far less ruthless than mine. "It's why I can't tell him what I want. My father would probably murder me the moment I did."

Eva doesn't say a word to the contrary. "Shall we stop dwelling on this and get some pizza at Fratelli's?

My stomach rumbles in response. "Hell yeah." I eye the beautiful lilac dress she's wearing. "Yes or no to the dress?"

Eva glances at it in the mirror. "I love it. What do you think?"

I nod. "It's beautiful. I'm sure Oak will love it." I wink, still finding a little odd calling Principal Byrne by his first name, but Eva always refers to him naturally by his first name.

Eva blushes. "Okay, I think I'll get it." Her attention moves to the dresses I tried on and hated. "Are you sure you don't like any of those?"

I nod. "Positive."

"We can continue shopping after lunch."

"Sounds good."

It's amusing how much Eva has changed since I met her. The girl I met not long after the start of the academic year was timid and shy. Certainly not a girl who enjoys going shopping all day for dresses. Hell, she hardly owned any dresses. She has come out of her shell since she arrived.

We pay for Eva's dress and then head down the main

street toward Fratelli's pizzeria. They do the best pizza in town. Once we're in, they seat us near the back and we order a bottle of wine to share, using our fake IDs.

"So, how is everything with Coach?" Eva asks.

Heat slams into me as I know she means him constantly trying to get me into his bed, but that ship sailed months ago. "What do you mean?"

"Is he still being an asshole?" She looks up from her menu and I try to compose myself.

I shake my head. "Not so bad." It's a brief answer, as I fear if I talk too much, I'll reveal the truth.

"He's stopped trying to get you in his bed?"

I nod. "Yeah, thankfully. I guess persistence paid off." I don't enjoy lying to my friends, but telling her I gave in and slept with him would bring up questions I can't answer. Why didn't I fight back? And the reason is he blackmailed me. Anita has remained silent about it, which I never expected. Maybe she's scared I'll break more of her bones.

"I guess so," Eva says, as the server approaches our table.

"What can I get you?"

"I'll have a pizza alla salicia, a pizza marinara and a basket of garlic bread."

Eva stares at me with wide eyes. "All for yourself?" she confirms.

"I'm not sure why that surprises you after two semesters of seeing how I eat."

She laughs. "No, I'm not sure either. The Margherita for me, please."

The woman serving us looks at us like we're crazy. "Sure, coming right up." She gathers the menus and walks away.

Both of us burst into laughter. "I think you freaked her out with your order," Eva says.

I shrug. "Couldn't care less."

She laughs and tips back her wine. "Thank you," she suddenly says out of the blue.

"What for?"

"For allowing me into your group and being so welcoming to me. I've never been happy like this before. I was always miserable."

I smile. "It's nothing. We're happy to have you." I pause for a moment. "At first, I must admit I felt like Nat was taking you under her wing because we were missing Giorgia this year. I felt like she was trying to replace her, if you get what I mean?"

Eva nods. "Yeah, I can understand that."

I shake my head. "When I met you, that quickly changed. No one will replace Giorgia. You just added something new to our group."

"I'll toast to that," Eva says, holding up her glass.

I clink mine against hers and we fall into comfortable chatter about day-to-day things. All I can think about at the moment is seeing Archer. I hate to admit it, but that man has clawed his way beneath my skin so deeply I'm not sure I'll ever get him out.

I CAN FEEL Archer's eyes on me as I polish off my fifth slice of pizza that evening. Pizza twice in one day is an overload of carbs, but right now I don't give a shit.

"You can eat as much as me," he muses.

"And your point?"

He shakes his head. "No point, it's an observation." He sits up straighter and opens up one box, grabbing his fifth slice to keep up with me. "I can't believe you went to Fratelli's for lunch and didn't mention it when I suggested ordering pizza."

"Can never eat enough pizza in one day."

He laughs and takes a bite.

"Plus, this is American-style pizza and Fratelli's is Italian. They're totally different."

He sits back and watches me with a flicker of amusement dancing in his dark eyes. "Right, not similar at all."

It's funny how our sense of humor aligns so perfectly. Archer's never serious and I rarely am, except for when in competition and then we both get serious.

"How about a movie?" I ask, glancing at his huge flatscreen TV on the wall.

He runs a hand through his dark hair. "I'm not that into movies."

"So why do you have such a huge TV?"

He arches a brow. "For sports, of course."

Typical man.

"I love playing sports but watching." I pull a face, as it's not my kind of thing.

He tilts his head. "Maybe I can get you into it."

"Maybe I can get you into watching movies."

"Perhaps." He grabs his beer and takes a swig. Silence falls between us as he doesn't move to switch on the TV. And so to break it, I ask a question that's been on my mind for a while.

"Why did you run from your family?" I blurt out.

His entire body turns stiff. "It's not something I normally talk about." Archer's Adam's apple bobs as he swallows hard. "But I guess I know your secret, so only fair I share mine, right?"

I nod. "Right."

He stands and goes over to the fridge in his open-plan kitchen, grabbing another beer. "Do you want one?"

I shake my head. "I'm good, thanks."

"Where to start?" He looks at me. "My family is in control of Dublin and has been for many years before I was born."

"Ireland?" I ask, totally shocked as Archer has no accent at all.

"Yeah, the accent is confusing, isn't it?"

"A little," I confirm.

He sits back down next to me, shifting to the side to look me in the eye. "I did something that led to a target on my back."

"What?" I ask.

"My father had remarried to a younger woman about two years before I fled."

I roll my eyes. "I think I know where this is going."

He actually looks hurt and shakes his head. "She was always suggestive toward me from the moment she came into our house. I was fifteen years old when they met. And

within a short space of time, she touched me inappropriately." He shrugs. "Now I'm not saying I wasn't up for it. I
mean, what fifteen-year-old boy is going to say no to hand
job from a beautiful twenty-four-year-old woman?"

I wonder then if that's why he's always been such a
man whore, sleeping around. His previous experience with
women, particularly at such a young age. No matter
whether he was willing, that woman shouldn't have
touched him. He was a minor.

"In Ireland, the age of consent is sixteen, and I was a
couple of months off that age, anyway. She didn't think it
was wrong, I guess." He grinds his teeth. "And that turned
into a full-blown affair until a couple of weeks before my
seventeenth birthday when my father found out the truth."

There's a weird look in his eyes that I can't quite deci-
pher. "I was at a soccer match that afternoon and
returned to my room to find Fiona on my bed in a pool of
her own blood with her throat slit and a note."

I can tell it's difficult for him remembering it as the
look in his eyes is haunted.

"It said *I know what you've done.*"

And within a few seconds, I'd thrown all my most
important possessions into a bag and climbed out the
window, ran and never looked back.

"So they blamed you for something she started?"

He nods. "Yes, but I knew it was wrong. She was my
father's wife, for fuck's sake."

"It's not as bad as selling your whole family out to
their biggest enemy, though, is it?"

"It's different."

"Did you have any siblings?"

"A younger brother, who's now in line to take control of the Monroe Clan. It would have been me."

"And you wanted that life?"

He looks thoughtful as he considers the question. "I did at the time, but I wouldn't change what I've found here for anything. Oak gave me a safe place to escape, and I'll forever be in his debt." Archer reaches for me and places his hand on my leg, squeezing softly. "As a veteran, I have some ideas about how you can pull off escaping from your dad at graduation."

I stiffen at the mention of the plan I've tried so hard to keep a secret, even from my best friends. "I don't need ideas. I told you no one is going to know but me."

He tilts his head. "But I can help you, Adrianna."

"I don't need any help," I say. All my life I've had barriers from everyone and anyone and they aren't about to come down for this man.

There's a flash of hurt in his eyes, but he shrugs it off. "Suit yourself. Have you got it all sorted out?"

I don't have it sorted it out, but no one can know my plan. If anyone does, it leaves me vulnerable to being caught by my family. "I'm not sharing my plans with anyone," I say simply.

His jaw tenses. "How can you act like this?"

"Like what?" I ask.

"As if what we have together means nothing."

I might be lying to myself if I say it means nothing,

but there's no way I'd admit it to him. "It means nothing. It's just sex."

The hurt in his eyes takes me aback, as it's intense. "You don't mean that." This is what I wanted. To get my revenge on him for forcing me into the sack. And yet now that moment is here, it doesn't feel very good.

"I mean it," I say, sticking to my guns as I won't back down, not after all that he has done.

His jaw clenches. "If that's true, then walk out of that door and tell me it's over."

I stand, glaring at him. "Are you saying I'm free to go, or is this a trick?" Rage builds as he's acting like a self-centered asshole for expecting me to tell him I care about him. "Up until now, I've assumed I've had to spend time with you to ensure the truth doesn't leak. Is that no longer the case?"

I can see the hurt building in his dark eyes. He's trying to mask it, but he's not very good at hiding his emotions. It's something I've noticed about him for a while now. "Yes. If you don't want to be here, leave."

"Perfect," I say, grabbing my rucksack. "I've been hoping you'd say that for fucking months." I turn to leave.

He growls and stands. "You're a liar, Adrianna!"

I turn toward him with narrowed eyes. "You are an idiot!"

His face is practically as red as a tomato right now with rage. "I know what I felt. I know you feel something for me."

"No, what you felt was me doing what I had to do to keep the truth from spilling about my plans." I look him dead in the eye. "And that's what I've done. Now my duty is fulfilled. Good fucking riddance."

I walk toward his door, but he grabs my wrist and yanks me back toward him. His eye full of pain. This is what I wanted and right now it feels good to see him hurt, because I'm angry that he expected anything other than contempt from me. He deserves even less.

"Don't do this, baby," he pleads.

"I'm not your baby or baby girl." I tear my wrist from his. "Now leave me the fuck alone and go find another student to fuck like you always do." I storm out of there, my heart pounding from the adrenaline racing through my veins. It's insane how angry he can make me. As I march through the courtyard and back toward my dorm room, the anger wears away with each step I take.

It's over.

I just broke up with Archer Daniels, and a part of me wishes I hadn't. A part of me wants to go back and admit that I do indeed have feelings for him. But that's too dangerous to admit, because he isn't a part of my plan, and the plan is all that matters. At least, that's what I thought.

28

ARCHER

I slam the fridge door and Gav arches a brow. "What's up with you?" he asks, shaking his head. "Normally, it's me stomping around and slamming doors."

I shrug. "Can't I have a bad day?" It's been two weeks since I last had Adrianna in my bed and it's driving me insane.

He chuckles. "Yeah, it's just funny, as you are always being an asshole when I'm in a bad mood. Maybe I should return the favor."

"Well, you seem to be in an oddly good mood." I unwrap my meatball sub from the deli up the road and bite into it. "Maybe the universe is fucking with us both."

He nods. "Perhaps."

I eat my sub in contemplative silence, which seems to bug Gav as he keeps glancing in my direction. Funny really. He moans when I speak too much and now he's unnerved by my silence.

"Seriously, what's the problem, Arch?"

"What? I'm just not in the best of moods."

"I'm not used to you being so quiet," he complains.

I shake my head. "I can't win with you. I'm either chatting too much or too fucking quiet. You can't have it both ways, can you?"

Gav runs a hand across the back of his neck. "You're right. I'm being as much of an asshole as you usually are."

"Exactly." I know that's his way of apologizing, but I've never heard the guy say sorry in his life.

I polish off the rest of my sub in silence and then go to the fridge to grab a can of coke. A dull headache is forming in between my eyes. It's been like this every day since the argument, perhaps because I drink too much every single night. The only way to stop myself from making an embarrassing move and turning up at her door is to drown my sorrows in booze.

Perhaps I'm more like my father than I realized. He was a drunk, although only after we lost my mom. He loved her, but the guilt he carried for her death drove him deep into despair. After she died in a hit that was intended for him, he became violent and distant.

"Has Oak mentioned dinner to you?"

"Dinner?" I ask, turning to face him.

He nods. "Yeah, him and Eva are going to cook a meal for us Saturday night."

I shake my head. "No, but I haven't seen him since yesterday morning."

"He told me this morning. Are you going to be around?"

I nod. "Yeah, I've got nothing better to do."

"That explains the bad mood, then. Did Adrianna finally kick you to the curb?"

Rage floods through me as he's being an asshole. "Fuck you."

"Woah, I think I hit a nerve."

"You really are being a dick."

He smirks. "Good, now that you know how it feels, you might think twice about being one yourself." He stands and buttons up his jacket. "See you later."

I watch him as he walks out, my fists clenched. He's not wrong. Perhaps I shouldn't wind him up when he's in a bad mood. The difference is he's in a bad mood at least fifty percent of the time, and I'm practically never in one.

Adrianna has screwed with me in a big way. I throw the empty coke can in the trash and then head out of the staff room, turning left toward the gym. As I round the corner, my body turns tense.

Adrianna is standing by her locker in the corridor, looking as beautiful as ever.

I watch her for a moment, desperation to break the ice clawing at me, but I don't know how to approach her. And then, by a stroke of luck, a bang from inside a nearby classroom startles her, and she drops her bag, the contents spilling across the floor.

I walk over and drop to my knees to collect some items.

When she glances up, our eyes lock, but she doesn't say a word.

Once I've got everything on my side of the corridor, I pass them to her.

"Thanks, Coach," she murmurs, her cheeks flushing.

"You're welcome." I swallow hard. "How have you been?"

She looks me in the eye. "Fine. You?" It's a short and clipped answer and I hate how much it stings.

"Not so good."

She clenches her jaw. "Thanks for the books." She turns away from me, but I won't let it lie.

"Why won't you return my texts or calls?"

"Because I said all I needed to say in your apartment." She doesn't turn to look at me.

"I know I was an asshole, blackmailing you into having sex, but are you still insisting that you didn't enjoy it? That you felt nothing?"

She spins around and looks at me. "Yes, now leave me alone."

I slam the palm of my hand into her throat as rage takes over. "I don't believe you."

Her nostrils flare and I feel her heart rate quicken beneath my skin. "You should."

"I can tell that you feel something for me, no matter what you say." I squeeze tighter. "The way your heart rate increases every time I touch you like this." I move my lips close to hers, but don't kiss her. "The way your eyes dilate every time I choke you."

"You're talking about sexual things. It doesn't mean I have any emotional feelings for you."

I growl. "Sex and emotions go hand in hand."

She laughs. "Tell that to the man who's slept with countless students over the years. Did you feel something for all of them, too?"

She's right. Sex has never been linked to emotion for me. It's been an outlet. A way to blow off steam. And in that moment, I realize Adrianna feels the same way I felt for all those girls. She feels nothing but desire.

I release her throat and take a step back. "No, I didn't."

"Then why do you expect me to feel anything for you?" She tilts her head slightly. "Is it because most of the young girls you sleep with end up having feelings for you?"

I swallow hard as Adrianna is right. Many of the students develop feelings for me and yet I carry on, knowing it's not going anywhere. Knowing that in the end I'll hurt them.

"I've got a class to get to." She shoulders her bag. "Thanks for helping with the stuff I dropped."

"No problem," I say, allowing her to walk away. As I know that she's in the right and I'm the one out of order, but it doesn't make it any easier watching her march off. There's a part of me that wants to demand she fulfill her end of the bargain and return to my apartment every night until she graduates, but it's not worth the pain she inflicts.

I finally know what it's like to be the one that actually

gives a shit in a relationship. I have to say I'm not fond of the sensation.

Two more weeks pass by with Adrianna ignoring me entirely after the encounter in the hallway, and it feels like I'm being torn apart. Time is slipping too quickly through my fingers. She only has five weeks until graduation. I want to forget about it and pretend like I don't have feelings for her, but it's impossible.

Every time I see Adrianna, she acts like nothing has happened. As if we didn't spend the better part of the academic year together in such an intimate capacity. They say men aren't in touch with their feelings, but Adrianna is as cold as ice to feel nothing.

Instead of looking forward to senior gym class, I dread it. And it's about to start right now.

"Everyone select your partners," I instruct, keeping my eyes anywhere but on Adrianna.

Adrianna pairs up with Camilla, thankfully. I didn't want to see her wrestling with any guy. Combat training today is going to involve getting pretty close with partners and I think I'd snap if I saw Nik rubbing up against her.

"You know the moves you need to practice. The same ones we did last week." Ever since Adrianna and I fell out, I've not bothered with doing the demonstrations myself. Instead, I show them the moves I want them to practice on video, as the idea of demonstrating with anyone other than her is unappealing, and yet it's too awkward between us.

The class grumbles a bit, but then gets on with it, practicing their moves. I walk around, giving instructions to people absentmindedly. And avoid Adrianna and Camilla like the plague, no doubt to Adrianna's delight.

"Coach, can you help me with this?" Camilla asks.

Fucking great.

"What?"

Camilla's brow furrows. "This move where you are supposed to put your arm around your opponent's leg and take them down?" She's demonstrating it all wrong, as her arms are too low and not in the right position.

"Yes, but that's not how you do it."

Camila nods. "Explains why I can't budge Adrianna an inch."

I glance at Adrianna, meeting her gaze. "I'll show you."

"You were doing this," I say, crouching down and grabbing Adrianna's leg in the same way Camilla did.

Adrianna shudders, visibly affected by my touch. And I notice the way her eyes shut for a moment and her lips purse; Lips that I have been longing to kiss for four long weeks.

"How do you expect to bring your opponent to the ground with no pressure?"

Camilla shrugs in response.

"You need to grab Adrianna's leg higher up here." I demonstrate, struggling to ignore the desire slamming into me being this close to her. "And then once you're at this point, you trap her leg between your legs like this." I trap her leg between mine and then put pressure downward so that she bends her other leg. "And force her to bend her other leg before doing the turn like this and taking her down." I take her down and throw her to the mat, and the images that flood my mind are beyond dirty. All the times I've had her on her back like that for me come rushing back.

Adrianna stares up at me as my hand remains on her knee. Her cheeks flushing as if she remembers the same moments too. And it feels like she's the only other person in the room for a few seconds as I'm mesmerized by her.

"That makes sense," Camilla says, approaching.

I clear my throat and release Adrianna's knee, glancing at Camilla. "Good. Now you try."

"Okay."

Adrianna stands in front of Camilla, while Camilla does the move, albeit clumsily.

"Perfect, that was a hell of a lot better." I clap my hands and try to ignore the stare Adrianna gives me. "Keep up the good work."

Camilla smiles. "Thanks, Coach."

I walk away from them, knowing at this rate with five more weeks left until graduation, I'm going to go insane having to be around her but not able to touch. My hands feel like they're burning from being on her for that short time. Adrianna has infected my blood and I fear there's no cure.

29

ADRIANNA

*J*ust as the bell rings, Coach approaches.

"Adrianna, can I have a word?"

I stiffen at the sound of his voice. I've been trying to avoid him since the encounter we had in the corridor.

Camilla lingers, a look in her eyes that says shall I stay.

"I'll catch up with you later."

She shoulders her bag. "Sure, see you later."

It's impossible for me to admit that I feel something for him. I don't know how or why I feel anything but hatred toward him, but unfortunately, I do. And so the only way to avoid dealing with that is by ignoring him.

I grab my bag and turn to face him. "What's up?" I ask, trying to seem as detached as possible.

His jaw is clenched, and there's tension running through his body. "I want to call a truce."

A truce.

I wonder what exactly he means by that.

"It's been awkward between us ever since… Well, you know." He clears his throat, looking uncomfortable. "Can we clear the air?"

"There's no air to clear."

He shakes his head. "That's not true. I want things to go back to how they were before."

"Before what?" I snap, unable to contain the anger. "Before you blackmailed me?"

He nods. "That's what I was hoping, yeah."

He has some nerve, but I must admit, it's been awkward during class. "Fine. It can return to how it was. Me hating you."

"You never hated me."

He's right. Hate is a strong word, but he infuriated me.

"No, but I wouldn't say I liked you very much,"

He smiles. "I'll take it. Not being liked isn't as bad as being hated." His dark eyes bore into mine as if he's looking right into my soul.

That one look ignites a powerful desire inside of me I wish wasn't there. I clear my throat. "If that's all, I'll see you around."

He grabs my shoulder and forces me around, slamming his lips against mine forcefully.

I tense, because this isn't supposed to be happening. We're supposed to be finished. He's not blackmailing me anymore, so I'm kissing him of my own free will.

The moment that thought enters my mind, I break away from him. Deep down I want to keep kissing him. I want to get out of my head and ignore the fact that I have feelings for this man. Feelings that won't go away, no matter how hard I try to bury them.

"Adrianna," he murmurs my name, keeping hold of my hips. "I need you once more." There's a rasp of desperation in his voice. "Please."

"Are you begging me?" I ask, a sudden sense of power washing over me.

His jaw clenches. "Perhaps."

I hate the rush I get at the thought of him begging me to fuck him. It's an attractive prospect.

"Maybe I'll consider if you're really convincing," I say.

He glares at me, and I instantly like this turn of events.

"Please let me fuck your heavenly pussy one last time, baby girl."

I run a hand through the ends of my hair. "Hmm, I'm not that convinced you really want it."

He growls and I can tell that my toying with him is going to drive him insane. A prospect I enjoy the idea of.

"How about on your knees?" I suggest.

"Adrianna," he says my name in warning.

"No? Okay, I'll leave then." I turn to leave, but he grabs my wrist and spins me around.

And then he drops to his knees. "Better?" he asks.

"Let me hear you beg."

"Adrianna, please let me fuck that perfect little cunt and make you come on my cock one more time."

"Okay, since you asked so nicely, but under my terms."

His body turns tense. "What terms?"

"Strip and lie down on the gym mat over there."

His eyes narrow.

"Or, I can leave."

He grunts in frustration, but then does as I instructed.

I watch as he reveals his muscled body and that beautiful tattoo on his chest. And then he pulls off his pants and briefs in one move, before lying down on his back on the mat, propped up on his elbows. "Now what, boss?"

I tilt my head. "Stroke your cock for me."

He wraps a hand around his thick length and strokes himself, and I've got to admit it's a beautiful fucking sight. Especially as he's doing it because I told him to.

Slowly, I walk over to him and take my clothes off as I go, teasing him. It's clear in his eyes that he's barely controlling himself from standing and taking me by force. Admirably, he manages to resist. Once I'm at the mat, I'm totally naked. "Lie back for me."

He lies back and I straddle him so that the underside of his cock is lying flat against my soaking wet entrance. And then I slide up and down the length of him, coating him in my arousal. At the same time, I play with my nipples, keeping eye contact.

"Don't tease me, Adrianna. I can't handle it."

"What's the magic word?"

He bares his teeth. "Please."

I rise up and crouch over him, because I'm probably feeling as desperate as him right now. His cock springs free and then I impale myself on him, hard and fast.

"Oh fuck," I say, the sensation so good.

Archer groans. "That's it baby, ride my cock."

I set my hand on his chest as he tries to sit up more and place his hands on my ass. "Hands free today, Archer."

His eyes narrow. "Please."

I shake my head and then move my hips slowly, grinding myself on him.

"Adrianna," he growls.

"Yes?"

"I'm warning you."

I glare at him. "Who's in control?"

A muscle pops out at the side of his forehead. "Adrianna."

"Perhaps I'll leave then." I use my hand on his chest to push myself up, but he sees it coming.

"No fucking chance." He grabs my hands and uses his weight to flip me over, so I'm beneath him. And then the beast is let loose, like the night he came to my dorm room. He's an animal as he pounds into me so hard it feels like he's trying to break me.

I moan, because while it was fun teasing him, this is what I really want. Him fucking me like I'm the most desireable thing in the world, which makes little sense to me. I've never been the beautiful girl that everyone fawns over, like Camilla or Eva. And yet he wants me in a way that's addictive.

Every time he slides back into me, it builds that pressure deep within, driving me toward insurmountable pleasure the harder he thrusts. I've never felt anything like it as he ruts into me with all his strength.

I watch him as he fucks me. His muscles straining under the exertion. That beautiful tattoo doused in sweat as rivulets cascade down his chest.

He grunts like an animal as he increases the tempo once again, leaving me breathless and in shock at how hard he's fucking me. There's nothing gentle about this. It's pure, animalistic mating and I hate to say I love it. I should tease him more often.

No. I can't think like that.

This is a one off. He wants me one last time, and that's all this is.

"Choke me, Archer," I moan, knowing nothing makes me come quicker than his rough palm against my throat, cutting off my airways.

His eyes narrow, but he does as I ask, wrapping his palm around my throat and restricting the flow of oxygen. The head rush follows and I feel tears prickle my eyes as he pushes a little harder than before, perhaps because I teased him so much.

It's all too much as a giant wave of pleasure washes over me. My pussy tightens around him and it feels like it pulls him deeper inside of me. I convulse beneath him, partially because I can't breathe, which only heightens the intensity of my orgasm.

White lights flood my vision, and my brain literally short circuits for a few minutes. I almost wonder if I passed out for a second, until my vison recovers and Archer is continuing to fuck me through it, chasing his own release.

"God damn it," he growls. "You come so well on my

cock, I can't hold out. Fuck," he roars. And I know he's about to come as his cock swells inside of me. And then kisses me, trying to drown out the sounds he's making.

After all, we're in the fucking gym in the middle of the day. Anyone could walk in. My heart skips a beat at that thought, as we've been so wrapped up in each other, we wouldn't have noticed.

I feel his cum start to drip down my ass crack and I hate how dirty and yet good I feel.

"Take it all, baby," he groans. "Such a good girl."

"Archer," I gasp his name.

"Yes, baby?"

I shake my head. "Nothing. I…" It's impossible for me to swallow my pride and tell him I made a mistake. Tell him that I want to continue this thing we have going on.

I push at his chest, but he doesn't move.

"We should probably get up, as the door isn't locked."

Archer presses his lips to my shoulder. "But if I take my cock out of you, that means it's the end."

"Perhaps," I say.

He looks into my eyes, a flicker of hope igniting. "Are you saying you would consider round two another time?"

I shrug. "Maybe, if you're really nice to me."

He bites my collarbone, sending a thrill right to my core. "I'm always nice to you, baby girl."

I shudder as he licks my nipples then, his cock hardening inside of me. "Seriously, Archer! It's the middle of the day."

"Does it look like I give a shit? I have a free period and no one is booked to use the gym."

I shudder, gazing into his eyes. "Fine."

He smirks and then starts to move in and out of me. A look in his eyes that tells me I'm in for one hell of a ride for the remaining thirty minutes of this period. I doubt he'll let me leave even a minute before.

ARCHER

I walk out of the front entrance of the academy, and every muscle in my body turns rigid.

Damien Vazquez, Adrianna's father, is getting out of an armored SUV. I try to keep my cool, continuing my path toward the woods down by the ruins, where evidently I'd hope to bump into Adrianna.

Oak mentioned only yesterday that Adrianna was being pulled from the academy early, but I didn't know it was going to be this early. I feel panic rise inside of me as I really thought I had longer to figure this all out. There's no way I can let her go that easily, and yet trying to force her to stay when her father is here is suicide.

Damien Vasquez is renowned for being the most ruthless cartel boss of all time. He is insane and bloodthirsty, which means if someone gives him a reason, he'll take it.

The air is warm at this time of year as spring closes in on summer and it's the perfect weather for a stroll by the stream. Adrianna needs to know that her father is coming to take her early from the academy, but she wasn't in her room and won't reply to my texts, which isn't anything new since we had that argument during spring break.

When I get to her special spot, I'm thankful when I see her sitting on the stone I found her sitting on before. Her head is in her hands and I've never seen her look so small before as I approach.

"Am I interrupting?" I ask.

Adrianna's dark eyes find mine, and she shakes her head. "No, have a seat." She looks at the rather uncomfortable looking rock next to her. I'm surprised she doesn't make any kind of smart remark.

"I'm okay standing. What's up?"

"My father is here to bring me home before graduation, even though I told him I'm not leaving the academy early."

"Yeah, it's why I was looking for you. And I text you about three times this morning. Oak told me yesterday that your father intended to pull you out before graduation. Although I didn't know he was coming today."

Her expression turns serious. "I assumed you wanted to talk about…"

"About you and me?"

She nods.

I shake my head. "No, I wouldn't risk being burned again. It's just sex, I get it." I narrow my eyes. "However you did say you wouldn't mind continuing, right?"

She looks at me and nods. "Yeah, I'm sorry. I was so harsh during Spring Break."

Her apology is something, but it changes nothing. It

doesn't mean she feels something that she insists she doesn't. Even after having sex after combat training. It's hard to believe that she doesn't feel the same, but I'm done trying to convince her otherwise.

"You sure you don't want to sit?"

I swallow hard and move to sit next to her, even though it's hard being this close to her after another week apart. It's been a week since that hot sex after combat class, and ever since all I can think about is touching her again. And yet she's ignored my texts and calls, no doubt regretting giving in. It's four weeks now until graduation. "What are you going to do about your father?"

Her lips purse together. "I don't want to face him. I fear he might have learned the truth."

"How?" I ask.

Adrianna shrugs. "I don't know, but you found out, so it can't be that hard."

I nudge her shoulder, trying to break the ice. "Are you saying I don't have skills?"

She doesn't seem in the mood for jokes, as she turns her attention back to the flowing stream. "I'm saying I don't want to go to Mexico. I told him that on the phone that I can't leave the academy early, and now he's here." She shakes her head. "My father has never been here, not even when I was first enrolled at ten years old."

I clench my jaw. "And that's why you think he knows?"

She nods.

"There's only one way to find out, baby girl." I forget completely that she's not my baby girl anymore. When we're together, it's so natural. Adrianna doesn't seem to notice, too preoccupied with her father's arrival.

"If he knows, he'll kill me." She looks vacant as she stares at the flowing water. "Family or not."

"I don't believe that," I say, knowing that despite the Vasquez Cartel being one of the most ruthless, blood is blood.

Adrianna may have betrayed them, but she did it because her family won't respect her wishes. She's too headstrong to be married off to someone who will boss her around. Hell, she should lead the damn cartel. I've never met a stronger woman than her.

"You don't know my father."

I shake my head. "No, I don't. Although I've heard the rumors about him."

"The rumors don't do him justice. The man is savage and you don't want to get on the wrong side of him." She shuffles her feet on the rock. "He killed his cousin last year for betraying the cartel."

"I get the sense that his daughter might be more important to him than his cousin."

Her brown eyes find mine. "Perhaps, which means my betrayal will only hurt him more."

She's right. It'll hurt him more if he's found out, but I don't suspect he has.

What reason would he have had to investigate his own daughter?

"I doubt it has anything to do with the Estrada Cartel." I run a hand gently across her back, noticing the way she shudders at my touch. "You're probably being paranoid."

Her eyes narrow. "I'm not paranoid. He's never been to the academy in the eight years I've been going here."

If she's in danger, I'd stand in his way. "Do you want me to come with you? I can intervene if something goes wrong."

Her nostrils flare. "No, you'll wind up dead if you try to get in the way of my father and what he wants."

I smirk. "I'm glad you care what happens to me."

She shakes her head. "I don't need your blood on my hands." It's said in a detached way, but I find it hard to believe that she truly feels nothing, even if she said it when we argued.

"I've missed you, Adrianna. Not just the sex."

Her eyes flash with a modicum of emotion, but it's gone quickly. "I guess I've missed the sex too, but that's all."

I laugh at that, as at least it's something. "Does that mean you'll consider coming back to my apartment tonight? You did suggest you might be up for a second round last week."

Her cheeks flush a pretty shade of pink. "I might not even be here."

I sense that even Damien Vasquez can't force Adrianna to do something she doesn't want, unless he has something he can blackmail her with. "Here's the deal. If you get taken home, then you won't come to my apartment, but if you get to stay, then you come at eleven o'clock and we'll celebrate with a bottle of champagne."

She nods. "Fine. I can't say no to champagne." Her lips purse together. "Will there be food?"

I laugh. "Of course. I'll order us pizza from Fratelli's."

Adrianna cheers up a little. "I can't wait... As long as I'm still alive."

"Sure you don't want me to come and face him with you?"

"My father would kill you if he knew that we slept together."

Silence falls between us. "Admit that you would be a little sad if I died. Surely you'd cry at my funeral, right?"

She rolls her eyes. "Stop being an idiot." There's a whisper of a smile on her lips, but she doesn't let it break. As always, she's tough to crack.

"How long do you intend to hide here?"

Her lips press together in a straight line. "Preferably until he leaves."

I chuckle. "I don't take your father as a man who gives up easily."

"No, he doesn't." She pauses a moment. "Fuck, I'm going to have to just face him, aren't I?"

"I think so, baby." I lean toward her, grabbing her chin, and press my lips to hers. "Don't worry. He won't hurt you."

She rolls her eyes. "You don't know that."

She's right. I don't know that. And the fact is, my father would have murdered me if he'd got his hands on me, that I'm sure of. He wouldn't have left Fiona alive, so why would he leave me alive? And yet all these years I've told myself he would have, even though I know it's not true, because it's too painful to think that he wanted me dead.

Adrianna stands. "I best find out if my father intends to murder me."

I tilt my head. "If it's any consolation, I noticed he didn't really look in the murderous mood when I passed him at the front entrance."

She sighs heavily. "I'm not sure it helps. I just hate talking to him, and if he's here, it can't be good."

I stand too and step toward her, pulling her close and kissing her lips softly. "Sorry, I have been dying to do that for a week."

She smiles then. "Is that right?"

I nod. "Yeah, it's all I could think about." My hands tighten around her hips. "Well, kissing and other things." I let my lips move lower, skating gently over her neck and then collarbone. "Fuck, I've missed you so damn much."

She puts her hands on my chest and pushes me away. "Seriously, I've got to see my father. He doesn't like being kept waiting."

I kiss her once more. "Okay, see you tonight."

"I don't know how you're so sure." She walks away, and I watch her.

She's insane if she thinks I'm letting her face him alone. I'll follow and stay within earshot to intervene if her father tries to hurt her.

"Have you heard the news?" Luca asks, looking smug. The kid's more annoying than me and that's saying something. Ever since he started after Spring Break, he's been driving most of the staff mad.

"What news?" I ask.

He smirks. "Adrik Volkov murdered Hernandez Estrada last night. The entire city of Chicago is in chaos."

My body turns numb as that means Adrianna's deal with them is off. And if anyone had any record of it, it may come back to bite her in the ass. "Why do you look so happy about that?" I ask, as it makes no sense. If the city is in chaos, it's not good for the Morrone family.

He runs a hand through his dark hair. "It means there's an end in sight to the war."

My brow furrows. "You're literally speaking in oxymorons. Chaos doesn't bring an end to anything."

Luca shakes his head. "Now that's where you're wrong."

I sigh heavily, unsure whether I have the time or patience for this. My feelings for Adrianna have been consuming my every waking thought. I followed her and made sure that things didn't go wrong with her father. Thankfully, she was wrong. They had a peaceful conversation and he left within thirty minutes. Now, I sense I know the reason he was here. The chaos in Chicago must have spooked him.

"Did you hear me?" Luca asks.

I blink twice and shake my head. "Sorry, I was in my own world."

He rolls his eyes. "Adrik Volkov has created enemy number one in Chicago, which means there are already talks of our family sitting down with the Callaghans and Volkov Bratva to broker a truce and work against Adrik."

"So you mean it's going to unite you against the cartel?" I confirm.

Luca nods. "Yeah, and three against one is good odds."

I don't mention the fact that the Estrada Cartel is one of the most powerful in the world and neck and neck with the Vasquez Cartel, Adrianna's family. The Morrone family, Volkov Bratva, and Callaghan Clan may well be formidable opponents but not for the Estrada Cartel.

"How does it even work?"

"What work?" he asks.

"A Russian running the cartel's operations in Chicago."

Luca shakes his head. "Don't ask me. I'm not sure Adrik is right in the head, to be honest. I doubt he's hashed out the details."

Gav comes into the staff room then, and I'm glad, as I am not interested in discussing Chicago mafia politics with Luca Morrone. Especially not as it throws Adrianna's chance of escape out of the window with Hernandez out of the picture.

31

ADRIANNA

*M*y plan to get my revenge on Archer is backfiring.

Why the hell do I feel so excited whenever I see him?

And when he touched me earlier by the stream, he was trying to comfort me, but his touch ignited butterflies fluttering in my stomach and made my head spin. He keeps talking about feelings and how he wants us to continue after I graduate, which is insane.

I can't work out if he's only saying it because I've never admitted I want him. All the while, I've made sure I keep detached and cold, even when he talks about his feelings.

As I walk into the academy, I'm ambushed by my father. "Where have you been?"

I cross my arms over my chest. "I went for a walk. Is that a crime?"

He sighs heavily. "I'm here to take you home."

My brow furrows. "But what about the academy?" I ask.

He yanks my wrist and drags me into an empty classroom, slamming the door behind him. The anger in his expression makes me wonder if he knows the truth. Is it possible that he, too, has found out about my deal with Hernandez Estrada? "America is dangerous right now, Adrianna."

"Dangerous?" I confirm.

He nods, running a hand across the back of his neck. "Yes, last night, Hernandez Estrada was murdered by Adrik Volkov. It has caused unrest and chaos both here in the states and back home in Mexico."

I shake my head. "How am I in danger here, attending a secret academy miles from any of those places?"

His jaw clenches. "You realize you attend this school with several enemies, Adrianna? Elias Morales is related to the Estrada family."

"Yes, but what does it have to do with us?" I ask, wondering what his problem is. "We are the Vasquez Cartel and had nothing to do with it."

"We may have given the boy a push on our end."

I swallow hard as I stare at my father. "A push to murder the leader of the Estrada Cartel stateside?"

He nods, paling a little. "And if they find out, they'll target you."

"If who finds out, though? If Adrik runs the cartel, who will come after me?"

"Hernandez may be dead, but his sons still live and word is they want to take back their throne."

I sigh heavily. "If you covered your tracks adequately, then they're no threat to me. I'm not leaving."

"Adrianna Elena Julieta Vasquez," he booms, glaring at me. "You'll do as you're told."

I clench my fists by my side. "No. I'm eighteen years old and I'll see out the end of the semester here. I won't be torn from my last year at the academy because of fear."

I'm surprised when he suddenly calms down and looks me dead in the eye. "That's because you're a Vasquez and you're right. We don't run in fear." He nods. "I agree. You'll see out the last few weeks of the semester here and graduate, but you'll return home as soon as school is finished."

Little does he know that this may be the last time I ever see him. I will not return to Mexico to be sold off like a prize mare. Somehow, I have to disappear just after graduation before they can haul me back home. The logistics of which I'm still trying to work out.

I walk up to the door of Archer's apartment, my heart thumping at a hundred miles an hour.

Am I crazy for being here?

Perhaps. I knock on the door and wait a few moments and then I hear the thud of footsteps descending the stairs. Archer opens it and smiles at me with a smile that could stop most women's hearts. "You are here."

I smile back at him. "I didn't get murdered."

315

"I'm glad," he says, stepping aside to allow me in.

I pause for a moment, knowing that now I'm coming to him of my free will rather than because he's blackmailing me. I'm not sure how to feel about that. It changes everything.

His brow furrows. "Are you going to stay there or come in?"

I purse my lips. "Still trying to decide."

He laughs and grabs my hand, yanking me into the apartment and against him. "Don't be an idiot."

"I'm normally the one saying that to you."

He leads me into his apartment, where he has a table set with candles alight. "I was prepared since I hadn't heard of any murders on campus." There's a bottle of champagne on ice and three pizza boxes on the table.

"Principal Byrne told you, didn't he?"

He shrugs. "I have my ways other than Byrne, Adrianna." Pulling out my seat, he gestures for me to sit down. "How did your meeting with your father go?"

"Well." I shuffle in my seat. "It had nothing to do with my betrayal, although I'm in the shit."

"I heard about Hernandez."

My brow furrows. "From who?"

"Luca Morrone."

"Of course, it affects the Morrone family." I nod. "Well, it means my deal with him is off."

"Yeah, I figured that. Does it mean you can't go through with your plan?"

I don't feel comfortable discussing it with him, but I

realize that there's no reason for me not to trust Archer. He wouldn't gain anything by ratting me out. "No."

"That's good." He nods at the boxes next to us. "Help yourself to pizza."

I open the nearest box and grab a slice, shoving it into my mouth. As always, I'm starving. It helped that I spent two hours in the pool this afternoon, trying to blow off steam after the encounter with my father.

"I have missed this," Archer says.

I swallow hard. "Me too."

His smile is heartbreaking and I hate that I can't open up to him. Even though he was an asshole for black-mailing me, which he admits, there's this part of me that wants to embrace the feelings I have for him.

"I love Fratelli's," I say, grabbing a second slice. My attempt to direct conversation elsewhere.

Archer nods. "It's good, for sure. What's your favorite food?"

"There are way too many to decide."

"Okay, what about a favorite type of food, like Italian or Asian?"

"Mexican hands down." I shrug. "I maybe Mexican and that makes me biased, but I love a good tamale or burrito. Italian is close second, though."

Archer smiles. "I'm like you. I love all foods, but for me you can't beat a well-cooked rack of ribs. What did you think of the ribs at the diner?"

"Delicious," I reply.

He looks at me then in a way that makes my heart rate speed up. I don't like the sensation, as it makes me feel odd. "Back to the fact I've missed you. When I say that, I don't just mean the sex."

"Archer," I say his name in warning.

He holds his hands up in surrender. "I know. I won't start that argument again. I'm just saying I enjoy spending time with you, even out of the sack."

I sense he won't let this go in the long term. "Fine."

His eyes narrow, as I know he was hoping I'd reciprocate the feeling.

I take another slice of pizza, needing to distract myself from this odd sense of dread sweeping over me. I don't have any control over what's happening now. It's the first time I've felt like this and I don't like it.

"Are you okay?" he asks.

I nod. "Yeah, I feel a little woozy."

"The champagne maybe?" he asks.

I nod, but I know it's not that. It's this sickening feeling that I actually care for Archer. No matter how much I try to push my feelings away, the more time I spend with him, the stronger they return.

"Why don't we sit on the sofa?" he suggests.

The half-eaten piece of pizza sits on my plate and for the first time in a long time, I don't think I can eat it. "Sure."

I stand and walk over to the sofa, slumping down on it. The dread still lingering over me like a dark rain cloud threatening to break open and drown me.

"Are you sure you're okay?" Archer asks.

I shake my head. "I've got a bit of a headache."

His brow furrows. "You didn't drink that much champagne."

"Maybe I'm getting sick."

He sits next to me and places a hand against my forehead. "You don't feel warm." He pats his lap. "Come here."

I do as he says, even though a part of me wants to resist.

Archer's powerful arms wrap around me and he holds me, his lips nuzzled against my neck softly.

I hate that him being like this only makes that sensation worse. "You know, I really don't feel great. I think I should go back to my room and sleep."

"No way am I letting you go anywhere if you're sick." He shifts me off his lap and stands. "I'll look after you here. Come on."

I swallow hard as he holds a hand out to me. And yet I take it despite everything.

He leads me into the bedroom and gently undresses me. Normally, things would take a sexual turn right about now, but I can tell every touch isn't intended to arouse but soothe instead.

It makes my chest ache as he pulls back the sheets. "Get in."

I climb into the bed, snuggle beneath the warm comforter.

"Is there anything you need?"

"Maybe some water?" I suggest.

He nods. "Of course."

I place a hand against my forehead as he walks out of

the room. For a while, I've known that my plan to get him to fall for me has gone wrong. Because I've been falling for him too, despite everything.

He returns with the water and places it on the night-stand. "Anything else?"

I shake my head. "No, thanks."

Archer strips off and I hate the way I instantly heat at the sight of him half naked, as if I don't have control of my urges. He gets into the bed and pulls me against him so my head is on his chest. "I'll look after you, baby girl, don't worry."

I swallow hard, as the fact he's being so caring is what's worrying me. He needs to return to being that arrogant asshole who won't accept no for an answer.

"Thanks," I murmur.

He pulls my chin up and then kisses me. A kiss that is soft and gentle, but sets my world ablaze. I am stuck in my head. "I'm sorry. I don't feel like it right now."

He shakes his head. "I know. Just because I kiss you it doesn't mean I expect sex."

I nod in reply and go to turn over when he grabs my hand and squeezes. "Adrianna." He looks into my eyes with such meaning it only makes the dread tighten around my heart. "I love you."

Those three words hit me hard. The moment I hear them, I tense. No one has said those words to me before, not even my family. And instantly, I feel my shields locking into place as I clench my jaw. "Are you insane?"

My response wounds him. I see it in his eyes.

"No, I care about you. Don't pretend this means nothing to you."

It doesn't mean nothing to me, but I don't have space for anyone else. I've always been alone in this world, and that's how it has to stay. I shake my head. "I can't do this right now, Archer. I thought I was clear about what this was."

I lie down and turn over so that he doesn't see the tears building in my eyes. There's no way to break the steel around my heart. I'm a lost cause and I don't deserve his love, even if actions at the start of our relationship were questionable.

I love him too. I think that's the sickening feeling in my stomach. I just can't admit it, not to him or anyone.

32

ARCHER

I stumble out of Gav's cabin as drunk as hell, knowing that if I don't speak to Adrianna, I'll lose my mind. It's been one week exactly since I told her I love her in bed. And we've gone on as if nothing ever happened.

It's hard to believe that Gav is actually dating a student, but right now, I can't focus on that. All I can focus on is getting Adrianna to see reason. She belongs to me and I don't just want her for this year. I want her indefinitely.

She wants a way out of her life with her family and I can offer her it here at the Academy with me.

Oak has hidden me from my family for enough years, which means he can hide her, too. I walk up the path from Gav's cabin in the woods toward the lights surrounding the huge stone building I call home. Instead of heading to my apartment, I unlock the door into the main building from the courtyard and make my way through the corridors toward the girl's dormitories.

Once I get to Adrianna's door, I try to stop myself from swaying and knock on it, waiting impatiently for her to answer.

The moment she opens the door, she tries to slam it in my face, but I block it with my foot and force it open. Even in my inebriated state, I'm quick enough.

"You need to listen to me."

Her nose wrinkles in disgust. "You're drunk."

"And whose fault is that?"

Her brow furrows. "Not mine. You're the idiot that drank too much."

I step inside and grab her throat. "You're the reason I'm drinking, Adrianna. I told you how I felt and you blew me off."

"And?"

Pain claws at my chest as I stare into her eyes, wishing she weren't so cold. "How can you say you feel nothing?"

She sets her hands on her hips. "How could I feel anything for a man who blackmailed me into sleeping with him?" There's a glint of amusement in her eyes, as if she is enjoying my torment.

"You're as stubborn as a mule."

Her brows furrow. "I think you're talking about yourself."

"No, I'm talking about your stubborn insistance that this means nothing to you, when clearly it means more than you let on."

Her jaw works. "I can't be dealing with this right

now." The way she says it, it's clear something other than my turning up here frustrated her.

"Do you want to talk about it?" I ask.

Her brow furrows. "About what?"

"Whatever's bothering you."

She bites her lip before nodding and stepping to one side. "Yes, but only talk."

I arch a brow suggestively before taking a step.

She puts her arm out in front of me to block my path. "I mean it. Talking only."

I hold my hands up. "Okay, you got it."

And then she lets me into her room, glancing each direction of the corridor before shutting the door.

"What's up, baby?"

She grits her teeth together. "It's getting close to graduation."

"And?"

She releases a shaky breath. "And my father says he's going to attend, which means I need a clever plan to slip away before he can take me."

I smirk, as she should have come to me with this sooner. "I'll get you out."

"No, I can't rely on anyone but myself."

I walk toward her and cup her cheek gently in my hand. "You can keep telling yourself that, but the truth is you can rely on me."

She looks up into my eyes. "How can I rely on a man who blackmailed me?"

"I'm telling you that you can rely on me. Why the fuck would I screw you over?"

Her lips purse together. "I don't know." I sense she isn't used to trusting anyone.

"Seriously, Adrianna. Let me help." I need to help her as I need to know her plan. She's so pigheaded. It wouldn't surprise me if she disappeared forever and I couldn't find her. It's the only way to ensure I keep tabs on her.

"Fine, you can help."

I smile, relief coursing through my veins. "Good, as I have quite a few ideas."

"Such as?"

I sit on the edge of her bed and pat my lap for her to come and sit on it.

Her eyes narrow, but she sits anyway.

"Your father is coming to graduation, and that's a complication, but not the be all and end all. I mean, you dictated to your father before, so do it again."

"What do you mean?"

"Tell him that you're going to celebrate with your friends. They're all going to be celebrating, right?"

She nods. "Yeah."

"Then tell him to book a motel and you'll leave with him the next morning."

A crease forms in between her brows. "I'm not sure that'll work, but I can call him beforehand. It's an option, I guess."

"Well, tell me your ideas."

"Honestly?" Her throat bobs as she swallows. "I don't have any. It's as if I've spent so long trying to plan this escape that anytime I try to think of how to execute it, especially with my father at my graduation, I come up blank."

I shake my head at her sheer stupidity for trying to shun my help. "And you didn't want my help out of sheer stubbornness?"

She nods, looking a little ashamed.

I laugh. "You never cease to amaze me."

"Good," she says, smiling.

"Call your father in the morning and request that he book into a hotel for the night of your graduation so you can celebrate with friends. And that you'll leave with him the following morning." My eyes narrow, as I assume her father isn't someone who takes direction well. "If that fails, we'll think of something else."

Adrianna draws in a deep breath. "Where will I go after the celebration?"

"Leave that aspect to me. I'll plan the entire thing for you."

Her lips purse. "No one should know where I'm going, as it'll mean you're vulnerable to interrogation from my family."

I've every intention of going with her, but I don't push that. Until we're free and to a safe place, I won't broach the subject. And once the heat dies down, we'll return here to the academy. "Why would your family think to interrogate their daughter's gym coach?"

"You're right. I'm being paranoid." She rolls her eyes. "God, this is stressful."

I chuckle. "Maybe what I found out tonight will keep your mind off of it." I realize the moment I say it, I assume Gav and Camilla's relationship is a secret. "I don't think I'm supposed to tell you, though."

She shifts in my lap so that she's straddling me, her arms around the back of my neck. My cock gets impossibly hard beneath her. "You can't say that and not tell me."

I kiss her lips gently. "No, I guess I can't." I tilt my head, wondering if she knows anyway. "Maybe you already know."

"Know what?"

"Who Camilla is in a relationship with?"

Her brow furrows, which is answer enough. "Camilla isn't in a relationship with anyone."

"That's not true."

"Who is it?" She asks.

"Gav."

Her eyes widen and she looks in utter shock. "No way, she's too sweet for him."

I would have thought the exact same thing. Camilla Morrone comes off as innocent to a certain extent, certainly not the kind of woman I pictured Gav with. To be honest, I don't know who I can picture Gav with. "I went down to Gav's place tonight and kind of crashed their romantic dinner. They seemed pretty annoyed, actually. I was very drunk when I arrived, much drunker than I am now."

"Why would they be annoyed?"

"Because I crashed his dinner and insisted I stay."

She rolls her eyes. "You idiot. Of course they would be

annoyed. If someone did that to us at dinner, how would you like it?"

I would be pissed as hell, because I'd be wanting to fuck Adrianna mid-dinner, most likely. Gav's probably the same. "It wasn't my best hour, but alcohol can make a man do stupid things. But back to the point. Camilla Morrone and Gavril fucking Nitkin!" It's crazy because he's a sadist, which means Camilla isn't so innocent. She's got to be a masochist.

"Yeah, that's crazy. I mean, she said something about trying to bag him after Eva got with Oak." Adrianna shakes her head. "Even though she's getting into a lot of trouble lately, I thought it was a joke. Explains it, really."

I grab her chin and kiss her, thrusting my tongue through her lips as an overwhelming desire sweeps over me. When we break apart, we can hardly breathe from the intensity of it.

"What was that for?"

"I wanted to kiss you. Is that a crime?" I ask.

"No." Her arms tighten around my neck and this time she kisses me. My cock is straining to break free. I need to be inside of her already. It's been too long since our makeup sex in the gym almost two weeks ago.

I stand and lower her to the bed, kissing a path down her neck and lower again to between my breasts. All she's wearing is a sexy nightgown that's rather skimpy. "I've missed this," I murmur, slipping the straps off of her shoulders and exposing her beautiful breasts. "I've missed these." I run the tip of my finger gently around my breasts, making her nipples harden. "I've missed every fucking part of you." I look her dead in the eye. "Did you miss me?"

The surprise in her eyes is clear, and she's not quick to react.

I can't help the smile that curves onto my lips. "I knew it."

"Knew what?" She asks.

"You missed me." I kiss her before she can contest the fact. And she doesn't fight me, because she knows it's true. She missed me and whatever this is between us. However, Adrianna being Adrianna, when we break apart, she shakes her head.

"You don't know what you're talking about."

I kiss her again. "Your lips say one thing, but your eyes give you away."

"Fine, I missed you," she admits.

At long last I get some emotion from her. "Good, because I'm not going to stop fucking you from now until graduation." And hopefully after, but I know not to push my luck right now. The last thing I want is to get into another argument with her.

"Shut up and kiss me," she says, grabbing my collar and yanking my lips to hers.

And for once I do as she says, as there's no way I'm passing up that opportunity. I need to be inside of her right now, and preferably never leave. This is where I belong.

33

ADRIANNA

*A*drenaline has been racing through my veins since I woke this morning.

It's sickening, but today is the day. Graduation is this afternoon and then I'll go out to celebrate with my friends.

My father agreed to my plans and told me he'd booked into a hotel twenty miles away in the nearest city, as he's above the little inn in town and the motel near here. It actually makes the plan easier, as he won't be nearby when I make a run for it.

After the celebrations are through, Archer and I will disappear. Our friends will know that I've left for good, but not where I'm going. No one knows that, not even I do. I've let Archer figure the entire thing out and where I'm going to go.

It's been hard trusting him in this way, as I've always relied on myself. He can't disappear with me, though. He has a life here at the academy, and so he's going to set me up with my new life and then leave. That's the part I've been trying to avoid thinking about entirely.

I'm not sure how I'm going to say goodbye to him.

"Hey, you wanted to talk to me?" Camilla says, sticking her head through the door into my dorm room.

I nod. "Yeah, I sent a text to Eva and Nat, too. They'll be here soon."

Camilla smiles and drops onto the sofa next to me. "You look troubled."

"Do I?" I say, swallowing hard. "I guess I am, and it has something to do with what I'm going to tell you guys."

Camilla groans. "Why do people always insist on waiting to spill the gossip?"

I shake my head. "You need to learn the meaning of patience."

She grunts and shoves me playfully in the shoulder.

Eva appears next, looking a little surprise that I've left my door open. "What's going on?"

Camilla pouts. "She won't tell us until Nat arrives. Where the hell is that girl?"

"Probably under the sheets with her bully."

Camilla frowns. "I'll still never understand how that happened."

"I don't think either of us will." I glance at Eva. "Although, Eva saw it coming a mile off."

Eva shrugs. "Fresh perspective, I guess."

"Fresh perspective on what?" Nat asks from the doorway.

I swallow hard, as I know Nat hates it when we talk

about her relationship with Elias. It's clear that she's embarrassed that she even gave Elias a chance after everything he's done.

"Gone girl," I lie, giving Eva a look. "She saw it only a few months ago and noticed things I never noticed, that's all."

Nat nods. "So, what's this all about?"

"Close the door," I instruct. "I have something I need to talk to you about."

Eva sits on the sofa on the other side, while Nat closes the door. She goes to join Eva, all my closest friends, except Giorgia, staring at me expectantly.

"I'm running away after graduation."

"Running away?" Camilla asks, frowning at me. "Why?"

I swallow hard. "I can't stay in Mexico and be married off to someone. It'll literally kill me."

Nat straightens. "I always thought you loved this life. Life as a part of the mafia."

I nod. "I do, but what kind of life will I have once I'm sold to some tyrant who sees me as nothing more than a breeding machine?" I swallow hard. "Just like my mom."

"We have more in common than I first thought," Eva says.

Camilla clears her throat. "Well, none of us wants that life. We've all avoided marriages we didn't want." She gives me a pointed look, and I wonder if she knows about me and Archer after he turned up drunk at Gav's cabin. After all, I know about those two, but I've not told her. I've been waiting for her to break the news.

"Except for Adrianna is going off alone. The lone wolf," Nat says.

I wonder if that's what they think of me. A loner. Someone who wants to be on their own.

"Are you going alone?" Camilla asks, and by the look on her face, she's suggesting I might still be fucking Archer, even if she's never brought it up.

I nod in response, as while Archer's helping me, I'm not leaving with him. "Yeah."

"Where are you going to go?"

I wince. "I can't tell you. At least not until I'm settled."

Nat frowns. "How am I going to send you an invitation to the wedding?"

"Just tell me where and what day and I'll be there."

"It's happening August twentieth on the Isla Mujeres."

"Oh," I say, shaking my head. "I'm not sure I'll be able to come to Mexico after fleeing from my family."

"Elias' family runs the island. We could fly you in direct on one of their jets. There's no way your father would find out."

I nod. "Maybe. I'll find a way to get in touch before then."

Nat looks a little sad. "So we won't be able to contact you at all?"

"Not until everything dies down."

"How long will that take?" Eva asks.

It could take a good few years for my father to call off a hunt, as long as I make it that long without being caught. "Who knows? It depends how determined my father is to catch me."

"This sucks," Camilla says, unshed tears in her eyes. "So after tonight, it could be goodbye for years?"

I swallow hard. "I don't have the answers, but you can't tell anyone. Not even your partners." I glance at Eva and Nat. "It's really important that until I've left, you say nothing."

"Got it," Eva says.

Nat nods. "Of course."

Camilla sighs. "I'll try, but I'm very bad at keeping things from Mia."

I give her a pointed look. "You literally have to keep your mouth shut until tomorrow morning. Is it really that hard?"

She purses her lips together. "No, I guess not."

Nat laughs. "You know how hard it is for her to keep her motormouth shut."

Camilla grabs one of my throw pillows and chucks it at Nat's head.

"That was uncalled for," Nat says, grabbing it and throwing it right back.

Eva shakes her head. "Is this turning into a pillow fight?"

"Why the hell not?" I say, grabbing one and throwing it at Eva.

Eva gasps. "That is it, you're going down, Vasquez!"

I laugh and we all descend into silliness as we chuck pillows around the room at each other. This is exactly

BIANCA COLE

what I needed. A bit of mindless fun to take my mind off
of the task ahead tonight.

My father stands at my door half an hour before the
ceremony.

"Hey, Adrianna." He looks at my outfit. "You look
well."

I swallow hard. "Thanks for coming." I glance down
the corridor. "Where's mom?"

He shakes his head. "Your mother couldn't make it."

It hurts a bit, I must admit. Out of the two of them,
I'd expect my mom to be here over my father. She may
not have ever been emotionally supportive, but she's
always been a little less cold than him.

"Oh, is she busy?"

"No, but I don't enjoy traveling with your mother. You
know that."

I clench my jaw. "I know that." He doesn't like to travel
with her because he likes to pay hookers whenever he stays
away from home. The man disgusts me, but my mother
isn't much better. Their marriage is a sham, and it has been
all my life. Exactly what I want to avoid by escaping, as that
was my future. My mom was married by arrangement to
my father, hence the toxic relationship between the two.

"Shall we get going then?" I say.

He nods. "Lead the way."

I clench my jaw and head down the corridor of the

dorms, which are bustling with people rushing to get to the ceremony, and other year students getting ready to leave for summer.

"This place is grander than I'd imagined. I noticed it when I was here last," he muses.

"It's nice here," I say.

"Yes, your dorm room looks more like a hotel room." He laughs. "I remember when you tried to beg me and your mother not to send you."

I nod. "I remember too." Every day I thank the heavens that my parents ignored me. It was rough, but as soon as I met Giorgia and Camilla, we hit it off. And not long after, Nat joined the three of us.

We complete the rest of the walk to the grand hall in tense silence. It's hard to believe how awkward it is between us, considering he's supposed to be my father. The man who brought me into this world. And yet he's like a stranger to me.

"Right. I think I've got to gather with the other students," I say.

He nods. "Go on then."

There's no wish of good luck or congratulations like most parents. Even mafia parents are generally more caring than mine, although often rather ruthless. I sigh heavily and walk toward my friends, who are already gathered together in the waiting area.

"Adrianna, there you are!" Camilla links arms with me. "Is your father here?"

I nod in reply. "Unfortunately, yes."

"You're still coming out with us to celebrate, right?" Nat asks.

"Of course. I wouldn't miss it for the world."

Oak clears his throat. It's odd thinking of him by his first name, but I've spent so much time with Eva and Archer, both of them calling him by his first name, that it's kind of become second nature. "I want you all in alphabetical order by your surnames. Figure it out. We're starting in five."

"Great, I'm near the end, then."

"We're all mixed up," Camilla complains.

"Oh well, good luck. See you after," I say.

We all part ways and get into our correct positions, which puts me next to Jack Whale, who is a complete bore.

"Hey, Adrianna."

"Hi, Jack," I say.

He smiles, but it comes off a little creepy. "Fancy seeing you here."

I swallow hard, as Derk Unwin comes to stand on my other side. Fuck's sake. I'm literally sandwiched between two boneheads.

Jack tries to talk to me, but I tell him I'm nervous and don't want to talk. It's the best way out of it. It feels like forever before they finally get to Derk, who hasn't said a word the entire time. I prefer it that way.

My heart is pounding as I wait for my name to be called, wondering what kind of expression will be on my father's face.

"Adrianna Vasquez!"

I step up the steps and onto the stage, my heart racing as I walk over to Oak, who's presenting the diplomas. Shaking his hand, I turn to face the crowd and the moment I see my father, my stomach sinks.

He's not even looking, typing away on his phone without glancing up to see his daughter graduate.

Why the fuck did he bother coming?

It's a question I doubt I'll ever know the answer to.

And then I spot Archer in the back, clapping frantically and beaming at me. It makes my heart ache that in less than twenty-four hours I'll be starting my new life without him.

34

ARCHER

I approach Adrianna, who's standing with all her friends. My nerves are fried, mainly because I'm practically kidnapping the princess of the Vasquez Cartel. Thankfully, I saw Damien Vasquez leave ten minutes ago in his armored SUV with two men. I'm pretty sure he hardly even said a word to Adrianna after the ceremony.

I clear my throat. "Adrianna, can I have a word?"

"Stil not giving up?" Natalya teases.

It's clear no one knows about us among her friends, except for Camilla, and that was my fault.

She meets my gaze and nods. I can tell from the look on her face that she's just as nervous as me. "Sure."

I nod toward the exit of the hall and she follows me out of it.

"What's up?" she asks, as I lead her into an empty classroom and shut the door.

"I wanted to double check you're all set for the plan?"

She nods. "Of course. I'm packed, only essentials and no tech."

"Good. And your father has gone. I watched him leave."

She purses her lips. "I don't even know why he bothered to come. He didn't say two words to me after the ceremony." Her throat bobs. "And while I was collecting my diploma, he was on his phone."

His actions hurt her. That's clear as day. Perhaps she clung onto some hope that he would show her he cared this once.

"Just more proof as to why I don't owe them a fucking thing."

I walk toward her and pull her close, squeezing her hips. "You don't owe them anything. You owe yourself the life you want to live."

I lean down and kiss her, knowing that somehow I've got to convince her that we belong together. There's no way in hell that I'm leaving her in my cabin to make her own way in life. Adrianna belongs to me, and I belong to her. Like two halves of the same whole.

"Thank you, Archer."

"It's nothing, baby." I kiss her again. "Did you tell your friends?"

"Yeah, they all know and won't say anything to anyone until I'm gone."

"Good. Shall we go and celebrate your graduation?"

She smiles at me. "Sounds good."

I want to walk back in there holding her hand, but she pulls away the moment we leave the classroom. It makes sense. She's not going to walk back in there and announce that she's been sleeping with me a good portion of the academic year.

Sighing, I follow her and we rejoin the group. "What's going on then?" I ask.

"The group of us are going to go for dinner and drinks." Oak looks at me. "You are welcome to join."

I nod. "Sounds good."

"Let's go," Oak says, glancing at Gav. "You going to drive too?"

He nods. "Sure."

All of us walk out front and I follow Oak to his car with Adrianna. The others go with Gav as his SUV is a six seater. Adrianna and I get in the back together and she shuffles a little in her seat as silence ensues.

"So, Adrianna, what are your plans for after graduation?" Oak asks.

She winces. "Not a lot, to be honest."

Oak's the only one in this car who's in the dark about the plan, but that'll change tonight. I need to break it to him and Gav that I'm going with Adrianna, as long as she agrees. Once we're at the restaurant, I'll take them both to one side and explain. It means he'll need a new gym teacher for a while, maybe indefinitely.

"How about you two?" Adrianna asks.

I slide my hand onto her thigh and squeeze, which results in her tensing up. She's obviously paranoid that Oak and Eva will see, but it's impossible. "Relax," I murmur.

She glares at me, which only makes me harder than nails.

"Have you got amnesia?" Eva asks, laughing. "I already said earlier we're spending the summer in Alaska. Except for the date of Nat and Elias' wedding. There's no way I'm missing that."

Adrianna shakes her head. "Sorry, I'm distracted. Alaska should be peaceful."

Eva pulls a face. "Yeah, not totally convinced about it, to be honest."

Oak shakes his head. "You'll see what you've been missing, Mrs. Byrne."

She smiles at him. "If you insist."

"You will. It's beautiful up there," I say.

Adrianna glances at me. "You've been?"

I nod. "Yeah, it's brimming with wildlife."

"Sounds nice. I'm sure you'll like it, Eva," Adrianna says.

Eva sighs. "Probably, it's just I've got southern blood. Maine is cold enough."

A comfortable silence falls between us, but Adrianna still looks uncomfortable as I keep my hand on her thigh, squeezing gently.

"Where are we eating?"

Eva turns and I quickly shift my hand off Adrianna's leg. "A new all you can eat buffet called Cosmo. It's meant to do all kinds of food, from Italian to Asian and Mexican."

I smirk. "All you can eat suits me."

Adrianna nods. "And me."

Eva chuckles. "I thought you'd like that idea, Adrianna." She turns back to face the front and I slide my hand back onto Adrianna's thigh.

This time, Adrianna swats it away and gives me a warning glare.

"Here we are," Oak announces.

He parks in the parking lot and he and Eva get out, but I grab Adrianna's hand briefly. "Cheer up, baby girl. In no time, you'll be starting your new life."

She smiles, but it doesn't reach her eyes. I wonder what she's thinking, but as always, she's a closed book.

———

I PULL my jeep off the main road in the middle of nowhere, driving down an unmarked track. It may be secluded, but I know the path to this place like the back of my hand. After all, I spent just under two years living up here in my cabin.

I notice Adrianna shudder.

"Are you cold?" I ask.

She shakes her head. "No, this place gives me the creeps."

"The creeps?" I never thought of it as creepy.

"Yeah, like maybe you're actually a serial killer and this was your elaborate plan all along."

I laugh, shaking my head. "You have a wild imagination." The woods open up to a clearing where my cabin is, and it's not just any old cabin. It's modern and sophisticated.

"Wow, do you own this place?" Adrianna asks.

I nod. "I bought it when I needed to remain low while my family was looking for me." It was a difficult time in my life. One fraught with loneliness and a little too much alcohol, but this place saved me. "It's actually how I met Oak. He owns a cabin near to here and we met while we were both hiking."

"And that's how you got the job at the academy?"

I nod.

"How did you afford all this?"

"When I escaped from Dublin, I had no plan, just a few belongings. But I had a lot of money in my bank accounts, which my father couldn't touch. It was enough to set me up for life, but the issue was that if I used it too soon, then my father could easily track me." I run a hand across the back of my neck. "However, before boarding a plane to American I wire transferred the money to buy this place to a friend who bought it in their name."

"That sounds complicated."

I nod. "The money has sat in those accounts dormant, waiting until I can find someone to pull the cash for me somehow." I tilt my head. "Gav has hooked me up with a Russian hacker he knows in New York who has ties at a banking institute which can move the money and hide where it goes, no questions asked."

Adrianna looks surprised. "Why do you need the money now?"

I swallow hard. "I'm hoping that you will allow me to come with you."

Adrianna stares at me for a few moments. "Are you serious?"

"Of course. I want to stay with you and help you build a new life." I pause for a moment. "Build a new life, together."

"What about the academy?" she asks.

"It's not as important to me as you are."

Her eyes fill with unshed tears, and for the first time she shows me some real emotion.

"Gav wondered why I wanted the money, but didn't ask questions. I told him and Oak last night I was leaving with you and hopefully not coming back for now, if you agreed."

Adrianna cries then, tears streaming down her face.

"Don't cry, baby girl," I say, wiping her tear away.

She swallows hard. "It's just that I have been dreading saying goodbye to you ever since we came up with this crazy plan."

My heart swells, hearing her finally admit that she does indeed feel the same way I do. "Took you long enough."

"I'm sorry. I've never learned how to deal with my emotions correctly." She laughs, but it's half-hearted. "I guess that's what happens when you are brought by criminals."

"To be honest, I'm not sure I ever did either."

She arches her brow. "Well, you're pretty in touch with your emotions, I'd say."

"With you, yes. As I know that we're meant for each other."

"I've been so terrible to you, though."

"You have, but I forgive you." I wink.

She shakes her head. "I'll never understand why you care about me."

"Then that's my job, to make you realize how amazing you are, inside and out."

"Don't be ridiculous." She blushes red, making me realize in that moment that she doesn't understand how special she is. Her family have treated her like garbage and never shown her any love. It makes sense why she would have such low self-esteem, despite being accomplished in practically everything she turns her hands to.

"Come on, let's get settled in." I get out of the car and pull the keys to the cabin out of my pocket before leading the way up the steps to the entrance.

When I open the door, Adrianna gasps. "This is more like a mansion than a cabin."

"I would hardly call it a mansion, but it's nice, isn't it?"

She spins around and smiles. "Yeah, beautiful." Instantly, her attention lands on the fridge. "When was it last stocked?"

"Yesterday. I paid someone to come in and bring supplies."

I laugh when she rushes toward it and starts pulling things out to make a sandwich. "I could eat a horse. Do you want one?"

A gunshot outside makes both of us freeze as Adrianna drops the food in her hands.

"What the hell was that?" I ask, despite recognizing that sound too well.

"Could he have found us?" Adrianna asks.

I swallow hard, wondering what we could have over-looked. "You ditched all your tech, right?"

Adrianna nods. "Left it all at the academy."

I narrow my eyes. "Is there anything you brought with you that your father gifted you?"

Her eyes widen as her hand moves to her neck, where a beautiful golden pendant hangs. "No way."

"Give it here."

Adrianna tears it off, breaking the chain and places it into my hand.

"Fuck," I say, the moment I notice the pendant has been badly welded back together. Throwing it on the floor, I slam my foot into it and it breaks apart at the weld, revealing a GPS tracking device. "It's your father."

"Fuck!" Her eyes go wide as panic sets in. "What are we going to do?"

Oddly, I feel calm. It could be the shock or the fact that my entire childhood they trained me to deal with situations like this. "Don't panic. Bedroom now."

She does as she's told, rushing into the bedroom, which evidently only has an east-facing window and the blinds are drawn. The gunshot came from the west, which means they'll be approaching on the opposite side of the cabin. "Now what?"

I go into my closet and crouch down to open the safe, pulling out a gun. "Now, I fight and get us out of this."

Adrianna shakes her head. "No, you could die!" She tries to grab the gun from me, but I dodge out of the way and dart out of the bedroom, locking the door.

"Sorry, I can't risk you getting hurt," I shout from the other side.

"Archer!" She bangs on the door frantically. "I'm going to fucking kill you!"

I chuckle. "You may not need to if I die in a moment." Cocking the gun, I turn and walk to face my maker. If I have to kill all the men out there, including Damien Vasquez, to protect Adrianna, I'd do it in a heartbeat.

35

ADRIANNA

Motherfucker.

I search the closet for something to pick the bedroom lock with. If Archer is facing my father and his goons, then I need to be by his side.

Another shot echoes through the air, making me tense. I work even harder to focus on the lock, knowing I need to get out of this room. Finally, the lock clicks and I'm thankful I took the class on safe breaking two years ago when it was being taught.

Quickly, I run out of the room and down the corridor, hardly thinking about what I'm doing.

My heart skips a beat when I see my father and Archer standing outside of the window, each pointing a gun at one another. "No." I rush out of the cabin without a second thought. "Stop!"

And then I see my father's two men shot dead on the floor. My eyes move to Archer and I wonder if he killed them, and if so, how?

How did he get the drop on two guys and still get his gun on my father without getting shot himself.

"Adrianna," my father growls, pointing the gun at me. "What the fuck are you doing?"

I freeze at the other end of his gun, knowing that he would without a doubt shoot me dead. "I'm not coming home to Mexico," I say.

He growls. "Like hell you aren't."

"I don't want to be married off to some mobster."

"No, you want to frolic around with a dirty man who's supposed to be your teacher." He turns his gun back onto Archer. "You should be disgusted with yourself."

Archer glares at him. "Well, I love her more than you ever fucking have, so I think it's you that should be disgusted."

My father cocks his gun. "Give me one good reason why I shouldn't shoot you dead right now."

Archer cocks his gun. "Because I'm the best shot for miles around."

My father's eyes narrow and I notice his hand is shaking a little. He hasn't shot a man for a long while, normally relying on others to do his dirty work. Unfortunately, the two he normally relies on are dead. I'm surprised he hasn't got more back up.

"I love him, Father. That should be reason enough."

My father glares at me. "Shut up! You can't love a fucking gringo."

Archer growls. "Don't tell her to shut up."

"You made a mistake, Father, coming here," I say.

His hand shakes a little more.

"When was the last time you shot a gun?" I move closer, knowing that it's been a lot of years. Even his cousin, who he murdered last year, it was an order. He didn't actually do the killing. "Twenty years, maybe?"

His eyes narrow.

"Did you know Archer killed a student's mother only last winter? She was threatening the principal of the academy." I glance at his men on the floor. "And by the looks of it, he killed your two best men pretty easily."

My father's hand shakes even more. "Only one of us will walk out of here alive!"

Archer doesn't hesitate as he anticipates his next move. His finger was ready to pull down on the trigger, but Archer was faster. And before my father even knows what has happened, the bullet has gone straight through his chest. His eyes widen as he drops the gun and falls to his knees on the floor.

A pang of grief hits me, but it's far outweighed by the relief that Archer is alive. The man was hardly a father to me.

I run into Archer's arms, wrapping mine around him. "I love you," I blurt out, unable to contain the truth any longer. He just saved both of our lives, that I'm sure of.

"I just killed your father."

"Better him than you. He would have murdered you. It was kill or be killed." I squeeze him tight, knowing that I've never felt like this about anyone before.

Archer's body is stiff with tension. "What the fuck are we going to do?"

I step back and take his face in my hands, looking him

in the eye. "Let's not think about it right now. There's always tomorrow." I kiss him. "Right now, we need to be thankful we're both alive and together."

He kisses me, thrusting his tongue into my mouth. "I love you more than anything." He bites my lip. "Hell, I just killed for you. And you are right. I know two guys who will help us clean this up."

My brow furrows. "Oak and Gavril?"

"Yeah, they have experience in it, apparently. I don't know the details, so don't ask."

"Come on, let's go inside." I take his hand and we both go back into the cabin.

Archer walks over to the GPS tracker and stomps on it a few times, ensuring it's destroyed. And then he walks over to the fireplace, which was obviously lit for our arrival, throwing it on the fire for good measure. "Is there anything else you have on you that could have a tracker inside?"

I think about it, trying to work out if I have anything else with me that my family gave me as gifts. They were never big on gifts, but on my sixteenth birthday, my father gave me that necklace. I thought it was a sweet, almost sentimental gift, but I should have known. He had an ulterior motive to keep track of his teenage daughter. "No, I'm certain. Anything else I have with me, I definitely purchased myself."

"Good." He walks over to me and kisses me passionately, making me moan. "Now I need to make love to you, or I might lose my mind."

Archer lifts me off my feet and carries me into the bedroom, kissing me frantically.

I think he needs this right now and so do I. The man just killed my father. It's too much to think about and this is an outlet to blow off steam. Neither of us can even contemplate the repercussions of what just happened outside.

He pushes me roughly onto the bed, nostrils flaring. "You are mine, Adrianna. Tell me who you belong to."

"You," I say, not an ounce of hesitation in my voice.

He tears off my skirt and then my panties like an animal, sliding his fingers into me without warning. "Always so wet and ready for me."

I arch my back off the bed, wanting him inside of me more than ever before. "Fuck me," I order.

He smirks. It's a cruel smile that makes my stomach churn. "I'm in charge." His hand wraps around my throat and he squeezes. "I decide when I fuck you or if I fuck you."

I moan at the thought of him not fucking me, as I need him so badly. "Please," I beg, not ashamed of it, not anymore. Archer loves me and I love him.

He leans down and bites my lip. "Beg harder, baby."

I groan as he continues to finger me, making me wetter. "Please, Archer, I need you so bad."

"What do you need?" he asks.

"I need you inside of me." I play with my nipples, which results in him grabbing my wrists and forcing them over my head. "I want you to fuck me so hard I can hardly walk in the morning."

He growls and unzips his pants. "You asked for it."

He releases his cock and stares down at me with those beautiful dark eyes, which almost look black in the dim light. I feel his cock teasing against my entrance, and then he thrusts inside of me with force.

"Mine," he growls like an animal.. "You are going to be mine forever, baby girl."

"Yours," I moan, agreeing wholeheartedly.

The lone wolf is no longer alone. I've found my alpha. My mate for life.

"Every part of you belongs to me." He pulls out and thrusts back in. "This tight cunt is mine."

I groan, arching my back as he goes as deep as possible.

"Your beautiful fucking ass is mine. And your hot mouth too."

"All yours," I agree.

He smirks down at me. "And that stone cold heart is mine too, isn't it?"

"Yes," I moan, wishing he wasn't restraining my hands above my head as I want to play with myself.

"You are perfect, baby." My nipples are so hard as he drives deeper, hitting the spot inside of me that takes me higher.

"Oh, fuck, yes," I cry, arching my back.

"That's it, moan for me." He

Archer bites my collarbone hard. "I'm going to fill you to the brim with my cum, baby." He pounds into me even harder than I believed possible and wraps his hands around my throat, blocking my airways. "Mark you with my scent."

I come apart so hard I see stars in my vision. "Archer!" I scream his name, unable to form any other words or thoughts as my world shatters.

"Fuck, your pussy is strangling my cock." He thrusts three more times and then comes apart.

I feel him shooting his cum deep inside of me, filling me to the brim. His cock twitching deep within me. It prolongs my pleasure as I continue to shake beneath him, knowing that this connection we share is deep and unbreakable in that moment.

His breathing is labored as he rests on me, head buried against my neck. For a long while, he doesn't move or speak, and I wonder if he's fallen asleep.

I poke him, as he's getting a little heavy. "Archer."

"Yes, baby?"

"You are crushing me."

"Shit." He rolls off of me, pulling his semi-hard cock out of me as he goes. "Sorry. I just never wanted to leave."

I shuffle closer to him and press my head against his chest, listening to the steady drum of his heartbeat. "I didn't think it would go like this." I glance up at him, pain clawing at my chest. "I thought we'd get away without any drama."

"I hoped that, but we couldn't have anticipated the tracker in your necklace." He frowns. "It's like he tagged you."

"As if I'm his property?"

Archer nods.

"I think he felt that way. That I was an asset to be sold to the highest bidder when the time was right."

He sighs and pulls me closer. "Well, I think I won, don't you?"

I nestle closer. "Yes, because I'm your property now."

"Forever, baby girl." He kisses the top of my head, and we fall into contemplative silence.

It's hard to feel anything much with the shock of what just occurred, and yet I feel how much I love him. That is a constant that can't be changed.

36

EPILOGUE

ADRIANNA

*A*rcher holds my hand as we pad barefoot through the sand, the sun just setting beyond the horizon and casting a warm, orange glow over the beach.

Natalya's wedding was beautiful. And even though I still can't believe she married the man that tormented her for years, I'm happy that she's happy.

"It's beautiful, isn't it?" I ask, stopping to watch as the sun dips slowly lower.

Archer smiles at me. "Shall we sit down and watch?"

I nod in response. "Sounds good." I sit down in the sand and he sits behind me, placing his legs on either side of my thighs and his arms around my waist. "This is nice," he murmurs into my ear.

I lean back into him. "It is."

"Did you enjoy the wedding?" He asks.

"It was beautiful, even though I still can't quite believe that Nat ended up with Elias after he was such a bully."

Archer moves my hair to the side and skims his lips

over the back of my neck. "Is it any different to you being with me after I blackmailed you?"

I stiffen at the reminder. "Not sure it's in your best interest to bring that up right now."

"No?" He asks, his arm tightening around me. "And what about you trying to break my heart? Shall I not mention that either?"

He has a point, but it's not like I was going to sit back and be bossed around without some kind of retaliation. He should have seen it coming.

"I guess we're even then?"

He kisses my neck. "I guess so."

"Do you think we'll ever get caught?" I ask, feeling more on edge than ever being back on Mexican soil. Even if it's not territory my family run, it's still Mexico.

Elias insists that his family will keep us both safe as the Vasquez Cartel wouldn't dare step foot in the Estrada Cartel's territory, at least not this deep into it. Even though Adrik may have taken control of the American operations, Elias' family still controls everything south of the border. They're working with the Russian, which is rather unconventional.

My father's disappearance did cause a stir, but no one knows what happened to him. We enlisted the help of Oak and Gavril for that, as apparently they had previous experience. Thankfully, it's assumed whoever made him disappear also had his daughter, which means I'm presumed dead.

He kisses my neck again. "No, I won't let your family find us."

"But you've had to give up so much."

"Have I? I don't think I have, to be honest."

"The academy, you love it there."

I can feel him tense a little against me at the mention of the academy. "I do and one day I hope we can return together, but for now we need to keep any ties between us and the academy at a minimum until the heat dies down."

"You've given up too much."

He bites my shoulder playfully. "I've given up nothing and gained the entire fucking world when you agreed to take off with me."

I shudder at the intensity of his tone. "You are crazy. Did you know that?"

"Perhaps," he murmurs, tightening his grasp on me. "Did you know there's a really beautiful cove near to here?"

I shake my head. "No, what are you suggesting?"

He chuckles. "You know exactly what I'm suggesting."

"It will be dark soon."

"Even better," he murmurs.

"How the hell are we going to see anything?"

He leaps to his feet. "Come on," he says, holding a hand out to me.

I take it and allow him to pull me up, lacing my fingers with his. I've learned since we've been together that it's best not to question him when he's like this. We walk further up the beach until we go around a headland and come to a cove which is lit with so many candles.

My attention moves to Archer, who is smiling.

"You were saying?"

"How did you do all this?" I ask.

He shrugs. "I wanted to do something nice for you."

I smile. "That's very sweet."

His hand tightens around me as he leads me to the table set for two.

I glance around. "Are we here to eat?" I ask, since the table is set with dinner plates and silverware.

"Yes."

"And where is the kitchen?"

Archer chuckles and speaks into a radio. "Ready for you."

The noisy rattle of an engine sounds as two bright lights appear from behind the cliff face.

"It's on the boat."

I arch a brow. "This is very fancy."

"Well, it's our first holiday away together, and I thought we could use a bit of a reward."

"A reward for doing nothing for three months in Alaska?" We ended up joining Oak and Eva in Alaska for the summer, since my father compromised Archer's cabin by finding it. We couldn't risk staying there, especially not after Archer shot him dead.

A man and a woman come toward us with silver platters.

"Oh, I'm starving."

He chuckles. "Don't say that if Gav is around. He has a problem with it."

"A problem with the saying?"

"Yep, I got told off at the diner when I said it."

I laugh. "Weird."

He shakes his head. "I think there's a reason behind it. Pretty sure Gav knows what it's like to be truly starving. He won't open up to anyone about what happened in Russia during his childhood. All I can assume is that it was pretty fucking awful."

"Oh, that's awful. I get why he wouldn't like that saying. It is said far too flippantly."

He tilts his head. "I agree, but it's just a saying."

The server comes over holding a bucket with a bottle of champagne. "May I?"

"Of course."

He pours us each a glass and sets the bucket down on a table against our table. The other server brings over two platters of food.

He sets down one platter and lifts the lid to reveal a load of tamales.

"Oh my God."

He smiles. "I know you love tamales."

"Yeah, they're one of my favorite." I grab one and put it on my plate.

"Taste them."

I take a bite and groan, as they may even be better than the ones my great grandmother made when I was little.

"And fajitas, right?" Archer says.

As he puts down the other platter to reveal a stack of made up fajita wraps. "Have I told you how much I love you?"

363

His smile widens. "Not nearly enough."

The other server who poured the champagne comes forward.

"Surely not more?" I ask.

He nods. "And last, chicken mole."

I practically fall off my chair, as this man knows me so well. Both of our appetites align in all aspects. To most, it would look like we're seriously pigging out, but this is just the right amount of food for us. "You are the best."

"Dig in."

I grab a couple of fajitas, two more tamales, and a heap of mole. And I just pig out. We both do, in comfortable silence.

Archer puts down his fork with a clang. "I think I'm done."

He polished off as much as me. Oddly, he looks a little nervous as he takes a sip of his champagne.

"I never thought I'd find a man as greedy as me."

"You're very lucky, aren't you?"

He hasn't lost his arrogance, but it's something I've grown to love about him. "I think you are the lucky one."

"Oh, I don't contest that, baby." He stands and walks over to my side, dropping onto his knees next to me.

"What are you—"

He pulls out a black velvet box and I'm pretty sure I almost go into cardiac arrest. "Adrianna Vasquez, will you marry me and make me the happiest man on this planet?" He flips open the box to reveal a beautiful baguette cut diamond ring.

I can't get my words at first as a well of emotion claws

at my throat, making it almost impossible to breathe. Finally, I make a sound, "Yes!"

He pulls the ring out of the cushion and slides it onto my finger. "Thank God you said yes. I thought I might have to blackmail you."

I shove him in the shoulder. "Don't be an idiot."

Grabbing my hand, he yanks me out of my chair and wraps his arms around me. "You are everything to me, Adrianna. I can't imagine life without you."

"Me neither."

He kisses me then and twirls me around under the stars to imaginary music. My heart feels so full it could explode. I thought I was destined to be alone forever. My upbringing had closed me off to the prospect of love or emotion. And yet through sheer pig-headed persistence, Archer broke my barriers down piece by piece, never giving up on us. For that, I'll be forever grateful.

He pulls me onto a blanket on the sand, kissing every inch of my body. "I love you more than anything in this world."

I smile up at him, knowing that somehow the man I hated so much less than twelve months ago is now the love of my life. "I love you, too."

And he kisses me again under the stars as the waves crash gently against the shore. In that moment, it makes it hard not to believe in fairytales and happy endings, even if our story was far from conventional.

THANK you so much for reading Playing Dirty. I hope you enjoyed Adrianna's and Archer's story.

For now, this will be the end of the Syndicate Academy series. I may revisit it in the future, but I've been struggling with this series creatively and I'm ready to start on something fresh. However, that doesn't mean there won't be familiar characters popping up in some stories coming this year.

THE NEXT SERIES I'm working on is Once Upon a Villian, and it's a series of dark mafia romances all of which are loosely based on popular fairytales or classic stories. This book has a release date set to May 31st, but I may well bring it forward.

PRIDE: A Dark Arranged Marriage Romance

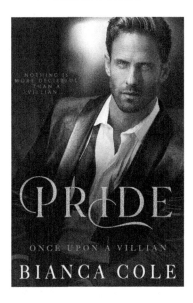

Deceitful. Arrogant. Cold.

Those are the three perfect words to sum up my husband to be.

After little deliberation, my parents decide Isiah Darcy is the perfect suitor.

He's rich, British, and the perfect ally for the Benedetto family business.

I can't stand him, but they don't care what I want.

He's stuck up and has little respect for women.

Once we're married, he makes it painfully clear I have no rights in his eyes.

I'm nothing more than a puppet.

A way for him to get what he's always wanted.

Revenge on my family for something that happened years ago.

My husband wants to tear my family apart.

He underestimates me, as I'll do everything in my power to stop him.

And yet all is not as it first appears as I get to know the villainous Isiah Darcy.

Pride is the first book in the Once Upon a Villain Series by Bianca Cole. This story is a dark arranged marriage mafia romance story with dark themes and certain subjects that may upset the reader. It has no cliffhanger, a happily ever after ending, and can be read as a standalone.

ALSO BY BIANCA COLE

Once Upon a Villian

Pride: A Dark Arranged Marriage Romance

The Syndicate Academy

Corrupt Educator: A Dark Forbidden Mafia Academy
Romance

Cruel Bully: A Dark Mafia Academy Romance

Sinful Lessons: A Dark Forbidden Mafia Academy Romance

Playing Dirty: A Dark Enemies to Lovers Forbidden Mafia
Academy Romance

Chicago Mafia Dons

Merciless Defender: A Dark Forbidden Mafia Romance

Violent Leader: A Dark Enemies to Lovers Captive Mafia
Romance

Evil Prince: A Dark Arranged Marriage Romance

Brutal Daddy: A Dark Captive Mafia Romance

Cruel Vows: A Dark Forced Marriage Mafia Romance

Dirty Secret: A Dark Enemies to Loves Mafia Romance

Dark Crown: A Dark Arranged Marriage Romance

Dark Reign Series Novella:

Empire of Carnage: A Dark Captive Mafia Romance

Boston Mafia Dons Series

Cruel Daddy: A Dark Mafia Arranged Marriage Romance

Savage Daddy: A Dark Captive Mafia Roamnce

Ruthless Daddy: A Dark Forbidden Mafia Romance

Vicious Daddy: A Dark Brother's Best Friend Mafia Romance

Wicked Daddy: A Dark Captive Mafia Romance

New York Mafia Doms Series

Her Irish Daddy: A Dark Mafia Romance

Her Russian Daddy: A Dark Mafia Romance

Her Italian Daddy: A Dark Mafia Romance

Her Cartel Daddy: A Dark Mafia Romance

Romano Mafia Brother's Series

Her Mafia Daddy: A Dark Daddy Romance

Her Mafia Boss: A Dark Romance

Her Mafia King: A Dark Romance

Bratva Brotherhood Series

Bought by the Bratva: A Dark Mafia Romance

Captured by the Bratva: A Dark Mafia Romance

Claimed by the Bratva: A Dark Mafia Romance

Bound by the Bratva: A Dark Mafia Romance

Taken by the Bratva: A Dark Mafia Romance

Wynton Series

Filthy Boss: A Forbidden Office Romance

Filthy Professor: A First Time Professor And Student Romance

Filthy Lawyer: A Forbidden Hate to Love Romance

Filthy Doctor: A Fordbidden Romance

Royally Mated Series

Her Faerie King: A Faerie Royalty Paranormal Romance

Her Alpha King: A Royal Wolf Shifter Paranormal Romance

Her Dragon King: A Dragon Shifter Paranormal Romance

Her Vampire King: A Dark Vampire Romance

ABOUT THE AUTHOR

I love to write stories about over the top alpha bad boys who have heart beneath it all, fiery heroines, and happily-ever-after endings with heart and heat. My stories have twists and turns that will keep you flipping the pages and heat to set your kindle on fire.

For as long as I can remember, I've been a sucker for a good romance story. I've always loved to read. Suddenly, I realized why not combine my love of two things, books and romance?

My love of writing has grown over the past four years and I now publish on Amazon exclusively, weaving stories about dirty mafia bad boys and the women they fall head over heels in love with.

If you enjoyed this book please follow me on Amazon, Bookbub or any of the below social media platforms for alerts when more books are released.

Printed in Great Britain
by Amazon